Praise for The Borgia Dove

I relished every word of *Borgia Dove*. Jo Graham paints these larger-than-life characters in a gloriously dynamic mural with grace and wit.

> — Sherwood Smith, creator of the Sartorias-deles universe,
> Nebula award finalist

Passion, intrigue, politics, and a papal election, all portrayed with Graham's trademark historical flair. I was planning to read this one slowly to savor every beautifully-chosen detail, but ended up finishing it in two days—I couldn't put it down.

> — Melissa Scott, legendary pioneering SFF author
> and winner of multiple genre awards

An insightful meditation on the rare alignment of true love and pure ambition—no one writes the Borgias like Jo Graham.

> — E. K. Johnston, #1 New York Times bestselling author

The Borgia Dove is a very sensual and sensuous book // Not just sexual and carnal pleasures, mind you, but the entire world is brought alive with all the senses in mind. // Graham's *The Borgia Dove* brings us into Giulia's world, life, passions and desires in a fully immersive way.

> — Paul Weimer, SFF book reviewer
> and Hugo award finalist

The Borgia Dove is an intelligent, action-packed fantasy of vivid characters and well-researched history, filled with so much life

I know I won't be able to read about Rome in this era now without hearing Giulia's voice and seeing it through her eyes.
— K.V. Johansen, author of *Gods of the Caravan Road*

Praise for A Blackened Mirror

Graham (*Black Ships*) recalls the legacy of Taylor Caldwell and Mary Renault in this smart series launch, humanizing history from the perspective of deeply imagined, unironically presented characters. //...this slow-building introduction to complex intrigue will please readers looking for vivid historical fare with just a touch of magic.
— *Publishers Weekly*

Ancient Greek and Roman rituals lie like a palimpsest beneath the streets of a Rome resplendent in full Catholic regalia in this tale of ambition, desire, intrigue and enchantment. La Bella Farnese is a compelling heroine, and author Jo Graham casts her Renaissance spell with a deft hand.
— Jacqueline Carey, award-winning author of the *Kushiel Universe* series

An addictively rich, vivid and lushly written Renaissance fantasy // Jo Graham's writing style is beautiful, as always, and her story-telling is utterly compulsive from beginning to end.
— Stephanie Burgis, author of *Masks and Shadows* and *Snowspelled*

Once again, Graham proves herself a master of historical fantasy—this time, the Italian Renaissance, portrayed in all its glorious complexity. Giulia Farnese is the ideal protagonist, ardent, ambitious, sharp of wit and tongue, willing to risk everything. I devoured the book, and cannot wait for the rest of the series.

> — Melissa Scott, legendary pioneering SFF author
> and winner of multiple genre awards

Jo Graham returns to magical history with a fresh take on some of Rome's most notorious. Witty and loving, with sharp edges in all the right places.

> — E.K. Johnston, #1 New York Times bestselling author

Jo Graham skillfully brings life in Renaissance Rome and Italy to life... // It is a highly enjoyable read, perfect for those who want to get to grips with the skullduggery of life in Renaissance Rome and the Curia.

> — Dr. Katharine Fellows, Oxford University, author of
> "Diplomacy, Debauchery and Devils:
> the ecclesiastical career of Rodrigo Borgia"

Jo Graham's *A Blackened Mirror* showcases the breadth of her writing talents... // Graham gives us a fresh and underappreciated perspective on the life and times of late 15th century Rome, with a strong heroine, rich worldbuilding and language; clever, refined and immersibly readable.

> — Paul Weimer, SFF book reviewer and Hugo finalist

Vivid characters, especially the charming and indomitable young Giulia Farnese herself, bring to life a story of conspiracy, intrigue, and Renaissance magic—Jo Graham's *A Blackened Mirror* is a wonderful adventure.

> — K.V. Johansen, author of the
> *Gods of the Caravan Road* epic fantasy series

Also by Jo Graham (selected works):

Black Ships

Stealing Fire

The Order of the Air (series, Melissa Scott co-author)

The Calpurnian Wars

    Sounding Dark
    Warlady
    Fortune's Favor

Memoirs of the Borgia Sibyl

    A Blackened Mirror
    The Borgia Dove

THE BORGIA DOVE

Being the Second Part of
the Memoirs of the Borgia Sibyl

Jo Graham

Candlemark & Gleam

First edition published 2024

Copyright @ 2024 by Jo Graham

For information, address
Athena Andreadis
Candlemark & Gleam LLC,
38 Rice Street #2, Cambridge, MA 02140
eloi@candlemarkandgleam.com

Library of Congress Cataloguing-in-Publication Data
In Progress

ISBNs: 978-1-952456-24-4 (paperback), 978-1-952456-25-1 (ebook)

Cover art by Alexael

Editor: Athena Andreadis

www.candlemarkandgleam.com

In memory of my daughter, Ashlee

1999-2023

Love is the thing that never ends.

There is written, her fair neck round about:
Noli me tangere, for Caesar's I am,
And wild for to hold, though I seem tame.

—Thomas Wyatt

The Borgia Family Tree in 1492

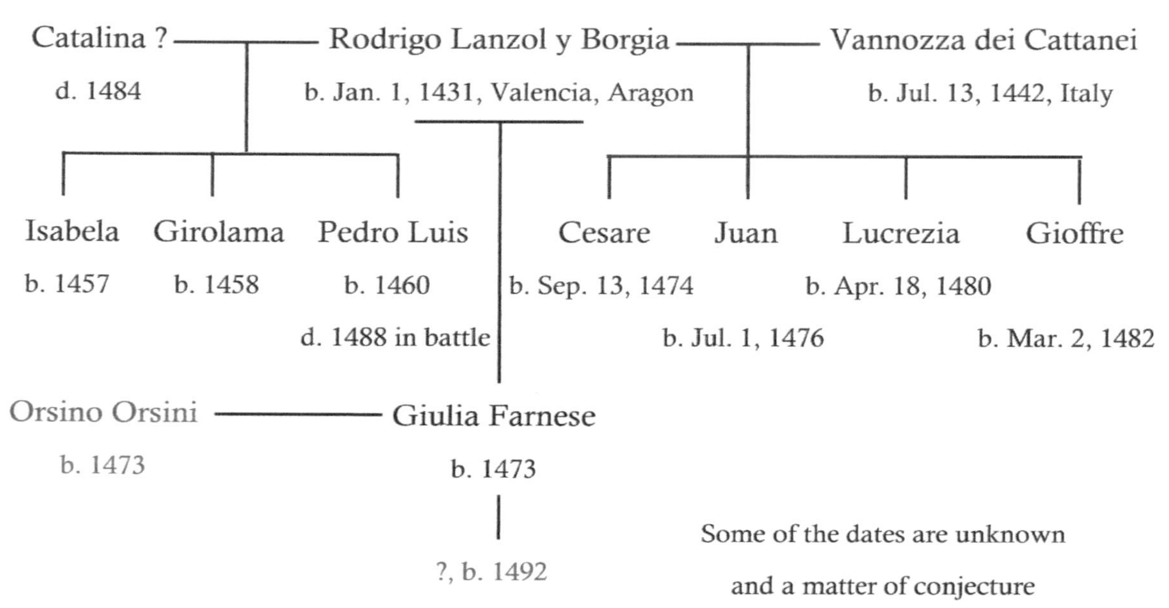

The Church Hours

As recognized in Rome in the 15th century

In the Renaissance, timekeeping for people in cities depended on church bells which were rung at specific hours of the day. A day began at sunset and went around until sunset the next day. Here are the hours as referenced in *The Borgia Dove* and all other works in the *Memoirs of the Borgia Sibyl* series.

Vespers: the Vespers bells rang at sunset, whatever time that was. In other words, what time Vespers is varied depending on the season. In Rome that's as early as 4:41 at midwinter. On June 22, the midsummer's eve of the last chapter of the book, sunset is not until 8:49 pm.

Compline: an hour after Vespers. Thus, "dinner after Compline" means anything from 6:00 to 10:00.

Vigil: two hours after midnight, so approximately 2:00 am.

Lauds: at dawn, which again means that it moves around. At midwinter, that's 7:02 am. At midsummer, it's 5:01 am. Thus, on June 22 if you come home at Vigil and are up for Lauds, you get three hours sleep!

Prime: an hour after dawn, generally the beginning of the working day.

Terce: the third hour, or two hours after Prime.

Sext: three hours later, so at midwinter it's about 1:00 pm and at midsummer at about 11:00 am, so noonish.

PEOPLE, PLACES AND THINGS

Borgia, Cesare: the oldest son of Rodrigo Borgia and Vannozza dei Cattanei. Intended for a career in the Church, he has been made Archbishop of Valencia though he is currently a student at the University of Pisa. He is about to turn nineteen.

Borgia, Gioffre: the youngest son of Rodrigo Borgia and Vannozza dei Cattanei. He is ten years old and lives with his mother.

Borgia, Juan: the middle son of Rodrigo Borgia and Vannozza dei Cattanei. He is sixteen years old and has just moved out of his mother's house to live with his father.

Borgia, Lucrezia: the daughter of Rodrigo Borgia and Vannozza dei Cattanei. At the beginning of *The Borgia Dove* she is twelve years old and lives with Giulia Farnese and Adriana de Mila a few blocks from her father's house.

Borgia, Pedro Luis: Rodrigo Borgia's oldest son by a relationship before Vannozza, he was killed in service to the Spanish crown four years ago.

Borgia, Rodrigo: Cardinal, Vice-Chancellor, and Dean of the College of Cardinals, he is a power in the Vatican despite being Spanish and a foreigner who is not connected to the ruling families of Rome. He is from Valencia, where he has amassed considerable estates and wealth. He is the patron of various Humanist and Neoplatonist writers, a notable collector of ancient art, and known for his lavish lifestyle. He is a member of the Humanist faction in the College.

Bracciano: a major fortress a day's ride from Rome held by the powerful Orsini family as the personal property of the head of the family, Virginio Orsini, known as Lord Bracciano.

Burchard, Johann: chronicler of the papal court

Caetani, Giovanna: now holding the castle of Montalto, she is the widow of Pier Luigi Farnese and the mother of Giulia and her brothers and sister.

Canale, Carlo: Vannozza dei Cattanei's husband

Carafa, Cardinal Oliviero: One of the leaders of the Humanist faction in the College of Cardinals, he is a Neapolitan nobleman who has served for decades. He is regarded as a leading intellectual with one of the finest personal libraries in Rome. However, he's made many enemies with his political positions and many consider him too radical to be elected pope.

Cardinal: the highest officials of the Catholic Church besides the pope, they are appointed for life to the College of Cardinals. It is their vote that elects one of their peers to be pope.

Colonna: one of the great families of Rome

Conclave: the mechanism by which a new pope is elected. When a pope dies, the cardinals go into conclave and vote on his successor. A 2/3 majority of the present and voting cardinals is required to win the election.

Condottiero: a mercenary soldier of purportedly noble birth who sells his sword and supposed military acumen to the highest bidder.

Cybo, Franchescetto: a Roman nobleman, the illegitimate son of Pope Innocent VIII

De Bastian, Giani: a young Venetian nobleman on the staff of the Venetian ambassador

De Michelis, Fiammetta: currently the foremost courtesan of Rome, and something of a celebrity in her own right. She became the concubine of Cardinal Piccolomini when she was thirteen, and he died two years later leaving her a fortune. Now twenty-eight, he has an elegant house in town where she entertains fashionably and lavishly and chooses her patrons according to her own tastes. She has befriended Giulia at Rodrigo's request.

De Mila, Adriana: Rodrigo Borgia's cousin, widow of Ludovico Orsini and stepmother to Orsino Orsini. She lives in Palazzo Orsini de

Ponte, a fine house not far from the Vice-Chancellor's Palazzo.

Dei Cattanei, Vannozza: once the foremost courtesan of Rome, she became the concubine of Rodrigo Borgia more than twenty years ago. They had four children together before they parted. She is now happily married to Carlo Canale and has a considerable business as a real estate manager and owner of a working vineyard.

Della Mirandola, Pico: a Florentine philosopher and thinker, student of Marsilio Ficino, and the teacher of Dionisio Treschi. He is considered one of the fathers of the western magical tradition due to his expansion of the teachings of Hermes Trismegistus into operative magic. He has currently been charged with heresy and awaits trial.

Della Rovere, Cardinal Giuliano: Papal Legate to France and one of the most powerful cardinals, he is considered a leading contender for the papacy when it next becomes vacant. He is a member of the Traditionalist faction but is considered by some members to be too much of an opportunist rather than a true believer.

Elissa: a friend of Fiammetta de Michelis, she is a courtesan currently without a patron.

Erythraean Sibyl: one of the sibyls of the ancient world, she was a series of women who served as an oracle in Asia Minor "from before the Trojan War" who foresaw both Alexander the Great and Jesus Christ. In *Black Ships*, this is the shrine of the Lady of the Dead that Gull would have been pledged to if she had not been born in exile.

Farnese, Alessandro: the oldest son of Pier Luigi Farnese and Giovanna Caetani, now twenty-two. His parents managed to afford a good education for him at the University of Pisa so that he could have a career in the Church. Two years ago he got a position as a Vatican clerk thanks to Cardinal Borgia and has worked in the Vatican's financial offices since then.

Farnese, Amadeo: the youngest son of Pier Luigi Farnese and Giovanna Caetani, he died in 1487 at the age of not quite two.

Farnese, Angelo: the third son of Pier Luigi Farnese and Giovanna Caetani, he is eleven years old.

Farnese, Bartolomeo: the second son of Pier Luigi Farnese and Giovanna Caetani, he is fifteen years old.

Farnese, Girolama: the youngest daughter of Pier Luigi Farnese and Giovanna Caetani, she is not quite five years old.

Farnese, Giulia: a natural seer, a young woman born with the gifts of the ancient sibyls, she is the oldest daughter of Pier Luigi Farnese and Giovanna Caetani and was married to Orsino Orsini in an arranged marriage three years ago. It was kept unconsummated to preserve her abilities as a virgin Dove for his kinsman, Lord Bracciano. Giulia thwarted Bracciano's plans and become the mistress of Cardinal Rodrigo Borgia two years ago.

Farnese, Pier Luigi: the former Lord of Montalto, father of Giulia and her brothers and sister. He had been a condottiero for many years before he inherited Montalto unexpectedly at the age of 39. He died of the summer sickness in 1487.

Ficino, Marsilio: a leading Humanist writer, founder of the Neoplatonist movement. He was the tutor of Lorenzo de Medici and now leads an academy of young writers and artists in Florence. Among other things, he has translated and introduced the writings of Hermes Trismegistus, and as such is the father of Hermetic magic in the western magical tradition.

Gherardi, Cardinal Maffeo: the Patriarch of Venice, he has recently been made a cardinal as a reward for years of good service to the Church. He is eighty-four.

Gonfaloniere: the title of the general in charge of the Papal Armies

Humanist faction: a faction in the College of Cardinals that favors the expansion of Renaissance thought, including the translation of ancient pagan writers like Plato and Pliny and their inclusion in the curriculum of the universities. The Humanists support the spread of printing and literacy.

Medici: the ruling family of Florence, merchant bankers and patrons of the arts

Miglio (plural, miglia): a measure of distance, about a mile

Montalto: a small fortress north of Rome along the ancient Via Aurelia near the seashore

Nepi: a fortress belonging to Cardinal Rodrigo Borgia as his personal holding

Osteria: a restaurant or tavern

Orsini: one of the great families of Rome

Orsini, Cardinal Giovanni: one of the leading members of the powerful Orsini family and a Cardinal of the Catholic Church

Orsini, Orsino: a young man of the Orsini family, son of the late Ludovico Orsini and stepson of Adriana de Mila. He was married to Giulia Farnese in an arranged marriage three years ago, but for the last two years has lived at the estate of Vasanello, a great country property that was deeded to him by Cardinal Borgia.

Orsini, Virginio (Lord Bracciano): head of the powerful Orsini family, he is the Lord of Bracciano, a substantial castle, and a wealthy landowner. He is also the Gonfaloniere of the Papal Armies, appointed by Pope Innocent as his military commander.

Pluto: the Roman god of the underworld, the equivalent of the Greek Hades. He is also called Father Dis.

Pope Innocent VIII: born Giovanni Cybo, he was elected pope five years before the events of *A Blackened Mirror* and has been in ill health for much of his reign. Part of the Traditionalist faction, he published the *Malleus Mallificarum*, which authorized the investigation and persecution of witchcraft, and encouraged the founding of the Spanish Inquisition.

Proserpina: the Roman goddess of the underworld, the equivalent of the Greek Persephone. She is the spring maiden who descends to the underworld and then returns over and over, thus creating the cycle of the seasons.

Riario, Cardinal Raffaele: one of the youngest cardinals, he had been made a cardinal at the age of 16 by his uncle, the pope before Innocent VIII. Now thirty, he's a patron of the arts and a solid member of the Humanist faction.

Sarfati, Chaya: a fifteen-year-old Jewish girl from Grenada, she has fled the Spanish Inquisition with her older brother and younger sister and is now in Rome illegally. She had hoped to be a teacher.

Sarfati, Mois: a young Jewish scholar from Grenada. Fleeing the Spanish Inquisition, he is now an illegal refugee in Italy with his two younger sisters.

Sarfati, Sincha: a twelve-year-old Jewish girl from Grenada, she has fled the Spanish Inquisition with her older brother and sister. She loves fashion and wishes she could be a designer and seamstress of fine clothes.

Savonarola, Friar: Florentine monk and preacher who is becoming a force in Florentine politics. He is extremely conservative and opposes the humanism of the Medici.

Sforza: one of the most powerful families of Italy

Sforza, Cardinal Ascanio: a member of the College of Cardinals from the powerful Sforza family, he is the brother of the Duke of Milan and the uncle of Prince Ferrandino of Naples, the King of Naples' grandson and heir.

Summer sickness: an endemic and serious disease, probably malaria

Tarocchi: a card game with four players that is the ancestor of bridge, but also the deck itself which is the precursor of the modern tarot deck.

Traditionalist faction: a faction in the College of Cardinals which seeks to limit the spread of non-Christian ideas, including ancient pagan books and art. They oppose the translation of ancient works and the expansion of printing and literacy.

Treschi, Dionisio: a Florentine scholar and would-be magician

Valencia: a city on the Mediterranean coast of Spain, part of the Kingdom of Aragon, Rodrigo Borgia's home city. He held the Archbishopric of Valencia for many years until he ceded it to his son, Cesare.

Vasanello: an estate north of Rome belonging to Orsino Orsini, Giulia's husband

Via Aurelia: the ancient Roman road going northward from Rome passing through Montalto on the way to Pisa

Xatavia: the small town outside Valencia where Rodrigo Borgia was born

Chapter One

Why does no one tell tales of what happened to Proserpina after she became Death's bride? Is it that she is no longer interesting once she is not a virgin? I would think that being the wife of a god would be worth a story.

I am neither virago nor virgin nor victim, so perhaps that renders me uninteresting as well. I am the consort of one of the most powerful men in the Christian world, and I have worked hard for it. *We* have worked hard for it despite all perils. I love my family, my friends, my God and my lover, though sometimes it is difficult to tell the difference between the last two.

If you would like a cautionary tale of suffering, my just desserts for my wayward acts, this is not the story you want. If you want to hear how we triumphed against a world set against us, against dagger and dark magic alike, read on.

It was a lovely day, the ninth day of June in the Year of Our Lord 1492. I sat at a little table on the balcony of my room, looking out across the city of Rome, across tiled roofs and gardens and streets, to the tower of St. Peter's Basilica against the sky. And tried not to gag.

Maria, our housekeeper, stood in the doorway with a packet

of papers in her hand. "Donna Giulia, I swear by day-old bread. Just a little of it; moisten it in your mouth and swallow a little at a time."

I looked down at the hunk of bread in my hand. It ought to be appetizing. Something ought to be. "My mother writes that I'll be done with this in a week or so." Cold sweat stood on my forehead despite the warm day.

"Your mother knows best," Maria said. "Young women carry most like their mothers."

"She had six," I said. "She ought to know." I looked resolutely out over the city as I put a piece of bread the size of my thumbnail in my mouth. "It will be over soon. And then I'll feel perfectly well. That's what she says."

I had missed my courses at the end of March and then again in April. By May it was clear that there would be a child, a not unexpected result of having had a lover for nearly two years. Indeed, the only question was why it had taken so long. Rodrigo did not seem to lack virility for all that he was much older than I. Certainly he had sired many children in the past, but one could expect him to slow down somewhat. Well, anyone could but he. Now that I was clearly gravid, he strutted around like the Borgia Bull in truth.

"I expect you will, Donna Giulia," Maria said. "I've brought a packet of letters up from the door guards. There are several for you." She put them on the table.

"Thank you, Maria," I said. "Would you mind bringing me pen and ink out here?"

"Not at all. You stay still." She went back into my camera while I opened the first of the four letters. It was a lengthy and overly polite letter from the aunt of someone my brother Alessandro had known at the university, extolling the thrift, punctuality, and honesty of her nephew who earnestly sought a position doing accounts in the Vatican if I would be so kind as to speak to the

Vice-Chancellor on his behalf.

I read it twice. I had never heard of the young man. I shook my head and put it aside to ask Alessandro about. Perhaps he had some idea if he was as honest and thrifty as advertised. Given that I had never met the woman or even heard of her nephew, I was not about to extend patronage to someone who might be a wastrel or a maniac.

Maria brought the ink and paper while I read the second. "Another bite, Donna Giulia." I glanced down at the bread. I had taken a bite and swallowed it without incident. I took another hopefully and read the second letter.

This one was even more perplexing, as it came from a man I had never met who stated that he had written a series of Petrarchan sonnets that he wished printed, and begged that he might be allowed to dedicate them to my lovely person. (And that I should pick up part of the printing costs, as a good patroness should.) It was at least easy to answer. I would like very much to read some of the sonnets before I decided whether to assist in their publication. I wrote it out, short and flowery, in very polite language without adding "And only an idiot buys a pig sight unseen." That was not how a lady corresponded.

The third letter made me smile, and I broke the seal on it with pleasure. *My dear Giulia*, it read, *I shall be hosting a little garden revelry on Saturday the 16th from dusk until whenever we're tired of it, with dancers and that sweet boy who plays the lute, Becchio or whatever his name is. It won't be half the city, my dearest, just a few close friends who will appreciate a rustic scene such as nymphs and dryads and shepherds and all sorts of rustic things.*

I reread that last sentence twice. It did seem to trip over itself.

I would be incomprehensibly pleased if the two of you would honor my little abode! I know you're breeding and have no taste for lamb, or ram either, but you could just drop in and sample the savories! All my love, Fiammetta.

It was certainly incomprehensible why her pleasure would be incomprehensible, and whether I had any taste for ram or not at present was not something I was about to discuss with Fiammetta. Pleasant company as she was, her discretion was not all that one might desire. And I wasn't about to let Rodrigo loose among the lambs under the circumstances. Still, if we dropped in early, her gatherings were always pleasant, and I did consider her a friend. Fiammetta was one of foremost courtesans in Rome, and she had welcomed me to her sisterhood warmly. I picked up a reed pen and dipped it to answer.

Dearest Fiammetta, thank you so for the lovely invitation! We will try to come. I hope I shall not be indisposed, but of course I cannot guess so far in advance. You know how it is. A hundred kisses, Giulia.

I did not have wax out here, so I simply folded it and put it aside, stretching like a cat in the sun. The bread did seem to be staying down. I tried a third piece.

The last letter was addressed in a familiar, flowing hand, and I broke the seal and unfolded it, a stiffer outer sheet over the inner, since it had come all the way from Florence.

Most Generous and Beautiful Lady, it read, *Once more I prostrate myself at your feet and pledge my undying affection for your interests. I write to you this 29th day of May in hopes of finding you well. I am very well myself, except for a certain pain in my knee where I twisted it, though that is of no concern to you, nor bears upon the subject of my letter.*

Dionisio Treschi was a dear and true friend, but he did take time to come to the point.

A very curious thing has come to my notice, and I bring it to yours. The other day a young gentleman recently come from Spain, whom I will call by his forename Mois, was introduced to me by a friend. He had escaped Granada, he said, with his two young sisters, having no idea if others of his family survived. He had brought with him certain valuable books the sale of which he hoped would provide enough money for him and his sisters to settle in some welcoming city.

Mois had heard that my old Maestro, Pico della Mirandola, was a scholar who would appreciate the books. However, as I have written to you before, della Mirandola has renounced all such studies and now attends only to the words of Friar Savonarola, even to the extent of burning his own works! Needless to say, I dissuaded Mois from taking these rare and possibly only copies of ancient texts to him! I am an honest man, Donna Giulia. I could not say that they were worth less than they are.

I raised an eyebrow. Dionisio could be excitable, but he did not tend to exaggerate to this degree.

They are very nearly priceless. I could not put a figure upon them. I told Mois so. His face fell, and he said that his sisters could not eat them. I said that I knew of a gentleman (and I did not name him!) who was both fabulously wealthy and who would appreciate these works and care for them as they deserve. If Mois wished it, I would contact a patron who could serve as agent for this most worthy gentleman. He agreed that would be best. And so it is with this in my mind that I write to you.

"But what are the books, Dionisio?" I said under my breath. "You have built up. Now tell me."

I hope that you will bring this matter to the attention of the august gentleman in question. One of them is written in the language of the Jews, of which I read but a limited amount. Mois says it is a writing on the nature of the universe, a Cabbalistic manuscript some two hundred years old. The other—Donna Giulia, I hardly know how to begin! The manuscript is very old, a scroll rather than a book. It is brittle. I did not dare to unwrap it far without recourse to a scriptorium and the best scribes who are accustomed to such old books. It appears at a guess to be a thousand years old or thereabouts, and to be a transcription made for the Roman Emperor Julian of the oracles of the Erythraean Sibyl.

I put the letter down and looked at it, putting the hunk of bread next to it on the table. "Really, Dionisio?"

When I saw it, I knew of its great worth, whether or not it is what it purports to be, simply based upon its age, its historical value and its condition. However, if it is the prophecies of the Erythraean Sibyl, a lost work from antiquity which is greatly to be desired, it is priceless. Madonna, I know of no one except the worthy gentleman you serve who could afford such a thing and who would care for it and conserve it. Friar Savonarola would see it on the fire, and he is not the only one. I beg of you, write to me in the affirmative so I may further this transaction to the good of all. Your loyal and loving servant, Dionisio Treschi.

I read the letter a second time. Then I reached for pen and ink. "Of course, Dionisio," I murmured. "What else would I say?" I had nearly finished my reply when Lucrezia came out. She wore a pink gown that complimented her coloring perfectly and was unconcernedly eating a small salami. I nearly retched. I could smell the salami from halfway across the balcony.

"Oh, sorry," Lucrezia said, hiding it behind her back.

"That doesn't help," I said.

"I'm sorry! I'll be right back!" She dashed back in the house to return without it a few moments later.

"I hope you haven't left that in my room," I said.

She went back in and was several minutes this time before she returned. "I forgot," she said. "Why does the baby hate salami?"

"The baby doesn't. Everything makes me ill right now. My mother says I'll feel better soon."

She slid into the other chair at the table. "My mother says she was never sick a day with me."

"Your mother is very fortunate," I said. I did wish Lucrezia had some judgment about telling everybody everything about everybody else. While Vannozza and I were certainly on speaking terms, I wasn't certain that I wanted my lover's former mistress of many years to hear every detail of my pregnancy.

Lucrezia glanced down at the letter from Dionisio. "What's this about?"

"My friend Dr. Treschi, who you may remember, is acting as agent for some valuable manuscripts he wants to sell your father," I said. Presumably Lucrezia did remember, as the events had been quite dramatic.

She looked up at me. "The man who conjures angels?"

"Yes," I said.

"Though it was you, wasn't it? Who actually called him?" Lucrezia inclined her head to the side.

"It was," I said. There was something that had bothered me at the time, but it had gotten lost in the chaos that night, and then Lucrezia had gone to the country with her mother and then it had been months later and it seemed pointless to bring it up. But now she had. "Did you truly see it?"

"Oh yes." She smiled. "The angel was beautiful. Just like a church window, all gold and light. It was quite amazing. Father says he didn't see it though."

I bit my lip. I wasn't certain what I'd seen, but I had definitely seen something. I had asked Rodrigo if he had seen anything as well. He had hesitated and then replied, "No, but I believe you did." That was the sort of answer that made one drop the question. And yet Lucrezia was perfectly matter-of-fact. "Are you going to call angels again?" she asked.

"I don't think so," I said. "I can't do things like that anymore."

"Because Papa forbids it?"

I shook my head. "I was what is called a Dove. That's a young woman who can see things in mirrors or be spoken to by spirits. But I am not anymore."

"Why not?" Lucrezia said curiously.

I put my hand over my belly. "My love, I'm not a virgin."

Her face wrinkled. "You have to be a virgin?"

"That is what I was taught," I said.

"That's stupid," Lucrezia said. "Men don't have to stop doing things if they fuck."

"Lucrezia, language!" I said. "Polite. Refined. Also men can't be Doves in the first place, so they're not losing anything."

Lucrezia sat up in her chair, folding her hands in front of her very precisely. "So virgins have all the ecstatic visions and talk to angels but can't be priests or cardinals. They can only be martyrs. Because being a martyr would be so much better!"

"My darling, I don't make the rules."

"I'm going to tell Papa that he needs to change that when he's pope," Lucrezia said.

"I don't think the pope makes the rules either," I said. "And it is far from certain that your father will be pope."

"My father changes every rule. Or breaks it," she said proudly. Which I couldn't argue with. It was not universally true, but it was certainly mostly true. He questioned everything as Lucrezia did, only with decades more experience and to better effect. No doubt at her age he'd been a holy terror. Lucrezia leaned against the rail. "If he were pope, would you still be together?"

"I certainly hope so," I said. At the very least there would be difficulties. Now we lived four blocks apart. Either I was at his house or he at mine nearly every day. It was a peculiar sort of domesticity, but it worked. How it would be managed if he lived in the Vatican, I wasn't sure.

"That was the thing Papa and Mama quarreled about," Lucrezia said matter-of-factly. "She says that she had no intention of being with someone she rarely saw who just dropped in stealthily to get it done. Carlo lives with her and they're together every day. She said she was never going to be a man's dirty secret when she didn't even have the man, and she'd have to be if he was pope."

"Lucrezia, your mother would not appreciate you telling me these things," I said. "You must learn discretion." I had guessed as much but didn't like to think about it. There would be some way to manage, surely.

"There must be something good about Papa being pope," Lucrezia said thoughtfully.

"Well, if he were pope, perhaps he could get Dr. Treschi out of trouble," I said, picking up the letter. "His maestro is charged with heresy and Dionisio is skirting charges himself. He would be in a great deal of trouble over the evening we were speaking of, if anyone knew of it."

"But it was to save Papa's life!" Lucrezia said. "And besides, Papa knows and he's a cardinal, so how does the Church not know?"

"Because your Papa knows how to keep his mouth shut," I said. "A lesson you could learn, Lucrezia. You don't have to say everything you know."

She sighed dramatically. "You keep saying that." She looked at me critically. "Don't you miss it? Being a Dove?"

"Sometimes," I said. "But I do not wish I were still a young maiden. I have traded one kind of power for another, as one does as one gets older. I would not like to be a holy virgin or a sister in a convent. I like my life."

"You have power?" Lucrezia put her head to the side.

"There are many kinds of power," I said. "And not all of them come with a title." I gestured to the letter. "I have the power to help my friend and his friends who need the books sold. That's important. And I hope I have the power to help your father's cause."

"How?"

"By cleverness and diplomacy. By connections and wit," I said. "There is an entire world that men barely realize exists, but the world of women moves all things beneath the surface."

"Like the queen on the chessboard," Lucrezia said.

"Your brothers can't play in that world, and I can. You will when you are old enough. It's not all swords and crowns and miters. Your father needs to sweep both boards to win."

"I don't understand what you can do that Cesare can't."

I sighed. "Cesare can never make the weak move." Her head tilted quizzically. "You know in chess sometimes you have to make a weak move to set up the board as you wish. Not every move can be aggressive. You can't attack unceasingly. You have to arrange your pieces with care, and sometimes that means not responding to a feint or withdrawing to a better position. Cesare is a young nobleman. Honor requires that he demand or threaten. He must always attack, never maneuver. He cannot conciliate or negotiate without appearing weak. I can. I can make the weak moves on your father's behalf because I am a woman and not subject to the requirements of a nobleman's honor. Your father will use us each according to our best purpose, just like pieces on the chessboard." I smiled at Lucrezia. "You will play on the board as I do before long. Ours is not the lesser board, my love."

She smiled, a perfect pink bow of lips that was the same expression as her father at his sneakiest. "I can't wait," she said.

Rodrigo arrived as Vespers rang, so we were four for dinner. Two years ago, when Adriana's son, my nominal husband, had been given the estate at Vasanello, she had moved from her suite to her late husband's larger one next door, so I had the rooms which had originally been hers. They were smaller than hers, but they had the balcony that I loved. We dined in Adriana's sala, Adriana and Rodrigo at the ends of the table and me and Lucrezia on the long sides, a very congenial party.

As usual, Silvia, our cook, presented a lovely meal, fettuccine in a cream sauce with new peas and Romano cheese, and a chicken fragrant with garlic and butter. It looked delicious. Unfortunately I was eating only the noodles, with a little butter to keep them from sticking together. My plate was very sad. Yet I knew better than to gorge on cream sauces and garlic that would simply make me sick.

Lucrezia was now a day student at a convent school for young ladies of good birth and returned home each day full of stories of her friends and their very mild adventures. I only envied her the opportunity a little bit. There had certainly been no schools for young ladies in Montalto, and when I was only slightly older I had lost my father and his care.

I had tutors now. Four days a week I gave my mornings over to the study of Latin, Greek, history, philosophy and theology, and was diligent in my studies. I had to run to catch up in this household. Rodrigo had graduated from the University of Valencia and then taken a law degree at Bologna. He had a library of more than three hundred books and had learned whatever he wished for decades. If there was any study I truly desired, I had only to ask, but there were gaping holes in my education.

I waited until Lucrezia had finished another amusing anecdote before I put in, "Rodrigo, who was the Erythraean Sibyl? And how were her oracles lost? I know of the Oracle of Apollo at Delphi, but I do not know the others."

He leaned back in his carved chair. "She was a prophetess in Ionia long ago—or rather a series of prophetesses, generations of women who claimed divine inspiration for their words. There was a shrine at a town named Erythrae supposedly from the time of the Trojan War." The candlelight glinted off his ruby cardinal's ring as he reached for his wineglass. "In ancient days there were eight sibyls, or perhaps ten, depending on which author was counting, who conveyed the words of the gods to men."

"And which god did she speak for?" I asked. "Apollo, as the sibyl at Delphi did?"

"Presumably," he said. "At least in later times. Though like Pythian Apollo, she may have originally spoken for the gods of the underworld." He gave me a little smile. "Persephone and Hades, whom we call Proserpina and Pluto."

I felt a chill at my back. I had once gone into a tomb and asked a favor of Proserpina, and he knew where it had led me: to him. "From the time of the Trojan War?" I said.

"Everyone always says everything happened from the time of the Trojan War," Rodrigo said. "Who's to know? But certainly it was a very old shrine in Herodotus' day. When the temple of Jupiter here in Rome burned in 83 BC, the prophecies of the Sibyl of Cumae that were there were destroyed, so the Roman Senate sent agents to other sibyls offering enormous sums of money for their books or to make copies of them. They brought back a copy of the prophecies of the Erythraean Sibyl, among others." He lifted his glass, looking at me over the gilded rim. "For more than four hundred years they were consulted by the Senate and Emperors alike until they were destroyed."

"Why were they destroyed, Papa?" Lucrezia asked.

"In a fit of overzealousness, like so many lost works," Rodrigo said. "Some of our Church Fathers believed that such pagan writings led people away from Christ. Or perhaps it was politically expedient at the time to be rid of writings that, if they had any accuracy, proclaimed the coming downfall of the Western Roman Empire." He took a sip, then put the glass down. "It's the same argument as today. Does ancient wisdom lead us to folly and should thus be suppressed? You will hear Cardinal della Rovere and the other Traditionalists making that argument now. This nonsense that the universities should be required to pair any non-Christian text with a Christian refutation! It's ridiculous. How would you have a Christian refutation of Euclid? Geometry is geometry."

"But it is not all geometry, is it, Rodrigo?" Adriana asked. "It seems this applies most to literature and philosophy."

"You support the freedom of the universities," I said.

"If truth cannot bear scrutiny, it is not truth," Rodrigo said. "I believe in the truth of the gospels and the mercy of Our Lord Jesus Christ. But if faith cannot be questioned, how can it be faith? Depriving ourselves of food for our minds is as harmful as depriving ourselves of food for our bodies." He shrugged. "Saying we will forgo all learning that is not Christian is silly. Will we go without double-entry bookkeeping because it was invented by Arabs?"

"And yet prophecy is somewhat different from bookkeeping," I said, "if it claims to be inspired by pagan gods."

"What are pagan gods but *daimones*?" he said. "Like unto angels, but neutral in form?"

"I don't think that's official doctrine," I said. It certainly was not, Dante aside.

"I find that very difficult to accept, Rodrigo," Adriana said. "Were not many Christians martyred in their names?"

"Assuredly," he said. "Every faith has its fanatics. Look at Florence. They have a friar who is preaching that all is vanity and that every household should give up their finest possessions so that they may come closer to God. God does not begrudge people footstools and carpets!"

"It seems to me," I said, "that lives of poverty and unhappiness more surely lead people away from God. Even an honest man will be tempted to steal when he is hungry! Even the most virtuous woman will lie down with strangers if she is starving. If we want people to be good, surely we must comfort them and protect them."

"And therein is the argument for charity," he said. Rodrigo looked at me, a little smile playing around his lips. "But that does not account for men like me, who have plenty and desire more. David was a king and yet stole Bathsheba."

Lucrezia put her head to the side. "Are you a very wicked man, Papa?"

"Only a little wicked," I said, and let Adriana change the subject as she wished.

After dinner he kissed Lucrezia goodnight and we retired. My suite was just down the hall and his hand was at my back as we went in and shut the door. "Are you still feeling unwell, Giulia?" he asked. "You ate almost nothing."

"I'd rather eat carefully and keep it down," I said. We went into the camera with my comfortable bed before the fireplace, now dressed with fragrant green boughs for summer. The balcony doors were closed but the shutters and curtains were open so that I could see the sky. I was tired of feeling unwell. Surely my mother was right when she said it would end soon! There was something else I'd meant to tell him. I began to undress while he did. What was it? "Oh, Fiammetta," I said.

"What about her?" Rodrigo asked. He was sitting on the other side of the bed.

"She's having a party next Saturday and asked if we'd like to come. I told her that we'd try, so don't make any other plans."

"Will you feel well enough?" He fussed with the pillows and covers, fluffing and arranging to his satisfaction.

"How would I know that now?" I lay down in just my camisa, my back to him, and he curled up behind me, his arm around my waist. Three months ago it would have inspired breathless desire. Now I appreciated his warm presence, but desire seemed elusive.

"Testy," he said without heat.

"I don't mean to be sour." I closed my eyes. "You could go without me if I'm not up to it." Which meant tossing him into a group of courtesans who would be delighted with his presence, the lambs Fiammetta had spoken of. It wasn't that I actually thought he'd prefer someone else, but I was hardly at my most attractive, retching and gagging and uninterested in bed sports.

"We'll see," he said. That didn't sound like he was eager to go.

I snuggled backwards with a little wiggle. He spread his hand against my belly. Quiet. Warm. "Rodrigo, what were your parents like?" Of course they'd been dead for years. I'd never meet them. And one day the child would want to know.

He didn't answer for a long time. Rodrigo rarely talked about his youth except in the most general terms. One would think he'd sprung full-grown as a Vatican clerk! And yet from the way he was a father to Lucrezia and her brothers I thought he must have had parents who loved him and taught him to love. I turned over so that I could see his face, settling down against his shoulder.

When he spoke, his voice was quiet. "I was the oldest of five of us, my younger brother and three younger sisters. My mother was very busy." He paused, as though recalling. "She had her hands in everything. She wasn't the kind of woman to leave her household to servants. She was everywhere, it seemed. My father saw to his own lands. Cattle, orchards…."

"Were you wealthy?" That sounded a lot like my own home at Montalto, which was not a great holding.

"No." He sounded amused. "Comfortable, perhaps. I was born in a little town, Xativa, a few miglia from Valencia. My father had inherited—I suppose I should call it an estate, but it was more of a farm. My mother's family were the Borja, a much more respectable family. Her brother was a canon of the cathedral of Valencia. I took his name, my mother's name, as one does in Spain if the mother's family is more distinguished, when I went to live with my uncle." His hand idly traced patterns on my skin. "My father was quieter. Gentle, really. He loved his lands."

"And his children?" I asked. I thought I saw the echo of that gentleness in Rodrigo when he was with Lucrezia.

"Yes," he said. He bent his lips against my forehead for a moment. "I was a very happy child. I loved learning. I loved pretending to be a knight on a perilous quest."

"Amadis de Gaula," I said. The well-thumbed book was in his library, a popular romance with all the adventure and long-lost relatives, convenient coincidences and sword fights one might wish.

There was a smile in his voice. "Yes. I was more interested in the perilous quest than winning the fair lady at that age. I thought a lady's favor was a fine excuse for an adventure."

"Well, it is," I said with a smile. Our hands twined around one another for a moment, then subsided with him stroking the back of my hand. He liked to touch me absently, constantly, as one pets a cat while talking.

"I imagine I was a lot like Lucrezia when I was a child," he said. "Sunny. Convinced that the world is a kind place where one is always welcome. Of course I learned better."

"I've thought you must have been like her," I said. I did not ask how he had learned better.

"I was intended for the Church, but that suited me. I liked my lessons and I liked the idea of seeing the world. I was ambitious."

I smiled. "Ambitious at that age?"

"I wanted power. How else does one gain power?" Rodrigo's voice was light.

"It is the best way," I said. "But what does a child want power for?"

"To order the world as he wishes, of course." Rodrigo's hand didn't stop caressing. "What else is power for, if not to make the rules?"

True enough. "And now you have power."

"It's much harder than it seemed then," he said. He raised my hand to his lips. "But the favor of the lady is more attractive."

"I will be Oriana to your Amadis at any time," I said, smiling.

"Complete with chaste adoration?"

"Not so chaste, was it? Didn't she bear him a child out of wedlock?" I said.

"There is that," Rodrigo said cheerfully. "I always preferred Oriana to Guinevere. Defiant, unchaste, stubborn as a rock."

"I do see you have a taste," I said, and settled back on his shoulder, drifting off to sleep while his hands traced meridians of unknown worlds on my flesh.

Chapter Two

iammetta's party was in a walled garden, a beautiful space which she had decorated to the greatest effect. It was dusk, Vespers had just rung; lamps hung from the trees, illuminating everything in a soft and enchanted light. There was a table laden with the Second Meal for people to graze upon as they wished while walking through her idyll, a lutist and a pair of female flutists performing beneath the colonnade, a space of lawn before them for dancing. Instead of chairs, she had arranged piles of pillows beneath the trees.

Rodrigo wore a doublet in saturated pink, and pieced sleeves, pink brocade and a matching solid cloth with gold on every seam, the vertical stripes making him look quite trim and handsome. I wore a gown in pink a shade darker than his over a camisa so fine the cloth was practically transparent where it showed on my sleeves. "You look like a rosa mundi," Rodrigo had said, speaking of the rich pink and white old roses out of tales of courtly love. That made me smile.

Fiammetta met us with both hands outstretched, a kiss on each cheek for me and one for Rodrigo. Her gown was apricot, a color that was beautiful with her red hair and creamy complexion. A decade older than me, Fiammetta had reigned in the night world for nearly fifteen years. She'd been fourteen when the previous Cardinal Piccolomini had installed her lavishly as his mistress. A year and a half later he'd died leaving everything he had to her, a vast fortune.

His family had appealed to the courts. He'd been in his seventies—surely he'd taken leave of his senses to disinherit the family he'd cherished for decades in favor of a wanton girl! The dispute had gone all the way to the Pope. He'd made a Solomonic decision to divide the estate between heirs. Fiammetta had merely gotten three houses, two of them palazzos in town and one at a vineyard in the country. She lived in the grandest of the palazzos, rented the other for good money, and also had the proceeds of the vineyard. In other words, she could choose her patrons as she wished, and she did so discreetly and temporarily. No man owned her.

She had welcomed me kindly to her world two years ago, I expect at Rodrigo's request. I did not ask either of them if they had been lovers. It was plain they were friends now, and if there were any more to it, they had had ample opportunity to discover that. In short, if she wanted him she would have had him already, so there was nothing to be jealous of.

"Oh my goodness! You look positively glowing!" she exclaimed, embracing me. Fiammetta smelled like orange flower water. "Rodrigo, look at this girl! Obviously you've made yourself very agreeable!"

"She's my sweetness," he said, lifting my hand to his lips with a little smirk. He did like his virility commented upon.

"Oh, you know he is agreeable!" I gushed back. "I am the most fortunate of women." It was a naughty little play on the Annunciation and they both laughed.

"Let me find a seat for the Virgin, then. Giulia, my dear, would under this tree suit you? It looks very comfortable," Rodrigo said.

Fiammetta turned to greet the next guest and we claimed a lovely stack of pillows under an almond tree, Rodrigo fussily arranging them to make a comfortable seat for me and inquiring after my health and comfort half a dozen times. If there was anyone who didn't know I was pregnant, they knew it now. If he'd hired a crier, he couldn't have announced it louder.

Of course this resulted in a stream of well-wishers, mostly sincere. Some of the men couldn't care less but wanted an excuse to talk to Rodrigo. He lounged beside me on the pillows like a sultan, holding court with a wine glass in one hand. A servant brought us a plate of savories, which I left to him. I wanted to enjoy the evening, not make myself ill; and while in the last day or two I had felt much better, I was not certain I was up to olive paste and oil-preserved fish. Then I did see something I wanted.

"Oh my goodness, Rodrigo!" I exclaimed, interrupting him. "Are those strawberries? Would you please, please get some for me?" At the table there was what appeared to be a big bowl of them.

"Of course. Anything for my lovely girl," he said with a little bow and excused himself to the gentleman he'd been talking to.

"Must be nice to have a cardinal at your beck and call," he said. He was a young man with cynical eyes.

"It is, rather." I simpered. I held out a hand. "Giulia Farnese. And you are?"

"Giani de Bastian, aide to the Most Illustrious Doge of Venice's Ambassador." He bowed over my hand quite correctly.

"And what does the Most Illustrious Doge desire of Cardinal Borgia?" I asked.

"He would like to know when Cardinal Gherardi's elevation will be published. The Pope raised him to the College of Cardinals in March. It is now June and he is yet to be listed or seated. Cardinal Gherardi is eager to join in consistory," he said.

Given that Cardinal Gherardi was eighty-four years old, one expected he was in a hurry! He'd been the Patriarch of Venice longer than I'd been alive, and Pope Innocent had raised him to be a cardinal as a sort of reward for decades of good service, a last honor more or less on paper to cap off a distinguished career. Whether he'd ever make the journey to Rome, or whether in fact the College would go into session before Innocent died were both good questions. However, when Innocent died the Doge no doubt wanted to ensure that Venice had a voice in the election of his successor, even if that voice were eighty-four himself.

"Alas, I cannot say," I said. "You know the Pope is unwell. I am certain that the College will meet at his pleasure when he is recovered."

Giani de Bastian nodded slowly. "Of course," he said. He looked as though he were phrasing his question carefully. "And if His Holiness should be taken from us? The Vice-Chancellor will support whom?"

"A worthy successor," I said. "There are many devout and honest men. I am certain he will support a cardinal who has the future of Our Mother Church firmly in mind."

De Bastian caught the key word: future. "Cardinal Carafa?"

"Cardinal Carafa is a great scholar," I said. I shrugged. "But there are other brilliant men as well."

"Certainly." De Bastian bowed. "I do appreciate your time and insight, Madonna."

"Naturally," I said, and let him take his leave.

Rodrigo returned with a bowl of strawberries, each perfect ruby fruit the size of my smallest fingernail. "Brought from Lake Nemi, so Fiammetta insists. Wood strawberries for my lady." He sat down beside me, putting the bowl in my lap. "What did de Bastian want?" he asked quietly.

I popped a strawberry in my mouth. It was an explosion of flavor, the first thing I'd tasted properly in weeks, absolutely luscious and luxurious. "To know if Gherardi will be seated before the Pope dies. And who you will support," I said softly.

Rodrigo smiled as though I'd whispered some endearment. The party swirled around us. "And you said?"

"Carafa, of course. But not committed."

"He does not think me *papabile.*"

I ate another strawberry. It almost melted in the mouth. "Of course not, my love."

"It's best not to show my hand too soon," he said. "The first horses out of the gate will be the ones tripped. Best to run steady in the pack. There's no need to be a target, and I know I can get Carafa's votes when I need them."

"Carafa wants a Humanist," I said. "That's more important to him than his personal ambition. If it looks like you're the Humanist who can win...." I put two more berries in my mouth. They were practically a sensual experience.

"I'll have his votes. Those are assured." He picked up a strawberry and fed it to me, smiling as my tongue touched his thumb as I took it. "There, my pet."

De Bastian looked back across the lawn at us, distracted from his conversation with another man. I bit my lower lip like a woman transported. If we were going to put on a show, best a good show. Cardinal Borgia was a voluptuary. As long as he had his pleasures and his women, he cared nothing for politics except where it convenienced him. After all, he'd been a cardinal for thirty-six years, longer than anyone else. If he'd never missed a meeting in consistory in thirty-six years except when away on official business, it was simply that he was a steady goer. A good Vice-Chancellor. A reliable coin-counter. A man whose vote mattered, perhaps, but hardly pope material. Not while feeding strawberries to his pregnant concubine. The Doge would no doubt have a detailed letter to this effect.

I settled back against Rodrigo on the pillows, his arm around my back. The musicians were beginning a new set. "They're very good, aren't they?" I said. We listened while I ate strawberries.

"They are. Are you sure you should eat the whole bowl?"

"It's the only thing that's tasted right in weeks," I said. "And

I'm feeling better." I closed my eyes, leaning back on his arm. The night air was soft and filled with music and the murmur of voices. The lanterns swayed a little in the gentle breeze. The pillows were comfortable and Rodrigo warm. I glanced up at him. He was watching the dancers, relaxed and at ease, smiling with pleasure, his other hand holding the bowl against my almost-flat belly.

I will always remember us this way, I thought. For a moment it was as though I stood a long way away, looking back. My breath caught.

"Are you ill from the strawberries?" Rodrigo asked, looking at me with concern.

"No," I said. The strangeness was gone. Just a pulse of fear remained.

He misunderstood the reason. His voice was comforting. "It will be well, Giulia. You're a young and healthy woman. There's no cause to think it won't go well. Of course it's natural to worry, but you and the baby will be fine."

I took a deep breath. That must be it. The natural fears of a breeding woman. "I know. My mother had six. She says it was always like this for her."

"So." He put the empty bowl on his other side. "Your mother knows what she's talking about. Do you want her to come and stay with you?"

I shook my head. "She can't possibly be gone that long. Bartolemeo is too young to manage on his own. I may ask her to come closer to time." My mother ran Montalto, of course. Though it was a small holding, Bartolemeo wasn't but fifteen. He wasn't able to handle things for months without her.

"As you wish, my dear."

I leaned back against him again. The lutist ended one song, the two flutists making pretty bows; three lovely young ladies joined him, laughing and demurring that they were terrible and it was silly for them to sing before he gave them the chord and they began, beautifully of course. They swayed together, voices in harmony, a performance that was clearly practiced for all they pretended it was spontaneous. They were younger courtesans, I thought, my age or younger, Fiammetta's protégées whom she was giving a chance to shine. Their performance was charming and very good.

As the rest of it was. I looked about at the groups seated under the trees, the servants with their impeccable, silent service, the courtesans with their schooled charm. It was all performance. Fiammetta created an idyll, a bucolic scene, a play that we could all walk into. The courtesans were actors on this stage as surely as the flutists, the lutist and the singers. Their rapt attention to a man holding forth on a book they hadn't read or the foibles of an artist they'd never heard of, the gentle hand to the sleeve as though admiring the arm within it, the pealing laughter at an old joke—it was performance intended to delight. It was the seeming of love, just as the sweet phrasings of the singers were.

It wasn't really love, of course. Frothy, beautiful, delightful, but ultimately no more than a dream, a fleeting pleasure conjured by players—real love is not so silken or smooth. I leaned my head against Rodrigo's shoulder and felt him smile, bending his head to brush his lips against my hair.

"My dear," I said, twining my fingers with his. I did not pretend interest in a discussion of whether Plutarch or Arrian's account of Alexander the Great was best or perform desire for his body. It was entirely real. And if art might improve physical pleasure, no more so than scholarship improved the joy one took in reading. After all, the more one knew, the better one could enjoy and appreciate the beauties before one, whether those were ancient statues, works of literature, or the lines of muscle and bone beneath flesh. Performance too can be joy. Rodrigo had taught me that.

The young ladies ended their song to a smattering of applause. They giggled, making bows with their arms around each others' waists. A gentleman I didn't know called out, "How about Elissa?"

He was looking at Fiammetta when he said it, and she smiled. "Elissa? Our celestial ornament?" Fiammetta looked meaningfully at a woman standing near a flutist, though she shook her head, demurring.

"Elissa!" someone else called. "Come on, Elissa!"

The woman was much older than I, perhaps thirty-five, with dark hair caught in elaborate braids and a gown of blue so dark that in the twilight it looked black. Her eyes were outlined in black against her pale face just as her white sleeves shone against the dark cloth. "Oh, no," she said, "I couldn't possibly."

"One dance?" the first gentleman said. "Put your hands together for Elissa!" I realized that he had been put up to it, probably by Fiammetta, and that this was all another bit of prearranged spontaneity.

Amidst applause, she stepped out in front of the musicians, who of course totally accidentally knew what to play for her. The music was sensual, the beat of the drums intoxicating, and one of the musicians handed her a tambourine which she took in her right hand, holding it quiet against her skirt, her head turned in profile, eyes closed. And then Elissa began to dance. It was slow, like a snake unwinding its coils. She moved very little but each step was deliberate, each movement of her arms, each flutter of the tambourine an exclamation. She showed nothing. No leg, no breast, but each movement was a huntress stalking her prey. The music supported her, lutist and drum, wild as something at a village fair, dark as the Etruscan tombs.

I glanced at Rodrigo next to me. He was watching with a little smile, and I felt a small, unworthy stab of jealousy. He hadn't looked at Fiammetta's protégées that way.

And yet there was something rather sad about the dance, more sad than seductive, as though the desire she invoked didn't touch her at all. She was dancing for them, not for herself. It wasn't just that following a group of girls half her age made her look old. She looked as though she'd done this too many times and this was just once more. I was still trying to find words for what I felt when the dance ended to thunderous applause. "Brava, Elissa," Rodrigo shouted once along with many others, then turned back to me, reaching for his wine glass.

"You know her?" I asked.

"She's been part of Fiammetta's circle for years," Rodrigo said, and took a drink.

"An excellent party, don't you think?" a voice said, and I looked up. Cardinal Ascanio Sforza looked down. Forty or so, with a smooth, bland face, he looked harmless enough. He wore blue instead of his cardinal's robes, the badge on his hat showing the Sforza arms of the snake devouring a child.

"Won't you join us for a moment, Ascanio?" Rodrigo said, sitting up straighter and gesturing to the pillows on the other side.

"For a moment." Sforza sank down gracefully, not spilling a drop of the dark red wine in Venetian glass in his hand. "Donna Giulia, my congratulations."

"Thank you, Your Eminence." If one were listing front runners for betting before a horse race, Ascanio Sforza would be in the third spot. He was a competent, ambitious man from one of the great families, a ruthless family eager to produce a pope. A dangerous man, whether enemy or friend.

He toyed with the stem of his glass. "I hear an interesting story. I wondered if you'd heard the same." He watched Rodrigo's face. "The Gonfaloniere intends to ask the Pope himself for extra troops to provide security in Rome this summer. Just in case, you understand."

There was nothing lazy or complacent in Rodrigo's face now. "That's very interesting." I felt a chill run down my back. The Gonfaloniere was Virginio Orsini, the lord of Bracciano, who had originally brought me to Rome for convoluted and unpleasant reasons of his own.

"I thought so," Sforza said. "Asking the Vice-Chancellor for money to hire men would be fruitless, of course."

"Of course," Rodrigo said. "We have plenty."

"But if the Pope himself were to order it...." He let his voice trail off. "In the event of unrest if the Pope were to die, it would be useful to have more men, wouldn't it? To prevent trouble."

"Or to intimidate those in consistory," Rodrigo said in the same tone. "Knowing that the Gonfaloniere's men controlled Rome."

"But it is difficult to speak against such a course, is it not?" Sforza asked. "After all, we all want to prevent unrest."

"And yet is it really necessary?" Rodrigo asked. "Aren't his troops already sufficient? That's an argument one could make."

"If more than one person made it...." Sforza took a sip of his wine. "Someone who was disinterested?"

Rodrigo smiled. "Am I disinterested?" I said nothing, just posed at his side, part of his persona.

Sforza spread his hands with a smile as if to say, *We all know who the front runners are, and I am one and you are not.*

"I'll have a word with His Holiness," Rodrigo said. "It is to no one's interest to have undue pressure on the electors. After all, we all want a fair vote."

"That was what I thought," Sforza said. He got to his feet. "Giulia, Rodrigo. Always a pleasure."

"Absolutely, Ascanio," Rodrigo said, and watched Sforza leave.

"Bracciano." I closed my hand on his.

"Easy, my sweetness." Rodrigo leaned back, settling me against him, my head on his shoulder and his eyes on the musicians. "I'm glad to know it, and now Ascanio owes me."

"Not enough," I said.

"Not enough. Not yet." He raised my hand to his lips as if he murmured some romantic thought. "But every favor goes on the account."

"If Bracciano has bravos all over the streets while you're locked in consistory to elect the new Pope, and all the cardinals know that they're shut in while their families are in Bracciano's power...."

"Bravos are one thing. Troops are another. I think I can stop the latter, if I've got Sforza on my side. Unnecessary expenditure, foolish waste of money and all that." He glanced sideways at me, as if to see if I was steady, to see if I feared Bracciano too much.

I made myself smile, as though he had indeed whispered something tender. "I presume you're sending Lucrezia and Gioffre to the country with their mother."

"As soon as I can," he said. "I'd thought two weeks from now, but sooner is better. Vannozza will want to be well out of town before he dies." He turned my hand in his. "You could go to Montalto."

I could. My mother would welcome me home, given the stream of money I'd sent northward over the last two years. Bartolemeo and Angelo and little Girolama had a good tutor. My mother had enough servants to make her life more comfortable and many little luxuries that made it more pleasant. And I would have my mother during my pregnancy.

And I would have my mother during my pregnancy. I was used to being my own mistress. I wasn't delighted about reverting to being her little girl. On top of that, I hardly wanted to abandon the field just before the battle I had prepared for. I wasn't that far along. I could surely stick to it. And Rodrigo. I had no illusions that Bracciano had tried to kill him twice and might again. If I fled and something happened to him, I would never forgive myself.

Besides all that, it mattered what I did. And that was the thing I could not forget. I smiled into his eyes. "I can do you no good in Montalto." He just waited. "If I were near my time, perhaps. But that's months away. I'll stay in Rome."

"Very well." Rodrigo kissed my fingertips, his eyes not leaving mine, as though I had said the most romantic endearment. And perhaps I had.

After a bit I went to find the necessary, stopping to chat with a few people on the way back. One of them was Cardinal Raffaele Riario, whom I had met on a number of occasions over the past two years. Barely thirty and member of the Humanist faction, he'd been invited to a number of intimate dinners at my house on Rodrigo's behalf. Tonight he looked splendid in yellow silk with pale blue ribbons on his sleeves. "Donna Giulia, always a pleasure," he said with a little bow. Unlike most cardinals who made at least a gesture in the direction of a correct clerical haircut, he wore his hair long and flowing on his shoulders like a poet.

"Your Eminence," I said with a smile that was entirely genuine. Riario had a gift of making everyone like him, unlike his surly cousin, Cardinal della Rovere.

"I didn't expect to see you tonight. I heard you were indisposed," he said.

"I'm feeling much better." I looked out over the crowd in the garden, now walking about and getting plates while the music had stopped. "And what are you reading today? You always recommend the most interesting works."

Riario laughed. "I have begun the *History of the Hungarians* by the Bishop of Lucera who has just returned from two years at that court. There is a great deal in it that I did not know and many worthy rulers whose lives are obscure to me."

"I know little of it myself," I said, "other than King Matthias Corvinus, who was a towering ruler."

"It is Queen Beatrice who commissioned the work," Riario began.

"Raffaele Riario," Elissa purred, coming up and twining her arm with his. "You're looking well."

"As are you, my dear lady," Riario said, attempting to bow with her holding onto him. "Your dance was lovely as always. Giulia and I were just discussing the *History of the Hungarians*."

"Are you from Hungary then?" Elissa asked, "I've heard you come from somewhere obscure."

"Alas, no farther than Tuscany," I said.

"Hungary is a fascinating kingdom," Riario said. "I once entertained a Hungarian musician who was a virtuoso on an instrument I'd never heard before."

"But you are a musician," Elissa said, "unlike Giulia, who does not sing a note."

"It's true I'm not a singer," I said. "Nor do I dance well, as you do."

"Practice makes perfect," Elissa said, holding tight to Riario's arm. "Raffaele, will you come meet this lutist? I think he'd be wonderful at one of your parties."

"Of course," Riario said, with a little nod to me. "Another time, then."

"Certainly," I said, and watched Elissa drag him off like a puppy on a leash. Fiammetta had come up beside me. "Why in the world does she dislike me so?" I asked in a low voice. "I've never done a thing to her. I barely know her."

Fiammetta sighed, looking out across the garden full of delights. "Because you have so easily what she wanted."

"Rodrigo?" I could hardly imagine Elissa in love with Rodrigo.

"Or any cardinal." Fiammetta's eyes were kind. "He's rich and his purse is always open. I expect she had him a few times several years ago, but it didn't stick. And you have it all. You're young and beautiful and lucky. Now you're having his child and he'll set you up for life. Look at Vannozza. She's got a beautiful house, investment properties, and a good business with the vineyard and winery."

"I haven't asked Rodrigo for investments," I said. I couldn't imagine being so crass, particularly when he gave me far more money than I could spend. "I'm not after his money."

The musicians began tuning up, a dance tune now, and couples scrambled laughing to form a set under the swaying lanterns on the trees.

"You can afford not to be," Fiammetta said. "And so can I, at this point in my life. But most can't. It's a business. You must have well-paying customers. I do my best to help my friends, but the truth is that most of them are going to wind up like Elissa. She's thirty-five and she hasn't made it. No rich patron who gave her a house, no nest egg to live on later, and she's running out of time. Sooner or later it will be the long, slow fall to the convent or the brothel. Or then the street." She pointed with her chin at the protégées who were giggling and asking men to dance. "You're a concubine, not a courtesan. You know who you're going home with."

I felt myself coloring. "Rodrigo, of course. But...."

"Giulia, I don't begrudge you good fortune. I've had some myself. But for you, this danger isn't real. It's one more illusion." She looked up at the softly lit lanterns. "Have some compassion for Elissa. She's never going to get Rodrigo or Raffaele or anyone like them."

"I do," I said. It was unutterably sad. I knew exactly why if she'd been with Rodrigo it hadn't lasted. He wanted someone who wanted him, not who pretended to because he was rich. I was not pretending. Of course he knew the difference. He had sampled all the world's delights and understood exactly how much joy could be had from virtuoso performance, but he wanted more. He wanted to be loved, not just to enjoy the illusion of it. "I will be kind, Fiammetta."

We left Fiammetta's house before midnight, four of Rodrigo's guards escorting us back to Adriana's palazzo. There were four already there. An entire set of rooms on the ground floor had been opened as a guardroom since the assassination attempt two years ago. Added to that, Rodrigo always had at least two when he was on foot in the street and so did I. It was unwieldy, but necessary. I knew he missed being able to simply walk around Rome as he used to. At least I wasn't instantly recognizable yet if I was not elaborately dressed. However, the princes of the Church were famous. Everyone knew his face.

My rooms were dark and quiet, the window shutters and balcony doors closed. I took off my gown and shoes and hose and opened the doors, going out into the warm night in just my camisa. The city was lit here and there with lights, the stars above bright in the summer sky like the lanterns in Fiammetta's garden. The moon was just rising, full and round. Rodrigo came out behind me, putting his arms around my waist, burying his face in the long fall of my hair. "Did you enjoy yourself tonight?" he asked.

"You know that I did," I said. "It's fun to play those games with you."

"You like being bad." There was amusement in his voice.

"I do," I said. There was something arousing about being just a little wicked, licking his fingers while he fed me strawberries and called me his sweet pet. "You'll stay?"

"It's late." It was only four blocks to the Vice-Chancellor's palazzo, but it was after midnight.

I turned in his arms, a sweet and tender kiss that turned passionate. Desire uncoiled deep in my belly. The last month I'd felt nothing, entirely unlike me, as though some part of me were missing. Now it came roaring back. Like strawberries, he was delicious. We went inside, the doors left open to the summer night. "Galatea," I whispered.

"Whatever you would like." He was smiling as he stepped back, watching as I pulled my camisa over my head and stood nude in the moonlight. The pale beams illuminated me as if I had been carved from marble. I spread my hands in invitation. "Exquisite," he said. Rodrigo walked around me, lifting my left arm so that it extended over my head, adjusting the curve of my elbow, the attitude of my wrist so that my fingers continued the line rather than curving over my head. I felt a frisson down my back at his touch, but did not move except as he moved me.

He came around, not touching, but judging the effect. I felt my privates throb. This waiting, this being seen, this being shaped, was utterly heady. "Your hair," he said. His eyes were hot and calm at once, arranging my long hair over my right shoulder, covering one dark nipple modestly, the full sweep of it below my waist.

And behind me again, a finger tracing my shoulder blade. "Weight on your left foot, right knee bent." I complied. "Lovely." Part of the game was that I did not speak, not until the end. I thought I knew which statue I was, Venus Genetrix. Utterly appropriate. His hand brushed against my hip as he turned, the casual caress given to a beautiful and precious thing. It made me gasp. I bit my lip.

He'd nearly made me move prematurely. He watched me with a sensual smile as he arranged my right arm, a modest curve of fingers before my privates as though I wished to conceal with opened fingers. "Beautiful." He trailed a touch across my belly, upward to my newly sensitive nipples, and I inhaled sharply. So sensitive. The lightest touch set me on fire. I almost lost my balance.

Rodrigo smirked. "One would think she was flesh, not marble. Statues don't generally tumble over when you touch them."

I couldn't answer. Not yet. He passed behind me again. For the longest moment there was nothing. Then he kissed my shoulder, a lingering, open-mouthed exploration to the back of my neck, gathering my hair out of the way, lifting it up gently to bare the nape of my neck. I could feel my pulse below.

I arched my back, leaning back involuntarily into him. The touch of his brocade doublet against my naked flesh, the warmth of his mouth, his hand at my waist so that I wouldn't fall…I closed my eyes. It was like a sensual dream half-remembered in morning.

And yet it affected him as surely as me. I felt his breath shudder as he ducked his face against my shoulder, the sculptor overcome by what he wrought. I didn't move. I just leaned against his solidity. His hand slipped around me, beneath mine, parting folds to touch sensitive flesh.

Now I did nearly fall over. I took a quick breath and heard him chuckle. "The most beautiful statue." Still holding me with his arm around my waist, he turned around me again, body to body, and kissed my lips.

A statue coming to life. I leaned into him, warm and hard against me, my left hand descending to twine around his neck, fingers tangling in his hair. "My Pygmalion," I whispered against his lips. It was quite a while before either of us could talk again.

Afterwards, we lay among the tangled sheets, body to body and heart to heart. My body still rang like a bell. The moonlight made a path across the room. I closed my eyes. "My sweet angel," he said, and laid his head against my shoulder, and sleep took us both.

I woke chilled and reached for him, but he was not there. The sky was gray flushing a little pink. Lauds must have rung. I turned over. He had put his long shirt back on and was kneeling on the other side of the room, his head bent over his hands. Lauds. I pulled the covers over me, trying to get warm again. The linen was soft, the room cool in the dawn.

In a few minutes the bed gave as he came back, crawling in behind me, fitting against me like spoon to spoon, his bare legs against mine. I laced my fingers with his around my waist. "What do you pray for and then come back to your concubine's bed?"

He didn't answer. I should not have asked such an intensely personal question. I turned in his arms, curling tight by way of apology. That was between him and God. I had no right to pry. And yet he did, his voice low. "What does Lucrezia say when she talks to me? She tells me of her day. She has petty complaints and stories that delight and things that flittered through her mind. She asks me for things she knows she won't get and explains why the things she has done aren't so bad, really." Rodrigo put his chin against my forehead as I lay on his shoulder. "All of that, I suppose."

Beloved son, I thought. *That is what you are to God. Loving father is what he is to you. Perhaps you are wayward or difficult but you mean well, an indulged child who is nevertheless a source of pride. Like Lucrezia, you are secure in love and favor.*

He craned his neck to see my face. "Giulia?"

"Just wondering," I said, "if it will change you when you win. When you are Pope." What would it be like to be the living embodiment of grace? What would it be like to be God's earthly habitation?

"I expect so." His voice was calm. "I don't know."

I closed my eyes. "And will you give me up? God has millions of people who love Him, and I have only you."

"No, I won't give you up." He kissed my forehead. "No, my darling. How would it be good or praiseworthy to hurt you, an innocent creature who has done nothing but love me?"

Not so innocent as that, I thought, nor so pure in motives as he wanted to believe, but I did adore him. And, I reasoned, if God didn't mind his unchaste life enough to deny him the papacy, He wouldn't mind if he kept it up! Rodrigo was Rodrigo, and surely the Heavenly Father knew that.

"You are going to win," I said.

"Such confidence in me." He sounded both amused and gratified.

"I know it in my bones," I said. Had I not seen, three years ago in the reflection in the water in Proserpina's cave, white slippers embroidered with pearls and gold?

Chapter Three

The next day I had an appointment with my new confessor, Father Donato. Rather than in one of the confessional booths in St. Peter's, it was in an office; Rodrigo did not want his business poured out in the Nave, and also I was hard on confessors. Father Donato was my fifth in two years. I had flatly refused to see the first again after he continued to insist I must submit to Orsino. The second had wrecked on the shoals of women, who should not pursue scholarship nor discuss scriptures as St. Paul had said they should be silent in church. The third had begged off after seven months claiming he was too ill to continue to see me. The fourth had requested lascivious and unnecessary detail to the point where I wondered if he were tending to his needs privately afterwards, and I asked Rodrigo to find another priest. Obviously, Rodrigo could not be my spiritual counselor himself. He could hardly be the cause of my sin and its forgiver at once!

By now I rather resented the entire business. Fiammetta was a more useful counselor. But Rodrigo was certain that biweekly confessions were necessary for my spiritual health, and quite determined that he would not be the cause of my soul's downfall for lack of twice monthly scrubbing. I had at least put him off from weekly, which was his own usual practice, so to my new confessor I went.

To my surprise, Father Donato was perhaps five years my

senior and quite handsome, with light brown hair and thoughtful blue eyes. Most middle-aged men would not want their concubine spending time in a private room with such a fetching young man, so the selection indicated that either Rodrigo trusted me implicitly or that Father Donato only preferred men. The office was small, one of the offices off the finance section, with sun coming in a side window onto a desk with a closed ledger, from which I deduced that Father Donato was more often employed as a bookkeeper than confessor. Thus he probably knew my brother, Alessandro, who was a finance clerk, a more senior position in the same department. I wondered if Alessandro had recommended him. *Poor man*, I thought. *Caught between the Vice-Chancellor and a senior clerk in his own department!*

I seated myself opposite him in another chair, folding my hands demurely. "I am Giulia Farnese," I said.

"Madonna." He had a little furrow of worry between his brows. "I am to hear your confession."

"Well, then," I said sharply. "How shall I begin? Do you prefer alphabetically or chronologically? Or in order from most serious to most venal?"

He opened his mouth and then shut it again, and yet his voice was mild. "However you prefer, Madonna."

"Then let me begin with the most obvious," I said, a sweet little smile on my lips. "I am the concubine of Cardinal Borgia and I am not the slightest bit sorry."

"You aren't." He looked a bit perplexed.

"How should I be?" I asked. "He is in every way the kindest and most amiable of men, and I love him with all my heart. I am no whore, Father. My marriage was a sham marriage left unconsummated for more than a year so that it could be annulled when a more advantageous match appeared for my husband. I have been with no other man besides the most generous and loving of protectors, who treats me with the greatest consideration. I do not repent of my actions in the least nor do I intend to change them." I folded my hands again. "There. You have pride and defiance both. So this is a rather pointless exercise for both of us."

His frown deepened. "So you won't repent and be absolved and then do it again?"

I put my head to the side. "Father, if I believed something was wrong, I would not do it. I do not believe that what I do is wrong, so I will not lie and say I repent when I do not. Surely God would not be deceived."

His blue eyes searched my face thoughtfully. "Why do you believe it isn't wrong?"

No one else had asked me that. I answered truthfully. "I don't believe God expects me to spend my life in an unhappy sham marriage."

"Your marriage could have been annulled, it seems," Father Donato said. "And you could marry someone else."

"But not the one I love," I said. "He may not marry. And so I am wife to him only in my heart. But I could be no truer companion, no more devoted partner, if we were wed. I will have no other, and I consider his happiness as he considers mine." I opened my hands. "I am here because he is concerned for my soul and wishes me to have a confessor to confide in who is not his."

Father Donato glanced aside. "And yet he's the Vice Chancellor and I but a humble priest."

"Short of having a cardinal as my confessor, it can hardly be someone of equal rank," I pointed out.

"True enough." He examined my face again. "And if you could marry this man, would you?"

"Of course," I said. "In a moment, if he would have me and could. And I do not see why it is not so. I have read enough Church history to know that in the early Church there was no requirement that priests be unmarried, nor is there now in the Eastern Church. Indeed, even in the West chastity was not required or expected for many centuries." He looked surprised, and I hurried on. "So this is why it is unwise to allow women to study history. It gives them defiant ideas."

I thought he was trying to suppress a laugh, but he answered thoughtfully. "And there are many marriages in the Bible which would not be allowed today."

"King David had many wives, yet we would not permit any sovereign today to have more than one," I said. "And who, pray tell, married Adam and Eve? Did they not simply cohabit in a state of nature as they wished?"

"As do many of the common folk," he said. "They do not ever marry in the Church but call each other husband and wife and live as though they were. I cannot find that so sinful."

"So I do not repent," I said. "And therefore you cannot absolve me, rendering this pointless."

"I was going somewhere," he said, holding up a hand. "There are rules, which are much less important than sins. Breaking a rule of the Church is not the same as a sin. Rules change. Rules are different from place to place. Every bishop in the world wrangles with petitions about whether someone can marry their half-second cousin once removed or their uncle's widow. The rules about that change all the time and one ruling supersedes another." He looked like Alessandro did when he was figuring out some thorny mathematical problem. "So do you think you could repent of not following a rule? That you are disobedient to the rules is a sin, but hardly a mortal one."

"As though this were only a rule?" I considered. It did lighten something in me that he took this seriously rather than upbraiding me. "I cannot be sorry for what I do," I said slowly, "but I can be sorry that I must break the rules of the Church to do it; at the same time I can think the rules are wrong, and that this is simply a rule imposed at the First Lateran Council in 1123."

"Then perhaps you can repent of disobedience," Father

Donato said, "And I will assign you prayers and grant absolution, without you repenting of your love for this man."

I took a deep breath. It did indeed ease my heart to be heard, and for him to agree that this was simply a rule. I had not quite put it that way to myself, and yet it was. Marriage had only been prohibited for priests for a little more than three hundred years, and that by the ruling of a council no different from the quarrelling prelates of today. I could disagree with them and still be sorry that I had to break a rule of the Church. "Yes," I said quietly. "I can do that."

"Then let us pray," he said, and I bent my head.

After confession, I thought that I might ask the archivists if they knew anything of the Books of the Erythraean Sibyl, since I was already in the Vatican. In the last two years Rodrigo had given me many beautiful things and opened many doors for me, but perhaps the one I loved most was the Vatican Library. One of the finest libraries in the world, it was a peerless collection of modern and ancient works, original scrolls a thousand years old cheek by jowl with chronicles of the last century and the latest printed works. If, like Ptolemy Soter, one wished to collect every bit of knowledge in the world, the Vatican Library had made the best stab at it.

Of course I had no business whatsoever setting foot inside. It was for serious scholars, churchmen and archivists, and the Vatican staff who cared for it. Even men of letters were admitted only by special permission. That a cardinal's concubine should use it was scandalous. Young women did not belong in libraries, and certainly not women of doubtful virtue. And yet the staff could hardly gainsay the Vice-Chancellor when he brought me with him. Wearing my most somber clothes, I stood with hands clasped like a penitent nun while he introduced me, explaining that by his own special permission I should be allowed to read within the library, though not of course remove any materials. The clerks had exchanged glances. Could I even read Latin well enough? Did I have the mental capacity to understand what I read? Traditional thought said no, though that was entirely stuffy and old-fashioned in Rodrigo's opinion. Lucrezia went to school and had tutors. Obviously even young girls had the mental capacity.

He showed me the system of the library, which books were kept where and what the shelving scheme was, splendid in his red robes, handing down a volume with gloved hands for me to examine. His eyes lit at my delight. As always, it pleased him to give pleasure.

The first time I returned without him, I had quaked inwardly. The silences, the stares, the horrified glances…. They did not forbid me, nor say anything that I could complain to Rodrigo about, but it was intended to be intimidating to be watched ceaselessly, a clerk standing four feet away while I read, not even pretending that he did anything besides stare at me. Therefore I read Thucydides calmly for more than an hour, my clean hands only touching the corners of the book. I do not remember what I read, but I read. And I returned a few days later to pick up where I left off.

After a week or two it paled to watch me sit at a table turning pages serenely. It was boring. They found other things to do. When Rodrigo asked me if I enjoyed it, I told him that I loved using the library. It would not help to have him shout at them. They would simply hate me more and resist more strongly women ever using the library. As it stood, it would be harder to deny the next member of my sex since the sky had not fallen from my presence. Better to simply wear away stone with inexorable water.

Two years later, my presence had become unremarkable. A clerk looked up when I entered, nodded at me, and returned to the book before him. I nodded back and made my way to the room of modern, printed works. It's always best to begin with the moderns and then seek their sources. Besides, the printed books were not locked up, and thus could be readily perused without requesting a specific volume be retrieved. I was not entirely certain which book I might need. After all, the Prophecies of the Erythraean Sibyl were lost.

To my surprise, Burchard was there, three books in his arms as he searched the shelves. He was the official chronicler of the papal court and in charge of the etiquette for many official functions. I had met him the first time I had come to the Vatican, a reedy, tall German with blue eyes and a perpetually distracted air. "Burchard!" I said with genuine delight. "How nice to see you."

He jumped, a guilty expression on his face. "I am returning books," he said. "Donna Giulia, what brings you here?"

He must have borrowed some to take to his own home to read in his leisure, hardly a terrible offense, though I supposed it wasn't entirely proper. I would certainly say nothing of it. "I am looking for information," I said, "and I am not certain where to begin. You are very knowledgeable. Perhaps you might direct me where to begin. I would like to learn about the Erythraean Sibyl."

"Which one?" Burchard asked.

I blinked. "Which one?"

"There were many women who filled that role over centuries. To ask for the Erythraean Sibyl is akin to asking for the Pope," Burchard said. "It's a title, not a person. Well, it's one person at a time, but who it is…you understand."

"I do," I said. "So we know who the sibyls were? As individuals?"

"Some of them. We do not have a full list, as we do of popes, but we have some names. There was Berossea of Babylon who was the daughter of the scholar Berossus, Erymanthe who foretold the Trojan War, and Herophile who predicted both Alexander the Great and Our Lord's Nativity. The last is one of the notable women Boccaccio detailed in *De Mulieribus Claris*, of course."

Burchard could be a little pedantic. "No, I have not read it," I said. "I have read *The Decameron*, but not his other books. *Of Notable Women*?"

"It is a collection of short biographies of about a hundred famous women from antiquity to the last century, his own lifetime." Burchard put the volumes he had been holding down on a table. "I'm sure it's here. There has been a printing in the last ten years. I'm sure we acquired it." He hunted along the shelves, then plucked out a volume and handed it to me. "This!"

I opened the good leather cover. My heart sank. The title page was beautifully engraved, the printing clear and dark. And in German. "In German," I said.

Burchard blinked. "Er, yes."

"Surely Boccaccio wrote in Italian," I said. "He predates the printing press, so perhaps there is a hand-copied volume." He was still looking at me. "I do not read German," I said. "Italian, Latin, some Greek and a little French. But not German."

"It's possible we have an Italian copy," Burchard said. "We shall find it."

"I am very grateful for your help," I said.

"It is nothing." Burchard led the way out of the printed room toward modern hand copied works. He glanced at me, a little twist at the corner of his mouth. "I presume His Eminence has need of it for some reason."

There was no harm in telling Burchard. "Someone has approached me to sell His Eminence a manuscript concerning the Erythraean Sibyl. Before I direct his attention to it or tell the seller that he would not be interested, I would know more about it."

"Ah!" That was a reason Burchard could entirely approve of. "His Eminence does collect interesting books."

"So I have discovered," I said. "But I do not want to waste his time. I appreciate your help."

"It should be here," Burchard said. And yet it wasn't. It was not properly shelved, nor on any adjoining shelf. Burchard searched with growing annoyance. "Someone has borrowed it," he said.

"That's the problem with popular authors," I said. Boccaccio's

Decameron was very entertaining. "People want to read them."

"Rather than leaving them quite properly in the library." Burchard was almost entirely solemn. I would have thought so if not for the twinkle in his eye. "Books should not be removed and read."

"As you never do," I said.

"Certainly not."

I sighed. "I wonder if I can find a copy to buy."

"That I cannot say," he replied, "but Christine de Pizan also discusses Herophile in *The City of Ladies*. I know that is in a popular print edition."

"Is it here?" I asked. Honestly, he could have said so to begin with!

"Alas, no," Burchard said. "The Vatican Library does not purchase books written by those of the female sex."

"Ah," I said tightly.

"Just so." Burchard said. "It renders the collection incomplete."

"I see that it does," I said. "Well, I will have to seek a copy from a bookseller." I wasn't surprised, just irked. If Rodrigo became pope, I expected that directive to be changed promptly. After all, the integrity of the collection required it. "Thank you, Burchard. You have helped me so much."

"It is nothing, Madonna," he said. There was that little smile again. "Remember me to His Eminence."

"Of course," I said, and took my leave.

A few days later Rodrigo informed Lucrezia that she was going to the country with her mother. Needless to say, Lucrezia was not happy.

"I do not see why I should go to the country if Giulia is staying." Lucrezia put her hands on her hips, meeting her father's eyes firmly. "Juan is staying."

"You are much younger than Juan," Rodrigo said. "Four years. And Giulia is a woman who can make her own decisions."

"If it's safe here for Giulia, it's safe for me," Lucrezia argued. "We live in the same house with Donna Adriana. If it's safe, there's no reason I can't stay. And if it's not safe, why is Giulia staying when she's expecting a baby?" She had a point.

"It is not entirely safe for me," I said. "But I have work to do on your father's behalf which I cannot do if I leave Rome."

Lucrezia rolled her eyes. "You're going to stab people?"

Rodrigo was letting me carry this myself, which I thought wasn't entirely fair. "I am going to persuade people and bribe people," I said, "and have conversations your father can't have when he's locked up in the Vatican to vote."

"While Cesare stabs people," she said.

"Nobody is stabbing anyone," Rodrigo said. "This is a papal election, not a grand melee!"

"Is there a difference?" Lucrezia asked, a smile on the perfect bow of her lips. "In a grand melee every fighter piles in and hits anyone and everyone until only one is left standing. He wins." It did bear a certain resemblance.

"Yes," Rodrigo said. "And I hit with money and influence. Not stabbing people. That's not how it's done."

I wasn't entirely sure that was true. Bracciano, the Gonfaloniere, had already tried to kill him twice. Rodrigo had sworn to return the favor at some future date. And yet I saw the point of trying to reassure Lucrezia that all would be bloodless. She was barely twelve. She needed to go to the country with her mother and her younger brother, Gioffre. Unfortunately she was bright and understood perfectly well that Rodrigo wouldn't send her if he were certain there would be no violence, even if he was more worried about city mobs in the interregnum than assassination.

I was frankly more worried about assassination. He was a big, scarlet-clad target, and he went around the city on foot with only a pair of guards most of the time. It would be easy for some accident to befall him. But what was the alternative? He hated traveling in a litter, and frankly it was no safer. On horseback would be better. Perhaps I could persuade him to ride more often. But that was not a conversation to have in front of Lucrezia.

"You are going to the country with your mother. There is no more argument," Rodrigo said sternly.

"There's always more argument," Lucrezia said. She usually wore him down.

"I am not hearing it." Rodrigo raised his voice, his own hands on his hips. "My decision is final. Your mother is taking you to the country and you are leaving tomorrow with her. There is no more discussion, Lucrezia."

Her face crumpled. "I hate you," she said. "You're so mean!" With that she fled to her room, her muffled sobs floating down the hall as she ran upstairs. He spread his hands helplessly.

"She is at a very uncertain age," I said. How could one explain the emotions of being a girl of twelve? I remembered the age too well myself and squirmed at some of the things I had said. "She does not really mean that she hates you. She means that you will not do what she wants."

"Giulia, it's not safe for her."

"You don't have to persuade me," I said. "I understand perfectly well. And I would not stay if I thought I could not manage. I will take every precaution."

"I've sent for Cesare," Rodrigo said. He paced around the sala, a model of nervous energy. He had waited for this for years. Now it had almost begun. "He's coming from Pisa."

My brows rose. "You are that certain it is time?" He had been reluctant to end Cesare's education until it was absolutely necessary.

"Yes." He stopped at the other end of the room. "It's time."

I nodded. "I will make certain Lucrezia gets off tomorrow."

"She has to go." He looked like he was wavering now that his temper had fled. Lucrezia really did have him wound around her fingers.

"Of course she does," I said. "She is twelve, as you've said. Lucrezia is too young. If you are worried about how she is taking it, I will go up and talk to her."

"If you would? I shouldn't have yelled at her."

"Lucrezia would try a saint," I said, coming over and kissing his cheek as I went to the door. "And you are not a saint."

"Hardly." The corner of his mouth quirked with amusement. As I went past, he swatted me on the bottom. I rewarded him with a very theatrical squeal.

Lucrezia was tossing clothes all over her room, two red spots high on her cheeks. The door was cracked but I knocked. "Lucrezia?"

"Come in," she said, throwing another gown across the foot of the bed and plopping down next to it. "Are you here to say Papa changed his mind?"

"No," I said. I closed the door behind me.

"It's not fair," she said. "I wish I were a boy like Juan."

"Juan is also four years older than you are," I said. "If you were four years older, your Papa would let you stay."

"If I were four years older, I'd be married and it would be up to my husband instead of Papa. But even then I couldn't do the sword-fighting parts," Lucrezia said. Her mouth pursed. "If I were a boy, I would be a prince. I'm smarter than Juan and I'm as good at chess as Cesare and my Latin is better. If I were a boy, I'd be the Gonfaloniere when Papa is pope. I'd rule cities and command armies!"

"I expect you would, my dear," I said. That was no more than true.

Her blue eyes fixed on me. "How can you be so sweet about it? Don't you wish you could be a prince?"

"Not really," I said. The words came out unthinking; I had never put it thus even to myself. "If I were a man, I would be a priest."

Lucrezia's mouth twisted as though that were the most boring thing she could think of. "Why would you want to do that?"

"So that I could know union with God," I said. "When I watch Alessandro or your father celebrate Mass, I envy that brightness. I wish I could feel what it is that moves them so. I wish I could be God's hand, even for a moment." I surprised myself with the longing in my voice. "I'm good enough in every way. I'm as good a scholar as Alessandro. I can dispute as well as any of your father's clerks. I'm as good at politics as Cesare. If I were a man, I'd be your father's protégé."

"But not his lover," Lucrezia said. "He's not interested in sodomy."

"That is true," I said. If he were, no doubt he'd indulge in it. "And I would miss what I have. One cannot have everything."

"One can try," Lucrezia said darkly. "Why can't women be priests?"

I sighed. "Because God made Adam in His own image, and Eve was an afterthought. Men are made in the image of God. Women aren't."

"Papa could change the rules." Lucrezia pursed her lips.

"My darling, your Papa can't change that, not if he were pope. Women can't be priests. They never have been, not in all of Church history."

"Ever? Anywhere?"

"I suppose they were once, in the old pagan religions." I carefully folded one of Lucrezia's sleeves, pale blue silk with matching ribbons. I wondered where the other one was. "The Vestal Virgins. The festival of the Bona Dea." I could think of some examples, certainly. "Cybele. Isis. They had female priests."

"Did they know that…thing you mean?" Lucrezia was a little vague on what I meant, or why I would want it.

"The embodiment of grace? I don't know," I said. "But that is
the thing I envy." I put my hand over my belly. "I don't want to be a
man. I suppose I do want to be a priest. But that is not possible, my
dear. I would be miserable in a convent and I would still not have
that." I laid her sleeve on top of her dress. "I certainly don't want
to be a cloistered visionary. If I were a priest, I would minister to
a congregation. Even a female saint, my dear, may not know the
sacrament of ordination, and that is what I crave."

Lucrezia looked at me blankly. Clearly such a desire had never
occurred to her.

"So we must all do what we can do," I said briskly. "What you
need to do is go with your mother so that you are safe until you can
enter the fray. It won't be long, Lucrezia."

"I hope not," she said. "I can't wait until I'm a married woman
instead of a child!"

"That will be soon enough," I said.

Naturally Rodrigo was too busy to take her to her mother's house,
and Adriana professed herself otherwise occupied, so I had to do
it. There was no animosity between me and Lucrezia's mother,
Vannozza, though I can't say that we were friends. She was my
own mother's age, and Cesare and I were contemporaries. She and
Rodrigo had ended several years before I met him, and she was
quite happily married to a man of her choosing, but I suspected
she thought me a fortune hunter, as so many others did. We were
cordial when we met for Lucrezia's sake more than Rodrigo's.

Her house was halfway across town, near the Church of St.
Peter in Chains, and Lucrezia sulked the entire way. Of course
Vannozza had to offer refreshment since the day was warm, and of
course I had to accept so as not to act as though I thought myself
her better; so we sat down in her restrained and tasteful sala, the

shutters open to the square below, drinking well-watered wine and making small talk.

"How is the little one?" she asked, an eye on my belly. "Lucrezia said that you were feeling better."

"Much better, thank you." I did wish Lucrezia had somewhat more tact.

"When are you due? You carry so nicely I wouldn't have known if Lucrezia hadn't told me." My gown was high-waisted, and it's true I wasn't showing much yet.

"The first of December," I said. "So I have a long way to go."

"A little more than halfway." She took a sip of her wine, her color high and flushed in the warmth of the day. Vannozza was blond like Lucrezia, but more honey than gold, with the pink and white complexion that artists so admire. "I hope Rodrigo's made good provisions for you."

"Yes, thank you." I cast about for a subject to change to. My financial relations with Rodrigo weren't something I particularly wanted to discuss. "He says he has no opinions about a name for a boy, so I will think of something. Though he doesn't like my father's name, Pier Luigi."

"Well, of course not." Vannozza looked at me over the rim of her glass. "That was the name of his son that died."

"Your son?" Lucrezia had never mentioned another full brother.

"His Spanish son," Vannozza said, and I kicked myself. Pier Luigi was of course Pedro Luis, the one who had been killed fighting for the Spanish crown the year before I met Rodrigo, the son of Rodrigo's first concubine. "He was named for Rodrigo's brother who was murdered."

"His brother was murdered?" I had certainly never heard that either.

Vannozza shook her head, offering me a plate of anise biscuits. I took one gingerly. "Not two years younger than Rodrigo. They came to Rome together with their uncle when he was made a cardinal, the only Spanish cardinal at the time. Rodrigo was for the Church, Pier Luigi for the sword. When their uncle became pope years later, he made Rodrigo a cardinal and Pier Luigi the captain of his personal guard. Well, and their cousin Luis de Mila was named a cardinal too."

"Adriana's uncle," I said. "I knew that connection."

"They were close, the brothers. Mind you, I didn't know Rodrigo then, and not for years after. But everything went to shit when their uncle, Callixtus, was dying. The mobs were roving around town calling for Spanish blood and looting the houses of Spaniards. I remember that part well enough." Vannozza took a sip of her wine. "Pier Luigi decided the game was up and decided to take the guard and try to get out to Civitavecchia and a ship to Spain. His own men mutinied on the way and murdered him. Knifed him and threw his body in a ditch. He never did have a Christian burial."

I shivered despite the warmth of the room. "And Rodrigo?"

She shook her head, a rueful little smile at the corner of her lips. "Went back to the Vatican. Said that if the mob would have him, it would, but that God would protect him and he wouldn't let his uncle die alone."

I could feel the cold horror of it, Rodrigo not so much older than I, and this terrible choice. "That was wisest," I managed.

"It wasn't wisdom," Vannozza said quietly. "He loved his uncle."

I felt the blood rush to my face. "I didn't mean...."

She shrugged. "Of course you didn't. But Rodrigo likes to pretend that he always acts out of some careful master plan that's so intricate and clever that no one else can possibly understand it. It's all some scheme in his own self-interest. It's not. Half the time he's just making it up, same as the rest of us." She took a biscuit from the little plate. "His uncle raised him from the time he was six. He'd been brought up in his house, not like Pier Luigi who had just come to Rome when he was a cardinal. Rodrigo was the son the old man never had. And he was more or less Rodrigo's father."

"Why was that?" I asked. Rodrigo never talked about his parents, not more than the snippets I'd managed to pry loose from time to time. I didn't like sounding ignorant to Vannozza, but the temptation to ask was too strong.

"His father was killed when he was six. Some kind of accident on the farm." She took a delicate bite. "It's the usual story. A piece of land that's all the wealth, a young widow with four children and one more on the way. Too many mouths to feed and no man of the family. Her older brother was a canon of the cathedral in Valencia. He offered to take the eldest to live with him. Raise him in town. Send him to school. The Church is a good career." She shrugged again. "It worked out."

"Yes," I said, and I could not say more. A family like my own, a posthumous baby who would never know its father, and the eldest sent away to school, to the Church, hoping he could pull the others up. Only Alessandro had been seventeen when he became the man of the family, not six. "Rodrigo was a baby," I said.

"He loved his uncle," Vannozza said. "So he went back and stayed with him as he died. Either God loves him or they were afraid to loot holy ground, but Rodrigo lived through it. And Pier Luigi died." Her eyes met mine. "Some might say everyone got what they deserved, the brother who was true and the brother who was false, but Rodrigo took it hard. He named his first son after his brother. But I expect he's thinking the name ill-fated now, and best not for that babe of yours."

"No, I'll not name a child Pier Luigi, though it was my father's name," I said, and let the conversation turn to other things.

With Lucrezia gone the house seemed quite empty, though we did have a small dinner for intimate friends in the Humanist faction each week, and Rodrigo entertained lavishly at the Vice-Chancellor's palazzo. Normally in summer things quieted down, but not this year. It was as though everything spun in a terminal frenzy. Soon the battle would begin. There were a limited number of opportunities beforehand.

My nineteenth birthday on July 22nd was celebrated with a fireworks show in Rodrigo's courtyard followed by a dinner for forty. There were Catherine wheels at the gates. Men stood by with buckets on the tile roof to douse the burning sparks, and the entire neighborhood turned out to watch the rockets crest over the roof and melt into flowers of gold.

I stood by Rodrigo applauding madly as each one rose, bursting in red showers, the smell of gunpowder filling the air. He knew I loved fireworks. The end of it was five rockets at once, breaking in blue and gold flowers as if Farnese lilies unfurled on a blue field. Everyone clapped, and I kissed Rodrigo on the lips. "So beautiful!" I said.

"Happy birthday, my darling." He put his arm around my waist, raising his other hand to cheer for the men who had set them off, a little old Florentine and his assistants. I imagine he was quite expensive.

As the clouds of smoke began to clear, servants went around outside the gates with trays of almond biscuits, while the guests for the dinner began to make their way inside. I had a dozen well-wishers vying for my attention.

Naturally, Alessandro was there. My brother was a clerk at the Vatican, a responsible—if in his opinion somewhat boring—job in finance. Still, it was a good position at his age. Rodrigo had secured it for him, of course. He was the Vice-Chancellor and all of the Vatican's money moved through him. Alessandro was still my best friend. I never ceased to be grateful that I had a brother who was so dear to me despite all the changes in our lives. While I had made many friends in the last two years since I became Rodrigo's concubine, none of them had known me before. I always felt a certain reluctance to confide. I was always aware that my thoughts and feelings were tempting gossip, not just to Fiammetta but to all the women I knew. I didn't want my relations with Rodrigo discussed in the same chatty, offhand way that they discussed others. It felt private, sacred even. I did not want daylight to fall on our underworld.

Fiammetta was not at my birthday party, however. She had sent word that she was "visiting a friend" and would be back a few days later. I didn't ask who. If she wanted the gentleman's name known, she would certainly tell me.

My other close friend was Caterina Gosette, whose lover was one of Rodrigo's clerks. He was young to afford a mistress but Caterina made light of it, telling amusing stories of life in third-floor rooms over a fishmonger's shop. She had a sister in Viterbo, however, and had left a few days before to stay with her until all this was resolved. "I won't see him a moment when they lock down, and it's safer to be somewhere else," she'd said. I couldn't disagree. After all, her Eugenio didn't have guards to leave with her! It only occurred to me after she left that I could have invited her to stay with me. Rodrigo wouldn't have minded and there was plenty of room.

There was dancing after dinner. We led off the dancing together, ten couples turning like stars beneath the painted ceiling, the Borgia bull ornamenting the coffers. The image of stars gave me an idea. Perhaps next year the theme of the Carnival masque should be celestial. I would mention it to Rodrigo. We had not done that, and it was an idea that would lend itself to beautiful costumes. If there was a masque next year. Who knew what would happen?

Rodrigo turned me neatly round him, smiling, one hand tucked at the small of his back, his posture straight. He was a good dancer.

He was, I thought, by far the handsomest man present, even if he was not young.

There was a servant in livery trying to catch his attention, and I sank into a curtsy as the music ended. He bowed deeply, glancing up. He saw the man as well. "Giulia...."

"Of course," I said. He was never entirely free of work.

He looked over my shoulder, beckoning to someone. "Here. Lead the next set." He lifted my hand, putting it into the hand of a young man who had just come forward, red doublet embroidered lavishly with gold, sleeves pieced with velvet. "Juan, be so good as to dance with Donna Giulia."

I curtsied as Rodrigo hurried off trying not to look as though he were hurrying. The music began again. "Donna Giulia." Juan Borgia bent over my hand, the first step of the figures.

"Just Giulia," I said. Lucrezia's middle brother had only turned sixteen, reckoned a man for all social purposes. He was very, very conscious of it. In fact, he'd probably had more to drink than was polite for his father's table this early in the evening, but when one is first allowed adult parties, one tends to overdo it.

"As though you were my stepmother." His voice was just a little too loud. He was going to say 'instead of my father's concubine' next, which was true but not polite.

"And you my baby boy," I said. "Shall I tell you to behave, little one?"

"You'll need Papa for that," Juan said. "Unless you'd like to spank me?"

"Clearly you don't need to drop your pants to show your ass," I said.

Juan laughed too raucously. Yes, he'd had too much to drink. No doubt he'd regret it tomorrow. If he made a fool of himself, Rodrigo would make sure he regretted it. "You're fast."

We turned, side by side as we began the processing steps. "And you're drunk," I said in a low voice. "It appears juvenile not to be able to hold your wine. Calmly, for the sake of your reputation." I smiled at him as we turned away and then back. "You have charm and money. Don't waste them." As it was, it looked like witty repartee. If he kept it up, he'd look obnoxious, and that would be noted. He straightened up, clearly attempting to imitate his father's bearing. He bowed over my hand on the turn gracefully, and I smiled. He could do well if he tried.

The set ended and I let him lead me from the floor. I looked around for Rodrigo, who was just coming back from the saletta. He stopped and said a few words to someone, but he was clearly distracted. I made my way over to him as smoothly as possible. "My darling, may I have you for a moment?" I led him around one of the columns, dropping my voice. "What's wrong?"

"I've had a messenger from the Vatican," Rodrigo said, his voice equally low. "The Pope has taken a turn for the worse. He collapsed insensible. He has been put to bed and the doctors called."

I took a deep breath. "Oh dear," I said. I looked out across the dance floor. The music played. Cardinals and courtesans, nobles and daring young wives turned like errant stars in their courses while outside these walls the world shifted. I could almost feel it like a murmur beneath, a rumble too faint for hearing. "Do you need to go now?" I asked.

He was looking as I was, his mouth tightening. "No," he said at last. "It will cause alarm. And there is nothing that being there will get me that being here won't." Rodrigo glanced at me. "Better to play it coldly."

I nodded. "Whatever you need me to do."

"I need you to look joyful," he said. The set was ending. He snagged a glass from the tray of a passing servant, stepping out into the middle of the floor. "Gentlemen, gentlewomen, and those of you who are not gentle!" A ripple of laughter ran around. "It is my very great pleasure to wish a delightful birthday to the brightest star in our firmament, La Bella Farnese!"

I smiled, turning left and right in my glittering gown as people applauded. Alessandro stood at the back, smiling over a woman's bejeweled head. "May the best of all things be yours." He bent deeply over my hand, his lips brushing the back of it, and people applauded again. He lifted his glass. "La Bella Farnese."

"La Bella Farnese." The toast was drunk, and I did my best to look modest.

"Thank you. Thank you so much for coming to my party," I said sweetly. "I love you all."

The night of the 24th Adriana and I dined alone. There was no moon. The city seemed to wait in a kind of breathless darkness, like the moment before a storm breaks. We kept beginning conversations and then letting them languish and trail off. And yet we did not leave the table but lingered, both of us reluctant to retire alone.

We both nearly jumped out of our skins when there was a banging at the street door. It was well after Compline. "There are guards," I said.

"Yes," Adriana said, sitting back down very deliberately. "Eight men in the house."

"And they will not open the street doors without cause," I said.

"True." She looked at me across the table. The fear in her eyes belied her calm voice.

And now footsteps on the stairs. I stood. One of the guards knocked on the door to the sala. "My ladies, Cardinal Borgia."

I nearly fell over. Adriana clutched the edge of the table. "Of course my cousin is most welcome," Adriana said.

He wore his full red robes, a billow of silk buttoned tightly at sleeves and neck, no doubt monstrous in the heat. I hoped that abroad in the city tonight, dressed like that, he had a full complement of guards with him. But he would. Rodrigo was not careless. He swept in, the guard closing the door behind him. "Adriana, Giulia."

I avoided nothing for Adriana's sake. I ran to him, gathered into his right arm. "Rodrigo, what is happening?"

"The Pope is dying," he said bluntly. "He has not spoken since last night, and before that he could take no nourishment except a little breast milk as one does for an invalid. He runs a fever." Rodrigo shook his head. "He has taken no liquid since yesterday afternoon and is not conscious."

Adriana nodded. "Not so much as another day, then."

"No." Rodrigo looked at me. "Rumors are rampant in the city. I hear from my own guardsmen that the story is that a Jewish doctor was called who killed a Christian infant and fed the Pope his blood. What nonsense! As though a bevy of Cardinals would allow such a thing! As though any doctor would do it!"

"Is there a Jewish doctor?" I asked.

He glanced at me keenly. "Yes. And it was he who prescribed the breast milk. It has more virtues than other milk, being our first food, and sometimes may cause someone ill of a disease to rally. But it is useless against these tumors in the abdomen."

"What will happen when he dies?" Adriana asked.

"We will go into conclave to elect his successor." Rodrigo paced across the room. "I believe we will wait several days. Cardinal Gherardi is on the road from Venice, and there is at least one more voting member who is expected to return to Rome. We will wait for them." His robes practically snapped around him as he walked.

"And in the meantime?" I asked.

He turned at the far end, looking at me. "You know what to do."

"The city…" Adriana began.

"Will be chaos." He came back to us, the three of us making a triangle. "There will be mobs. Looting. Fighting between various factions. I've just come from my palazzo and I'm returning to the Vatican. Once we go into session, no one can enter or leave the Vatican, certainly not us." He shrugged. "It will be days, possibly weeks, though hopefully not."

"I'm ready," I said. I had my instructions. Cesare had his. I had my plans with Alessandro. "Where is Cesare?"

"He's here in Rome. He and Juan are taking three donkeys laden with silver to Cardinal Sforza," Rodrigo said. His eyes were laughing. "For safekeeping."

"Ah," Adriana said.

"You'll hear the bells when he dies. Cesare will come to you when he has more information." I nodded. It was far safer for Cesare to chance the streets than me. "I'm leaving six guards here," he said. "And once we are locked in, the guards who escorted me to the Vatican will come here. I'll have no use for them there. Use them wisely."

"Of course."

"Are you sure that's enough guards?" Adriana asked.

"Unless you're planning to be invaded," Rodrigo said. "Stout house, all windows high or barred, solid oak gates. Ten men should be enough."

"You sent Lucrezia to the country," Adriana said.

"And should you wish to join her, take guards," Rodrigo said shortly. "Giulia, I've arranged for Alessandro to be one of the clerks who will be locked in. But he'll have a great deal more latitude than I do."

"We have a way to communicate," I said.

"Cesare can't be locked in. I need him outside." He took my arm. "So, me to Alessandro, Alessandro to you, you to Cesare. Yes?"

"Yes," I said, my chin up. "Whenever you go into conclave, we're ready."

"Good girl." He squeezed my hand. "There will probably be a few days when everything is in flux waiting on the absent members.

Stay off the street. If you need money transported, Cesare has men."

I nodded. "Rodrigo, be careful."

He smiled, and it was a wolf's smile. "My sweet, it's you who must be careful. You'll be out here with the mob. I'll be locked in with my worst enemies, all of us being very polite and praying at each other. Nothing worse will befall me than malediction. But you are out here."

With the Gonfaloniere and worse, I thought. Not all his enemies would be locked in. We were playing on two overlapping chess boards. "Cesare and I can do this," I said. "Your orders will be obeyed."

"It's not simply my orders," Rodrigo said. He drew me away from Adriana, leaning close as though to say something dear. "I can't know what's going on out here. You and Cesare will have to respond appropriately. I have every faith in both of you."

I took a deep breath. I knew how hard it was to let go of the reins and to simply trust us, but it was true that he could not know. "Will I see you again before the conclave?"

"I don't know." His eyes searched my face. "It depends on how long we wait for the absent members and what's happening. We could lock in tomorrow or a week from now. If it's days, I'll try to see you and Cesare." He took a step back. "I need to go now." He nodded briskly to Adriana. "Good night, Adriana."

"Wait," I said, and heedless of Adriana wrapped myself around him, drawing his face down to mine. He smelled of torch smoke and himself, and I kissed him like I'd never let go. Was this the last time I'd kiss him completely as himself? Or the last time at all? He enveloped me, a swirl of scarlet silk around me, his mouth hard on mine as though he would drink down a week's pleasure in one gulp.

And then he pulled back. "My Giulia." He put his hand to the side of my face, a single caress. "I must go."

"Good night, Rodrigo," I said, and he was gone, the guards coming to attention as he swept out the door and following him down the stairs.

I listened until I heard the street doors thump shut, the bar falling into place. Adriana was watching me with a curious expression. "You truly are devoted to him, aren't you?" she asked.

"Yes." Was that not obvious by now?

"You derive so much good from him," Adriana said. So many clothes, so many toys to be his plaything…. I almost heard the rest of the sentence.

"Is it not possible for self-interest and love to lie together?" I asked.

Adriana laughed. "Like politics and ideals?"

"Just so," I said.

Her face sobered. "One man will win. The others will lose. If he loses, it's not Rodrigo who will suffer, locked in under solemn guard. He plays chess as though he were the king, and if he sacrifices some pieces, that is the game."

"I am the queen, not a pawn," I said. "One does not sacrifice the queen lightly."

"Unless one must," she said. Adriana frowned. "Giulia, I am worried for you. Do you not understand that? You should have left for the country when you could, not stayed to do his bidding when you're breeding. He should have made you leave."

"He gave me a choice," I said.

"Which was no choice!" Adriana said. "He knows you, Giulia! He knows you will not be called a coward! He gave you a choice knowing what you would do for your own respect—his bidding, no matter how it endangers you. Is that an act of love?"

"To trust me as he trusts his sons, whom he loves?" I said. "He loves Cesare and Juan and does not send them away."

"They are not women and carrying his child," Adriana replied. She shook her head. "He does you wrong in this."

I knew she spoke from concern, and yet I would not let her sow these doubts again. I embraced her instead. "Dearest Adriana," I said. "I know you are worried for me. But I am perfectly all right. I will be safe here with you. Now let us retire and rest as we can. Tomorrow may be trying."

Chapter four

The quiet lasted through morning and into afternoon, all of Rome taking a deep breath before the plunge. Three hours after noon the bells began. St. Peter's was first, and then each church took up the mournful toll—the Pope was dead.

I went to the balcony, looking out over the city. Heat lay upon it. Not a cloud showed in the flawless blue sky. The bells rang over empty streets, closed doors and boarded shops. It was like some other place I had seen once, I thought, some great city in an unquiet dream. Darkness would bring pandemonium. I put my hand to my belly, feeling the slight movement like a ripple in a stream. Twenty-one weeks since I had bled. "There, my dear," I said to the child. "There. It is only the bells you hear. You are safe."

There was a movement in the street three floors below. Two men and two women hurried along, glancing constantly behind. They each carried bundles and burdens, one man leading, a hat with a drooping plume on his head. The other man followed, closely guarding the two women. They passed too low for me to see them further. Did they come to our door?

I frowned. I expected Cesare. Why would he bring two women and another man? And while there was something familiar about the man's gait, he did not walk with Cesare's confident stride. They did not reappear. They must be at our door. I turned and went out through my camera and sala, down to the vestibule. Yes, one of the guards was remonstrating with someone through the door.

"If you will simply tell Donna Giulia my name," the voice on the outside said, "I swear to you that she knows me!"

Our guard was having nothing of it. "So you say."

I came down the last stairs. A solid oak door with a bar was between us and the street. "What seems to be the problem?"

The guard turned. "Donna Giulia, there is a man here with several people who says he is known to you and would speak with you. I'm under orders to admit no one without permission."

His voice carried through the door. "Donna Giulia!" shouted the man outside. "It's me! Please let us in! I'll explain everything!"

"Dionisio Treschi," I said.

Adriana came in from the garden side. "Who is it?"

"A man who has worked for me and for the Cardinal before," I said.

"Please let us in!" Dionisio begged. "I have the thing you commissioned!"

The books. He was standing in the street with priceless books, today of all days. "Open the gate and let them in," I said. "But stand ready until I say."

"Madonna." The guards opened the door, one still ready with his halberd.

Dionisio Treschi scuttled through, followed by another young man and two women, one looking about her with a steady and appraising gaze, though she couldn't have been more than fourteen or so. The other was even younger, maybe twelve. The seller and his two young sisters, I thought. "Dionisio, have you lost your mind?" I said. "This is the least safe place you could have brought your friend and his sisters! Do you understand that the Pope just died?"

Dionisio sketched a deep bow. "Donna Giulia, allow me the great honor of presenting my scholarly colleague Mois Sarfati. And these are his sisters, Chaya and Sincha. My friends, this is Donna Giulia Farnese, the very great lady of which I have spoken.

And…" He looked at Adriana's stormy face and faltered.

"And Donna Adriana de Mila," I added. "My mother-in-law."

"At your service, my ladies," Mois Sarfati said with a graceful bow. He was perhaps my age, handsome and lean, with a neatly trimmed brown beard and an elegant manner at odds with his weathered workman's clothes. The two girls bobbed curtsies in unison.

"Dionisio, this is not the time," I said. "Do you realize you have endangered your friends by bringing them here?"

"No more so than we were all in," he said. He dropped his voice. "We barely got out of Florence with our lives. Do you think I would return to Rome if it weren't urgent?"

"You do know that Bracciano will hold the streets before midnight, like as not?" I demanded.

He winced. He'd left Rome one step ahead of Bracciano's assassins, and only with Rodrigo's help and mine. "Then we can't be in the streets. Donna Giulia, would you turn these maidens out into the streets tonight?"

"Of course not," I said. I looked at the two girls; the elder was watching me closely. She at least understood the stakes. "You are Dr. Treschi's friends, and you are welcome here as guests. I am merely concerned for your safety, given the uncertainty of the times. But of course you may stay. I have no thought of turning any of you off." Adriana stiffened. It was her house, and I dispensed hospitality as though it were my own.

"Donna Giulia, I have no words to thank you for your kindness," Mois Sarfati began.

The younger of the two girls looked faint. It was hot, and who knew where they had been today. "You may stand down," I said to the guard. "It's all right."

"Yes, Madonna." He looked amused. He had three little girls of his own, if I remembered rightly. Cardinal Borgia paid him well.

"Come upstairs to my sala," I said. "I will have water brought so that you may refresh yourselves. Dionisio…"

"Giulia, I will speak with you," Adriana said. "In the garden. Now."

"Of course, Donna Adriana," I said, wondering what could be the matter, other than the usual disreputable appearance of Dionisio, and the terrible timing. "If you will excuse me?"

"Of course, Madonna," Dionisio said with a deep bow.

I followed Adriana into the garden. "What's wrong?"

She looked at me incredulously. "What's wrong? The Pope has just died, there's the rumor that a Jewish doctor was feeding him the blood of Christian babies, there will be riots in the streets on any pretext, and you just invited a bunch of Jews to stay here as our guests?"

"Dr. Treschi is no Jew," I said. "He has a commission for Rodrigo. And how could I turn those girls loose into the streets tonight? There is plenty of room and it's no trouble or expense." The last was a turn of the screw. Rodrigo was paying the household expenses. Which meant I had as much to say about what those were as Adriana.

She stared at me. "Are you really so naïve?"

"About what? That those girls will be raped or killed if I put them out? I think I understand that quite well."

"That this is the last thing Rodrigo would agree to. If anything will destroy his ambitions...." Adriana paced around the fountain. "We cannot afford any breath of scandal!"

"How is it a scandal for me to have guests? They are the friends of my client." I felt Adriana was overreaching in her anxiousness.

"Your child will not appreciate this," she said, looking at my midsection. "He or she will have enough trouble. A Borgia bastard...."

"This child has been a Borgia bastard since conception," I said. "Which was some months ago. I have not noticed you having compunctions before." The child was definitely not Orsino's, my nominal husband. I hadn't seen him in nearly two years.

"I am going to Vasanello," Adriana said. She looked like she was near tears. "To stay with Orsino until this is over."

"Fine," I said. I was getting tired of this. If Adriana wanted to go hold Orsino's hand in the country, technically under Orsini protection, she could do so. This last bit didn't even make sense. "Four guards can accompany you. You can be outside the city before dark if you go now. The sun sets late in July."

She took a deep breath. Perhaps she'd thought I would beg her to stay. "Giulia...."

"Go, dear Adriana," I said gently. "Take four guards and go before nightfall. It will be safer for you in Vasanello."

She shook her head, a rueful expression on her face. "You have no idea. Rodrigo can be such a bastard himself." Adriana took a deep breath. "Yes. I will do that. Four guards will see me safe to Vasanello. I'll take Cecelia as my maid and leave you Maria."

"Thank you," I said. "And hurry, if you want to be clear by dark."

Maria was waiting just inside the doors as I came in from the garden shaking my head. "Pack Donna Adriana's things as quickly as you can. She's leaving for Vasanello immediately. And tell Beneo that I need a service for five upstairs in my sala as soon as possible. We should expect at least five for dinner, possibly more. And three chambers will need to be opened—perhaps the two on the third floor above Orsino's that are together for a young gentleman and his two sisters. The third could be the one next to the stair across from Donna Lucrezia's rooms for Dr. Treschi." It was a terrible lot of work on no notice. "Dr. Treschi is on the Cardinal's business," I said. "And the young ladies...."

Maria nodded. "I'd not send them off tonight either," she said. "If I may be so free, Donna Giulia."

"Well, then." I rubbed my hands on my skirts. "And His Excellency Cesare Borgia may arrive at any time. Let me know the moment he does."

"Yes, Madonna."

I ran back upstairs, stopping at the top to compose myself before I entered the sala. The baby moved, an eager little nudge as though it were curious. It was hard not to imagine it as a smaller Lucrezia.

Dr. Treschi and the three Sarfati were sitting stiffly in four chairs in the middle of the big room. The windows were open in hopes of catching a breeze through the balcony doors in the camera. Their bundles were around them on the floor as though they expected to pick them up and run. The gentlemen jumped to their feet as I entered. I gave them all my best smile. "Signori, Signoras, I am sorry to have tarried. Some small domestic matters. I am delighted to make your acquaintance."

Dionisio gave Mois a look as though to say, *I told you she'd let you stay.* "Donna Giulia, the honor and pleasure are ours," Mois said.

Dionisio bowed deeply with a confused look at my middle. "Are congratulations in order? To you and Signore Orsini? I have not met him but I am certain that he is greatly to be envied. I confess I had misunderstood..." There was no way to end that sentence.

I sighed. Dionisio always made a mess of things. "Signore Orsini is not to be envied. You misunderstood nothing." I felt a blush rising. Perhaps Mois Sarfati would not consider me a suitable influence for his sisters, but now he had no choice but to know things best left politely veiled.

The older sister, Chaya, looked at me closely. Fortunately, any further discussion was forestalled by Beneo arriving with a tray, carafes of wine and water to be mixed as one wished, and a plate of fruit since that could be quickly arranged on a platter without notice. I would have to thank Silvia, the cook, and tell her ten times how much I appreciated this. Right now she'd be running about madly since the number of people for dinner had gone from two to five at least, and sending anyone to the markets now wasn't worth the risk. Arranging a table and settling everyone with what they wanted took some time. At last I sat down again between Dionisio and Chaya.

"You have a lovely home, Donna Giulia," she said. Her brown eyes were very round in a sweet face. "The situation of it reminds me—" She stopped abruptly.

"Of your home?" I asked gently.

"In Grenada," she said. "I do not think I will see it again."

"I am sorry to hear that," I said. "I hope that in time you will come to love Rome as I have come to love it. It has beauties that speak to the heart, even if it is not the place your heart yearns for."

Mois made a movement in his seat. "I don't think we can remain in Rome," he said, "unless the Pope allows it. We are in the Papal States illegally and can be expelled at any time. And now you say the Pope is dead...."

"That is why the bells were ringing," I said. "His Holiness had been ill for a long time. He has died at last. As to whether the Pope will allow Jews from Grenada to live in the Papal States, it depends on who the next Pope will be."

Dionisio cleared his throat. "Of course I am of the party of Cardinal Borgia." Wise, considering he was trying to sell him an expensive manuscript! And that he owed him his escape from Rome in the business with Bracciano.

"Naturally," I said. "But needless to say, he cannot look at these books at present. He has gone to the Vatican and I do not know when he will be available, so you must wait on his pleasure." I smiled reassuringly at the two girls. "I feel certain he will buy the books if they are what Dionisio says they are. I would love to see them later myself. You are quite welcome to remain as my guests until he is able to look at them and come to an arrangement."

"That is more than kind, Madonna," Mois said.

Beneo came to the door of the sala. "Donna Giulia, His Excellency the Archbishop of Valencia is here."

Mois had jumped to his feet. "It is all right," I said reassuringly. "If you will excuse me."

"The Archbishop of Valencia is here?" Mois said to Dionisio as I went onto the stair landing. "The Archbishop?" He sounded incredulous.

I hurried down the stairs. Cesare was waiting in the garden, wearing plain leathers with no device. We were the same age, he and I, and had met on several occasions in the past, though he had spent most of the last two years at the university. He was a strikingly handsome man with his father's dark hair and dark eyes, though he had a swordsman's physique rather than a wrestler's. With two days' beard on his face and a sword at his side, he did not look like a bishop.

"Beneo, fetch water for His Excellency," I said, and drew him to the little table. "What has happened?"

"I don't need anything," Cesare said, waving dismissively to Beneo. "And you know as much as I. They haven't sealed the Vatican yet, so I've sent my man, de Corella, to see if there are messages."

"Your father was here for a few minutes last night," I said.

Cesare nodded. "I was at the Vice-Chancellor's when he left. He said he was coming here on his way to the Vatican."

"I have had no messages today either, so we both know the same nothing," I said. "What do you think will happen next?" We had not worked together before. Rodrigo thought we could. I was a little worried; many men had little respect for women and most saw me as a young and pretty face with no mind behind it. Still, he was Lucrezia's brother, Vannozza's son, and he had plenty of examples before him of women with intelligence.

Cesare paced around the table. He looked like a dog eager for a run who has been kept indoors too long. "They may lock down immediately, but I doubt it. Several cardinals aren't in Rome. The rules don't say they have to take the vote immediately. Soon, yes. But they're going to let all the cardinals who are out of town get back." He glanced at me. "But the chaos will start immediately. There were already some street fights last night. Juan and I had no problem, but we had several men with us." Rodrigo had said they were taking a bribe to Ascanio Sforza. Well, even a donkey load of silver wasn't worth tangling with Cesare, Juan and several other men unless one practically had an army! No gang was going to chance that.

"Was Cardinal Sforza happy?"

He shrugged. "I didn't see him. He was at the Vatican. If you hear from Papa before I do, tell him that we delivered everything as he said." Cesare glanced at me, ceasing in his pacing for a moment. "I've pulled forty thousand florins from the Strozzi Bank for bribes. They're not happy." He gave me a narrow smile. Forty thousand was enough to buy an estate with cash. I should imagine the bankers were far from happy. They preferred to deal in promissory notes rather than have large depositors require cash. "Do you need money?"

I shook my head. "I have ninety florins in the house. That should be plenty. I'd rather you handled the larger sums."

Cesare's eyebrow twitched. I was missing an opportunity to feather my nest, clearly. In the multiple moving parts of this election, I could easily keep a tidy sum without comment. And yet I had a month's expenses for the household in cash with more in the bank, and should I arrange a large transaction on Rodrigo's behalf, Cesare was supposed to pay it. Carrying around a ransom in gold seemed to be asking for trouble.

"Rodrigo said if they didn't lock down immediately, we'd try to meet here in the evening day after tomorrow. I expect that I'll have word before then," I said.

He nodded. "Send me word at the Vice-Chancellor's if you hear."

"I will," I said, and saw him out into the baking streets. Cesare strode away with neither a look to the right or left in the bright sun.

After dinner, when the table was cleared, Mois and Dionisio fetched two bundles. I had brought lead weights from the library and put two candelabras on the table so that it was bright enough to see well. Carefully, Mois brought out a book, a scroll, and what appeared to be part of another book—pages tied together but with no binding, though beautifully illuminated. He put the whole book on the table first.

"This is the Cabbalistic treatise I told you of," Dionisio said. "As you can see, it is written in Hebrew."

"May I?" I asked, and Mois nodded. I opened it carefully. The leather binding was tight, the pages clean and well-preserved. Of course I could not read a word.

"Does His Eminence read Hebrew?" Mois asked.

"Perhaps some," I said. I remembered that he had said that when he was a boy in Valencia he had gone to school with Jewish boys. Knowing Rodrigo, he had probably picked up something. He was insatiably curious. I turned the pages. "I feel certain he will be interested." I looked up at him. "I will leave it to him to say what he will pay. I do not know what is an appropriate value as he will."

Mois nodded. "Of course."

"And this is the prize," Dionisio said. He lifted the scroll carefully. Mois untied the linen which wrapped it. It was clearly fragile. I felt a chill down my back. A thousand years old, Dionisio had said, and I believed it. It felt so. Carefully, each of them taking an end, they attempted to spread it on the table, each unrolling one end a little bit.

"Oh, be careful!" I said. I leaned over it, trying to make out the faded ink. It was in Latin, of course, the hand difficult and the style of lettering not what I was accustomed to. Perhaps Alessandro had worked with documents this old, but I had not. Still, I could make out a few things. "*Annus mirabilis*," I read. "The year of wonders." I picked up a line pointer, its ivory tip just resting on the scroll. "In the year of wonders the mountains will echo with the tears of the dispossessed. The keeper of the keys shall die, and from the sea new worlds will rise revealed." I glanced up at Dionisio. "The keeper of the keys is the Bishop of Rome, the Pope." I took a deep breath. "This isn't just an old and valuable scroll of prophecies. You think that there are sections that are about today."

"That is what I think," Dionisio said. "I think the previous sections tell of the fall of Grenada. And now we stand…"

"…in the year of wonders. The prophecies of the Erythraean Sibyl." I glanced down at it again. "And yet the Pope has died many times over the centuries. There is a new election every ten years or so. And how should new worlds rise revealed from the seas? That is quite fantastical."

"The problem with prophecies is that often they are only clear in retrospect," Dionisio said.

"Yes, that would be the problem." I shook my head. The lengths Bracciano had gone to in hopes of finding out what anyone could guess…. A thought struck me. "Have you told anyone else of this?"

Dionisio shook his head. "Absolutely not. The moment I saw this I knew that Cardinal Borgia was the man to buy it. I wrote to you directly."

Mois winced. "I did discuss it with several men in Florence. I had the name of Pico della Mirandola, and I sought him first but did not find him. One of the gentlemen I talked to suggested I come to Dr. Treschi. He assured me he could arrange for its sale and I looked no further. But there were others I spoke to first."

"Well, hopefully they are in Florence and will stay there," I said. I could imagine that Bracciano, with his penchant for prophecy, would jump at the idea of getting a true prophecy of upcoming events. I straightened up. "Let us not try to unroll it further. His Eminence has a proper scriptorium with men who are used to such old books and who have the means to make a fair copy. I would not accidentally damage it."

Gently, they rerolled it and put it back in its linen case. "Do you believe His Eminence will purchase it?" Mois asked. He frowned. "It was the pearl of my father's collection in Grenada. But my sisters must be provided for, and these three books are the only ones we managed to leave with. Our funds are nearly gone."

"I am certain His Eminence will buy it," I said. "And for a fair price. He will appreciate it and preserve it as it deserves. You need not think you have failed your father by letting it fall into careless hands." I looked up at Mois, who sighed.

"That does take a weight from me," he said.

"I hope so," I said. "What is the third manuscript? Dionisio did not speak of a third one."

Mois put it on the table. "I hesitate to even offer it. It is only a partial copy and not so valuable. Dr. Treschi believes it is an alternate or corrupted copy of part of Plutarch's *Moralia*."

"Perhaps of interest to a scholar of Plutarch," Dionisio said. "But the *Moralia* are well known; it is only a few pages of *The Religion and Philosophy of Egypt*, and I would guess it isn't very old."

I lifted one of the loose pages, turning it so I could see it better. It was beautifully illuminated. A veiled woman, her belly large with pregnancy, looked back behind her as if afraid. The Latin hand was as neat as Rodrigo's, copied in exactly the same style, and quite easy to read. "When Typhon had done the dreadful deed, he dishonored the body in all ways, cutting it into pieces and scattering them as offal. Therefore the Wandering Goddess…" I stopped, glancing up at Dionisio. "Dea Peregrina?"

"An epithet of Isis," he supplied.

I nodded, tilting the page. "The Wandering Goddess fled in fear of her life, for she carried his child, and it was no longer safe in the city." A wave of dizziness came over me suddenly. It was as though I was gripped in horror, half-stunned with grief and yet desperate, like a pregnant fox run to earth. The world spun alarmingly.

"Donna Giulia?" Mois had caught my arm. "Are you well?"

"Perhaps you should sit down." Dionisio guided me into a chair. He took the page from my hand, laying it carefully on the table.

"With dog and cat," I said, "faithful to the end."

"What?" Dionisio asked. He knelt beside my chair. "Giulia?"

"I don't know!" It was simply a wave of horror, a wave of fear. "The city, the heat, the light without shadow…."

"Is she ill?" Mois said. He sounded frightened. "Should we call for someone?"

Dionisio shook his head. "She is…was…a Dove." He put his hand gently on my wrist. "Giulia, what do you see?"

"Nothing. I don't know." I didn't want to know. If it was a future, it was one that terrified me. Was it future? Past? My story or someone else's?

"Take a deep breath," Dionisio said. "Feel my hand on yours. You are here, not in that vision."

I opened my eyes. His face no longer swam. The room did not turn. I took a deep breath and another. My limbs still trembled with the need to flee, with grief so thick it choked my throat, but I could push it away. *It was simply an upwelling of sympathy*, I thought. *Because I am with child, I felt this distressed woman's plight so deeply.*

"Better?" Dionisio asked.

I nodded. "Yes. I don't know why…."

He gave me a sideways smile. "Neither do I. A Dove's abilities end with her virginity. Obviously."

"You mean there is something you do not know?" I asked. My head had stopped spinning. Deep breaths. I had too much excitement, too much exertion. I simply needed to rest. That was what had happened.

"Unfortunately," he said, and squeezed my hand. "You look yourself again."

"I'm fine," I said. "Truly." I felt the strangeness receding, though I did not look in the direction of the manuscript. "But perhaps I will retire. If you gentlemen will excuse me?"

"Of course," Mois said.

I got to my feet, perfectly steady now. "I bid you good night."

Perhaps I should eat something. I had not eaten much at dinner, nor drunk much water on a hot day. I made my way down to the kitchen.

It was not quiet. Our staff was much larger than it had been two years ago. Our cook had two assistants now and one of the maid's sons who helped with cleaning up. Beneo was still the majordomo. Maria had been promoted to housekeeper, and in addition to Cecelia who had gone with Adriana, there was my maid, Tina, and three young maids of all work. That made for eleven in the household, plus ten guardsmen who ate with the staff. On a normal day, the three family members were often augmented by various others. We entertained twice weekly as a rule, and Rodrigo was here two or three times a week. Often he sent word that he was arriving late and would turn up for supper well after Compline, which meant Second Meal for everyone at sunset and then dinner for me and Rodrigo three hours before midnight. Our poor cook needed two assistants to serve something like fifty-five meals per day, not counting breakfast trays and refreshments for visitors.

I entered the kitchen with an apology on my lips. "Silvia, I am so sorry! I was not expecting Dr. Treschi and his guests. Nor did I know in advance that Donna Adriana would be departing for the country."

Silvia gave me a fishy eye. "Jews in our house."

"The Sarfati family are gentlefolk from Spain," I said. "And they are my guests."

"I'm not going to cook any strange food."

"And I have not asked you to cook any strange food," I said. "We had your perfectly lovely duck for dinner and it was delicious." I decided to employ the thing that did give me some authority over someone three times my age who worked for Adriana, not me. "They are here for Cardinal Borgia. You know how he appreciates your food and always asks after you. Now he's going to be locked up for days or weeks, like as not, and we must do our best for his guests until he is free."

"Don't know why they can't be at his palazzo," Silvia grumbled. "He's got more servants."

"And his palazzo is likely to be looted if he wins," I pointed out. "That's why he's sent the women servants away. Do you think I could send two little girls Donna Lucrezia's age there under the circumstances?" Silvia was quite fond of Lucrezia. Everyone was.

"No, of course not." She wiped her hands on her apron.

"How are the streets?" I asked. I had not heard anything, but I had been on the second floor in rooms facing the garden.

"Quiet so far. We've got the kitchen entrance barred and the storeroom beyond it is locked." She gestured to the keys she wore around her waist. "And there are guards in the vestibule."

"I'll check with them in a while," I said, suddenly realizing that with Adriana gone I was the only one of the family in residence. There was no one senior to me. Everyone—servants, guards, and guests—all answered only to me. The guards could not report to Rodrigo at the Vice-Chancellor's palazzo four blocks away. I must command the men at arms as my father had. "Silvia, is there any bread and cheese left? I felt a little faint earlier, and I think I should eat something."

That produced a turnabout. "Of course, Donna Giulia! Sit down! I'll have everything for you in a moment."

I sat at one of the scrubbed trestle tables and she produced not only bread and cheese but a dish of olives and a bowl of the bean soup left from the guardsmen's supper. It was utterly delicious. Everything was either wonderful or disgusting these days. There was something comforting about eating in the kitchen. I chatted with Silvia while she put away the last of the pots the boy had washed, gossip of the neighborhood and such.

Maria came in as I was finishing. "The rooms are ready. I did Dr. Treschi's last," she said.

"You are a wonder," I said. "Maria, three rooms on no notice was unforgivable of me to ask."

"A well-run household should be able to do it easily," she said. "Without spending all day complaining." She glanced at Silvia. "It was no difficulty at all."

"I wish I could tell you what will happen," I said. They were, after all, the two most senior servants, given that Beneo was Silvia's husband and did as she said. "But I don't know. We may have more guests. We may have Signore Cesare or Signore Juan or their men. They may come at odd times or leave at odd times. We may even have the Cardinal if he is able to visit in the next days. And what will happen in the city...."

"I was here when the old pope died, Sixtus who was before Innocent. Not a pretty sight," Maria said.

Silvia sniffed. "I go back thirty-four years to when Callixtus died. I was new in service then, twelve years old, at the palazzo of Cardinal de Mila. That was madness." Her voice dropped. "We barred the doors but the mob broke in anyway. They hate the Spanish, no offense to Donna Adriana, being of Cardinal de Mila's blood. He wasn't there but it didn't matter." I felt a chill of horror, not so much at her words but her tone. "I heard the footmen yelling and then one of the maids screaming and screaming. I ran into the storeroom but there were no other doors. There was nowhere to go. I knew they'd find me. I heard the screaming stop with a gurgle and I knew they'd cut her throat." She was looking past me, at something beyond our sight. "There was a big barrel of dried beans that was nearly empty. I pulled the lid off and climbed in, the beans all around me to my knees, and dragged the lid back on. I crouched there in the dark—I don't know how long. Forever. Someone came in. I heard them talking. I tried not to breathe. But there wasn't anything valuable there. Strings of onions. Sacks of flour. Nothing portable and expensive. And so they went away again." She swallowed.

"And then?" I asked gently.

"Eventually it was quiet. Everyone but me was dead. I knew that's what it meant. I couldn't move. But eventually I had to." She looked at me. "You'll know, someday. You're frozen but sooner or later you come back. I climbed out of the barrel. The maid, Catie, was dead on the kitchen floor, her dress up around her waist and her legs apart like she wanted to take all comers, blood all around her. I pulled her dress down and closed her eyes and stuck the flap of skin back on her throat so it looked like she was just sleeping." Silvia spread her work-worn hands like she could still see the blood on them. "I thought I should go somewhere so I went to the hall. One of the footmen was dead there, his skull broken open. It was summer and hot. The flies had come. Everything was still. And then I heard a step."

I swallowed. "The mob?"

She shook her head. "Cardinal Borgia. He was wearing dirty plain clothes and he had a sword in his hand. He looked pale as a sheet, walking by himself among the dead. He turned round and I nearly fainted. 'Who are you?' he asked. 'One of the kitchen maids?' 'Silvia, Signore,' I said, and all I could feel at that moment was humiliation. I'd wet myself in the barrel of beans, you see, and to have the Cardinal see me like that…. Well, he took no notice. 'You're the only one I've seen alive,' he said. 'They're all dead.'"

I clasped my hands together tightly in my lap.

"'I know,' I said, and he came up beside me. 'Come with me,' he said. 'Come on now, you can't stay here.' 'I don't dare the streets,' I said. "I have a sword,' he said. He covered my eyes with his arm when we went through the sala, walking blind with him to guide me until we were in the street. It was so bright that it seemed there were no shadows. 'Where are we going?' I asked him. 'St. Peter's,' he said. 'It's a refuge.' We went there and he left me with some of the sisters from St. Cecelia's." Silvia cleared her throat. "I expect he doesn't remember me at all. I've changed a bit in thirty-four years. Just as well."

"So has he," Maria said.

"The mob hates Spaniards, is my point," Silvia said. "But this is an Orsini house."

"Yes," I said. I put one hand over my belly involuntarily. An Orsini house. Rodrigo had hoped it would be some protection, I supposed.

"We have ten guardsmen and stout doors," Silvia said. "So it's different this time. But you can't blame Donna Adriana too much for going to the country. It was her uncle's house, though she didn't live in it then."

"I understand," I said. Cold horror still gripped me, but I tried to be as matter-of-fact as Silvia was. I stood up. "I know I can count on both of you, and we will all come through this together. I'm going to check on the young ladies."

"You'll find their room in order," Maria said.

"I'm sure I will," I said, and went up four flights to the third floor.

I knocked softly on the door in case they'd gone to sleep, but it opened immediately. Chaya peered out the crack, then opened the door when she saw me. "I didn't mean to startle you," I said. "I wanted to be sure you and your sister were comfortable."

Chaya stepped back. "Please come in, Donna Giulia," she said in a low voice. "Sincha is asleep, but nothing wakes her."

I came in, closing the door quietly behind me. The room had been nicely aired, the small window open to catch any breeze. The double bed had one sleeping form in it, curled beneath the sheet. "If there is anything you need, please let me know," I said.

Chaya took a deep breath, glancing toward the window. "Everything is very nice, Donna Giulia." There were lights moving outside.

I went to the window. It was not quite on the same side of the house as my balcony, facing toward St. Peter's rather than having St. Peter's at the end of the balcony, and it was a floor higher, looking out across a wide vista of city. There were torches moving in the street some blocks away. They did not seem to be coming in this direction. It appeared they were going toward the river. Chaya stood at my elbow.

"I think they are going another way," I said. "Toward the bridge and the Vatican." Not toward the Vice-Chancellor's palazzo either—that was southwest and could not be seen from this window. She did not tremble. Who knows what horrible things she had seen leaving Granada. Supposedly there had been a truce, but surely taking a city after a long siege resulted in looting at least? I thought of Silvia's story and I could imagine. I would not frighten Chaya. I was older than she, and I was the host. "I think we are safe here," I said reassuringly. "And Cardinal Borgia has left guards to protect us."

"To protect you."

"Yes," I said. I took a deep breath. Best to be honest. "I am the Cardinal's concubine, and this is his child. I am sorry that Dr. Treschi has brought you to a house which may compromise your reputation. He should have thought."

"He said that you lived here with Donna Adriana, the Cardinal's cousin."

"Yes," I said. "And his daughter, Lucrezia, who is the age of your sister."

Chaya put her head to the side. "Then why would it be any compromise to my reputation? This is Cardinal Borgia's seraglio."

I blinked. "Excuse me?"

"The home of his women. His concubine, his daughter, his older cousin who presides over it. Why should it damage my reputation to be within the women's quarters?" Chaya looked honestly confused.

"I don't understand," I said.

"Jewish women often come and go within the seraglios of Grenada," she said. "My family are scholars, not merchants, but it is women who sell to women or teach them in all decency. If a woman wishes to learn or to have a teacher for her young children come in, it is usual that it be a Jewish woman. I have not taught in a seraglio myself because I am too young, but it is perfectly respectable. I expected to teach in a few years when I am married. Sincha and I can certainly be your guests in complete propriety." Chaya shrugged. "If anything surprises me, it is that you allow my brother and Dr. Treschi to stay. Your cardinal must trust your chastity as well as your judgment of valuable manuscripts."

"He does," I said. It was an entirely different way of looking at the world. I had thought of Spain, of al-Andalus, as a different country, but not realized that it was like looking at the world through a window facing another direction. And it was a world Rodrigo knew. He had grown up in Valencia and said that in his boyhood less than half its people were Christian. He lived in a Christian house, but surely he knew Chaya's world. It was not oceans away but city blocks, and scholarship crossed borders. The Cardinal's seraglio.

Chaya smiled. "When is the baby due?"

"The first of December," I said. I put my hand over it. "It seems like a long time."

"Do you hope for a son or a daughter?" Chaya leaned on the windowsill. The torches were definitely moving in the other direction.

"I hope for a son and Rodrigo for a daughter," I said. "So whichever it is, we will be well pleased."

She looked at me sideways. "Usually it is men who want sons."

"Rodrigo says he has a pack of sons and they're trouble enough. He'd like another girl." And yet I knew he would be equally delighted if it were a boy. He loved all his children. "His oldest surviving son is my age. That is the one who was here today—Cesare. You will see more of Cesare in the coming days. And his brother, Juan." As Rodrigo had said, it was far safer for Cesare to come to me than me to him.

Chaya nodded, storing up information that might prove useful. "I will pray for the safety and health of your baby, Donna Giulia."

"Thank you," I said, "And goodnight. I hope you rest well." I took my leave. Surely Jewish prayers could only do me good. *Prisca theologia*, I thought. And was not Jesus a Jew who had suffered at the hands of Romans?

Chapter five

Rodrigo's sons arrived first. Vespers had just rung when Cesare and Juan were shown in. I came down to greet them in the vestibule, Cesare looking past me into the garden where the little table was being set for Dr. Treschi and the Sarfati family. "We're dining there?" he asked without preamble, his left hand grazing the hilt of his sword.

"No, we're upstairs," I said. "That is for the rest of the household."

Juan bent over my hand more properly. "Donna Giulia."

"Signore Juan," I said, with a smile for him. He had something of the look of Lucrezia about him, though his hair was dark rather than blond.

"Is Papa here yet?" he asked.

"You are the first." I motioned to the stairs. "Would you care to come up to the sala?" He gave me his arm and we went up, Cesare following.

Beneo opened the doors for us. The sala was set up nicely, windows open for a breeze, with a rectangular table for five set in the center with a fine tapestry cloth. The wine was on a credenza behind, and Cesare took the decanter and swirled it in the light, looking for precipitants. *Always cautious*, I thought. It had been strained, so there should be no lees. Precipitants would indicate something added in powder form after it was decanted. He saw me watching and put it down. "I don't intend offense," he said.

"Of course not," I said. "You are careful."

"It's my job to be careful," Cesare said.

There were more steps on the stairs. "Father Alessandro Farnese," Beneo announced.

Alessandro wore a plain doublet and dark hose and like the others wore a sword, though he was also carrying a light hunting bow and quiver with arrows. "Good evening, Giulia," he said, coming to embrace me. "How's my nephew or niece?"

"Very well," I said. "What's the bow for?"

"You," Alessandro said. "Remember how Papa used to take us hunting in the marshes? I thought you might like something better than crockery. After all, it's a little unwieldy to throw pots out the window!"

I laughed. On one notable occasion I had hit an Orsini guard with a pitcher of water while he tried to stab Alessandro. "I am hoping it won't come to shooting out of the windows!"

"Just in case," Alessandro said, handing them to me. "I'll feel better if you have them, Giulia."

"How is it inside?" Cesare asked. "I've not been in the Vatican since yesterday."

"Tense," Alessandro said. "No one is certain when we'll lock in. Not till late tomorrow, certainly, because Cardinal Gherardi isn't here yet; and since he's eighty-four he's not burning up the road. But the Cardinal will know better than I what the plans are." There were many cardinals, but only one "the Cardinal" in this company—Rodrigo.

"Your sister hunts?" Juan asked. "Lucrezia doesn't."

"Lucrezia has been raised in the city," I said. "Alessandro and I grew up in the country. We used to hunt ducks in the marshes with our father."

"And our dog," Alessandro said. "Good old Fidelis. He was a good boy."

"He was," I said. "And a fine retriever, though he'd always give Papa a long-suffering look if he had to wade. He didn't like water."

Juan looked at the bow. "Can you hit anything with that?"

"You, at forty paces," Alessandro said.

"I'm wearing leather."

"You might live," I said with a smile. I had learned long ago how verbal tussles with brothers went. Never back down.

Cesare paced over to the window. "Where's Papa?"

"Here," Rodrigo said, coming in from the hall. He too was wearing plain clothing, though he did not wear a sword. He looked handsome and alert, his hair newly trimmed, his dark red coat a color that agreed with him.

I went to his side and put my arm around his waist. "Rodrigo."

He kissed me on the lips regardless of his sons, one hand on my belly. "Ready to join your brothers plotting?" he asked it.

"Not just yet," I said. I looked past him to the doorway. "Beneo, you may serve now."

One of the maids helped him, as there was quite a lot of food considering the markets were uncertain: fresh sausages cooked in wine and a lovely artichoke timbale, with all accompaniments one might wish. Once we were served, Beneo bowed his way out and closed the doors. Alessandro put pen and ink beside his place, ready to take notes if Rodrigo wanted them.

Rodrigo ate enthusiastically and I watched him. He never did anything idly. Whatever he aimed at, it was with passion, whether love or work or artichoke timbale. Cesare, however, was all business. "What's the vote count?"

Rodrigo spread his hands. "Five."

Cesare winced. "How many do you need?" Juan asked.

"There will be twenty-three cardinal electors," Rodrigo said, "when Gherardi arrives from Venice. A two-thirds majority is needed. So, fifteen."

"That's a long way to go," Juan observed.

"You're brilliant," Cesare said. "We would have never thought of that."

Rodrigo held up a hand. "And I've promised to support Cardinal Carafa on the first ballot."

"What for?" Cesare demanded.

"And he will support me," Rodrigo said. "We will vote for each other."

"To see how big the Humanist faction is," I said.

"Clever girl," Rodrigo said. "Yes, exactly. How many votes do each of us have? Carafa will throw his to me if it looks like I have a better chance of winning because he'll eat his zachetto before he'll let della Rovere or any of the Traditionalists win. I am guessing he's at five or six."

"So ten or eleven out of the fifteen," Cesare said. "That's better."

"It is. Now," he picked up his wine glass and took a sip before he continued, "Cardinal Sforza has three or four. Cardinal Orsini has three or four. Neither of them will ever support the other, nor will Cardinal Colonna support Orsini, though he couldn't care less about the Sforza or humanism or what the universities teach or any of the rest of it. So two axes—tradition and family power."

Cesare cleared his throat. "And then we come to France and Spain. I hear that the King of France has given della Rovere two hundred thousand ducats to assist in his campaign. Spain gave us only a quarter of that."

"And another fifty thousand to Cardinal da Costa of Portugal," Rodrigo said. He smirked. "Obviously the papacy isn't worth as much to Queen Isabella as it is to King Charles. And she splits her bets."

"She's spent a great deal conquering Grenada," Alessandro said.

"You'd think she'd have gotten good money out of it," Cesare said. "Looting the Alhambra ought to give her ready cash."

"Most of the Alhambra's treasures aren't ready cash," Rodrigo said. "One can't simply pass them around." He shifted in his seat. "Besides, she's thrifty. It's one of her great virtues. And she must present a dowry for her daughter to that other parsimonious soul, Henry of England. I don't think the Spanish crown is likely to donate further to our cause."

"We're out of time anyway," Cesare said.

Rodrigo nodded. "Agreed."

Juan looked quizzical. "Why is it worth that much to the King of France? That's a lot of money."

"Naples," Rodrigo said. "France has a tenuous claim on the Kingdom of Naples, but King Ferrante is a strong king, by which I mean he's bloodthirsty, ruthless, canny and has held Naples for more than thirty years. France doesn't dare press their claim while he lives."

"But he's an old man," I said.

"Just so." Rodrigo leaned back in his chair. "His son, Alfonso, is in his forties, but he's a scholar rather than a warrior. France thinks he'll be an easier nut to crack than his father. They mean to press their claim, by arms if necessary, when Ferrante dies. It will be much easier if the pope recognizes the legitimacy of their claim."

"And doesn't resist their passage south through the Papal States," Cesare said, taking a sip of his wine. "To get to Naples, an army would have to pass through the Romagna."

I felt a chill down my back. "Two hundred thousand ducats is a fair toll."

"If della Rovere wins. Which he won't." Rodrigo smiled. "We have voted that we will open the conclave on August 6, one week from today. Presumably if Gherardi is coming he will be here by then. So that is our time, dear ones. We must make the most of it."

"Bribe Sforza," Cesare said.

"Oh undoubtedly, but he's going high. I don't want to be the first bidder or della Rovere will start running it up out of his deep purse."

"Sforza and his three votes would get you to thirteen or so," I said. "And Colonna would get you to fourteen. Colonna ought to be bribable."

Cesare raised a finger in a gesture very like his father's. "If he can hold all Carafa's votes. Which he can't. He'll lose one or two, probably Riario at least. He's a Humanist but he's related to della Rovere even if he disagrees with him. He'll vote for Carafa but not Papa."

"Maybe, maybe not," Alessandro said. "He doesn't like him much."

"Is there any way to peel off any of della Rovere's votes?" I asked.

"There are one or two who might be more attached to their own good than his," Rodrigo said. "But most of them are ancient men who are attracted to his promises of returning to some past golden age of virtue." He shrugged. "Old men."

Juan laughed. "And you're a youth, Papa."

He looked at Juan over the rim of his glass. "The dreams of youth are strong, Juan, but they are nothing compared to the dreams of old men who are spoiling for a fight."

"Like you, Papa," Juan said.

"I've been preparing for this for thirty years. Nothing is going to stand between me and the prize now." He took a sip. "Young men can wait." He glanced at Cesare. "Perhaps someday one of you will take this up."

Cesare sighed. "One papal election at a time. What's my first job?"

"Colonna," Rodrigo said. "He needs money and he hates the Orsini. Benefices and raising the specter of Cardinal Orsini winning. We know Orsini can't, but Colonna hates him. So some lovely arrangements on his behalf...."

We went through the full list, all twenty-two cardinals one by one, with a strategy for each of them excepting Carafa and della

Rovere, twenty men to consider the weaknesses of. Money. Family. Pride. Ideals. *Everyone has something they will move for*, I thought. *The best of them will do what they think will help a cause they care about. The worst of them act in spite.* Rodrigo could promise most of them one or the other, or something between, but eight or so were immovable.

"Why do they hate you, Papa?" Juan asked. "More than their own self-interest?"

It was full dark now. The candles illuminated the table but not the whole room. Outside, the stars were just visible over the city through the cook smoke. Rodrigo leaned back in his chair. "Some of them believe me a wicked man. They may be right." He smiled at me. "Some of them hate Spaniards. That is their prerogative. They call us marranos and believe themselves descended from the Caesars." *Bracciano*, I thought, *and the Orsini*. "And some are simply frightened of the way the world has changed in the last forty years and believe that the Pope has the power to turn back time. Da Costa was born in 1406. He was three times your age, Juan, when Constantinople fell. And that was nearly forty years ago. He simply can't accept that the Turks are not going to be defeated by a crusade or that the printing press is not going to vanish." Rodrigo shrugged. "Della Rovere understands its power very well. That's why he fears it. He appreciates the art and wisdom of the ancients. That's why he wants to control it. That's an entirely different game. But he's very good at speaking the language of Traditionalists. Why not express sympathy for a new crusade? Even if it's never going to happen." He took a sip of his wine.

"We've got to get at least one of the eight," Cesare said. "Or run the table and get all of the other fifteen."

"One vote at a time," Rodrigo said. "Pluck the low-hanging fruit. No one is going to be close on the first ballot or the second." He looked at Cesare. "Colonna. Then Sforza." He looked at me. "Orsini."

I looked back in disbelief. "You think I can get the Orsini?"

"I do." Rodrigo put his head to the side. "You have great affection for the family which you have married into, and you fear that Ascanio Sforza will be elected."

"Bracciano will never..." I began.

"Cardinal Orsini does not always dance to Bracciano's tune. He won't let Bracciano's hatred of me give the papacy to the Sforza. That's the key to him. But for that to work, he has to believe Sforza is tying it up behind closed doors. That's a move further on."

"You see it all like a chessboard," I said admiringly.

"And I'm the knight," Juan said. "Cesare is the bishop, of course. What are you, Alessandro?"

"A rook, perhaps," Alessandro said.

"God help the pawns," said Cesare.

Cesare and Juan left shortly after to return to the Vice-Chancellor's palazzo where they were staying. Alessandro was going to remain overnight and I had prepared a room for him. I left him in conversation with Dr. Treschi and Mois Sarfati about rare manuscripts. Rodrigo was staying but wouldn't require a room. I drew him into my camera and shut the door. One candle was lit on the mantelpiece; the balcony doors and shutters were closed and the curtains drawn.

Rodrigo took off his coat and sat down to remove his shoes. "Where in the world is Adriana?"

I glanced at him in the mirror as I carefully unpinned my snood, its delicate net enhanced with tiny gold beads. "Vasanello."

"Vasanello!" He nearly jumped out of the chair. "What in the devil is Adriana doing at Vasanello? Why isn't she here? She receives a generous stipend to run this house."

I turned around. "She was terrified, Rodrigo. I told her to go. She wasn't making any sense."

"What do you mean she wasn't making sense? She is supposed to be running this house, not dropping it on you when you're breeding. And when you have other things to do." He had definitely raised his voice.

"Don't shout at me," I said. "Adriana can't hear you and the baby and I can."

"I'm sorry, sweet." He did in fact moderate his tone. "What is the matter with Adriana?"

I started unlacing my gown. One of the nice things about it was that it was infinitely expandable, certainly a useful feature at the moment. "She was already scared. And then when Dr. Treschi brought the Sarfati family, Adriana completely went to pieces."

Rodrigo looked at me quizzically. "The Sarfati family?"

"The manuscripts from Grenada." There had been so much going on I had not gotten around to telling him about Dr. Treschi and the manuscripts. "The ones that Dr. Treschi is acting as agent for. The sellers are the Sarfati family—a young scholar and his two little sisters from Grenada. They all had to flee Florence and so they're here. I know you'll want to see the manuscripts and I can hardly turn two girls Lucrezia's age into the streets right now." I got into bed wearing my camisa, plumping up the pillows and waiting for him. He didn't answer. He blew out the candle. "Anyway, I said they could stay and that when you were available, you would look at the manuscripts and make an offer. And Adriana completely dissolved. She said that I was doing something terrible to the baby! What in the world! Surely Adriana isn't the kind of superstitious woman who thinks having Jews near a baby is bad luck. That's ridiculous."

"No, I'm sure Adriana doesn't think that." He settled on his back, and I came to his side, my left hand against his chest, my head on his shoulder.

"And then she started ranting that I was naïve and you could be a complete bastard and that she was leaving. So I told her to go if she wanted to. Rodrigo, I don't know what is the matter with Adriana, but it was better for her to go under the circumstances. She seemed genuinely frightened." I undid the tie at the top of his shirt so I could rest my hand flat against his chest. I wanted his skin.

"Probably for the best," he said.

I craned my head to look at him, though it was too dark to see his expression. "What was that about?"

"You know Adriana can be easily upset." I had not noted any such thing in the past, but he knew her better than I did. Adriana seemed very good at protecting her own interests.

"I sent guardsmen to take her to Vasanello and come back," I said. "Perhaps she just lost her nerve. In any event, I know you probably don't have time to look at the manuscripts now, but I think you'll find them interesting. I certainly do."

"Then I will trust your judgment," he said. Rodrigo was being unusually quiet. Perhaps he was still weighing the votes for the conclave. I knew that he had another meeting the next day with a group of clients who would also be working on his behalf, but surely he could rest a few hours. There was nothing more to be done tonight.

I leaned up, putting my other hand on his chest as well, like a cat with both paws resting, claws just barely extended to knead. "It has been so lonely this week," I purred, "with no handsome priest in my bed."

That got his attention. "That sounds predatory."

I flexed my nails against his chest. "I feel quite predatory. Deprived. Hungry." Something about my state left me in near-perpetual frustration these last weeks.

"Do you?" There was a breathless catch in his voice.

"I do." I shifted, kneeling up to straddle his thigh. "And here's a pretty priest right here, ready to be sorely tried." I pulled my camisa over my head, letting my hair fall as my only garment. "Tasty."

His hand went to my leg. "Like a succubus."

"Just like a succubus," I said, my voice low. "Slipping into your room at night to torment your dreams. Only it's not a dream, is it?" I drew his shirt up, grinding against his leg. Oh, I had wanted that. Needed that.

"To wake to this…." One hand on my hip to guide me. "How could a man resist?"

"And you are not resisting, are you?" I whispered. "You lust. You lust for me. And I will have you." I ran my hand down his chest, following the dark line of hair to his groin. "You want me. You've dreamed of me. You can't help yourself."

"I can."

"You can't." I bent forward as much as my belly would allow, body to body, kissing him, nipping at his lips with my teeth. "I feel you. You want me." Rodrigo groaned, responding despite his pretended protestations. I teased, kissing and withdrawing, brushing my heavy breasts against him. "You can't be chaste. You have to have me. I am temptation."

"You certainly are," he said between kisses. I rose over him, grinding against his leg again. So good. So incredibly fast. It caught me by surprise, the deep rolling movement inside, as though my entire being gripped and released, so intense I nearly fell. I would have, had his hand on my hip not steadied me. I gasped, knowing he felt it. "Really?" he said. I was generally responsive, but going off like fireworks so quickly was much.

"I want you," I said. "I want more of you." I shifted my weight and took him, feeling the clenching going on and on.

Afterwards, I lay against his side, a sheen of sweat on our naked bodies. We would be cold when it dried, but for now the room was hot and close. He untangled part of my hair and pulled it back. "Three times?"

"You satisfy me." Only once for him, but hopefully he didn't feel deprived.

"Well." Rodrigo's voice was smug.

"Your succubus," I said. It was a very filthy idea.

"My cute succubus," he said. "With little bat wings." He ran his hand down my back as though stroking invisible wings.

"A cute little succubus," I said. "Just so hungry for a sweet young priest." I stretched under his touch. "But if she ever knew love rather than desire, she would know God and cease to be a succubus."

"That sounds like quite a long project." He kissed my forehead. "Saving her, really."

"By causing her to fall in love." We could have months of fun from that.

"A terrible sin, but if it saved her...." He said, gathering me closer against his side. "Aren't you cold?"

"Not yet. Are you?"

"Yes." He got the covers and pulled them up.

I snuggled down against his shoulder, yawning. "A cute little succubus."

"My confessor is going to have gray hair," Rodrigo said.

I winced, still reveling in the scent of his body, in the feel of us together. All senses seemed heightened. "Do you have to? Can't you just say, 'Father, I have known a woman carnally?' He must be used to that from you."

"It doesn't convey the full picture." He sketched in the air with one hand. "Perhaps, 'known a woman carnally with blasphemous fantasies.' Does that protect your dignity?"

"Yes," I said. "I'm sure you do give him gray hair. Tonight alone, Lust, Greed..."

"...Pride..." he said.

"...maybe Envy."

"Sloth, if I don't get up in the morning. I have a lot to do."

"I know you do." I rolled over, curling up with a pillow against my stomach, and he put his arms around me from behind, fitting together. "I'm glad you're here."

"I don't know when I'll see you again." He ducked his face against my shoulder. "Maybe not until it's done."

I laced my fingers with his. If he lost, we'd make the best of it. If he won, how changed would he be? It worried me, though it didn't seem to frighten him. He waited for it like an anxious bride, I thought, eager for the union and worried at once. *Dear God*, I pled silently, *please leave some of him for me. I do not deserve it, but I need it.*

"My sweet girl," he said, and we fell asleep thus.

The next day the city was quieter. Everyone had heard that the votes were postponed until all the voting cardinals were present. It was Tuesday, the last day of July, and they would not convene until the next Monday. It seemed that everyone breathed a sigh of relief. Markets opened. Everyone hurried out to do business before next week's crisis. *It is like a fever*, I thought. *It wanes during the day, but you know it will return with night.*

I sent everyone out to markets and errands while it was safe. The household needed a good many things. My tutor even managed to come, and I spent three hours pleasantly comparing Suetonius and Tacitus in text and content, and then studying a map of northern countries and their bishoprics and archbishoprics. I would look silly if I did not know where someone was from, and so I had resolved to learn where each seat was and something about it, even if it was as basic as *seaport, salt herring, St. Agnes.*

After my tutor left, I went down to the kitchen where there was the usual turmoil on marketing day. I told Silvia I would be no trouble, getting bread and cheese and a peach and taking them up to the garden so that nobody had to stop what they were doing and wait on me. I settled down quite comfortably in the shade with my lunch and my beloved volume of Plutarch which Rodrigo had given me. I had ordered a copy of *The City of Ladies* from Rodrigo's usual bookseller, but it had not yet been delivered. Hopefully it would, now that the city was quiet enough for people to be about their business. Since it was printed in three volumes it was quite expensive, but within my means. What utter luxury, to order books if I wished and know that Rodrigo would not object!

"I beg your pardon, Donna Giulia." Mois Sarfati had come out into the garden and now excused himself to me. "I didn't mean to intrude."

"It is not an intrusion," I said with a smile, putting the book on the little table. "You are welcome to join me. It's a beautiful day, and I am trying to stay out of the way of the servants, who have much to do." His sister had said it would be unusual for a man to be allowed in women's quarters, but surely even the strictest person could hardly object to conversing in a garden in full view of the household. I did not want to make him uncomfortable.

He sat down, glancing at the book. "You are reading?"

"Plutarch," I said. "And I have read it several times, so there is no suspense."

At that he smiled, for I had meant to set him at ease. "I apologize if I reacted oddly the other day when you said the Archbishop of Valencia was here," he said. "I thought you meant someone else, but the man who was here is much too young to be the man I had in mind."

"Yes, Cesare is probably younger than you are," I said. "Who did you think?"

Mois picked up the copy of Plutarch, turning it over in his hands. "About ten years ago...you know of the Inquisition, yes? In Spain? Founded with the patronage of the crown to purge the lands they have conquered?"

"Yes," I said.

"About ten years ago the Inquisition came to Valencia. They arrested ninety Jews and conversos on pain of death." He did not look up from the binding. "It was expected they would burn. The

Archbishop of Valencia appealed to the Pope. They were released and the Inquisitor relieved of his position and ordered to Rome. This ended the trials there to this day."

"And you endure such hazard always?"

"We did not in Grenada. We were safe. But no more." Mois took a deep breath. "I hope that we may find another haven. But if it was the same Archbishop of Valencia in your house, I wanted to speak with him and give him my thanks. He must have been a very holy man indeed."

"He is not so very holy, but you will meet him in my house," I said. "Cardinal Borgia was Archbishop of Valencia then, as his son is now. He is the man who will buy your books."

Mois looked astonished. "I did not know," he said.

"You did not know who my patron was?" I asked.

"Dr. Treschi didn't say. When we fled Florence—and that was touch and go—he said we went to the home of a great Roman lady who had been his patron in the past, who was the companion of a cardinal and could see that the books would be bought by him. He gave me your name, but not the cardinal's, and that only when we passed the city gates of Rome. We heard the bells toll, and he told us where to go in case we became separated in the streets."

So Dionisio had learned discretion. That was good to know. "It is common gossip in Rome, but I suppose you had not heard it in Florence," I said.

"No, Donna Giulia." Mois looked thoughtful, as though he considered whether or not to speak. "Do we hurt his cause by our presence here? I could not help but hear the lady's objections the other evening."

"I think you are the least of his worries at the moment," I said candidly. "The papal election hinges on many things, but you and your books are not one of them. I only regret that Cardinal Borgia does not have time to examine the books right now. I am afraid you must wait on his pleasure."

"We are happy to wait," Mois said. "And if there is any way we can thank you, please say."

"I shall," I said. After he had departed, I frowned down at the book on my lap but did not open it. A very holy man, Mois had said. He did not understand the world at all. A very holy man would never have the power to save the Jews of Valencia. He could only weep and remonstrate and say that it was wrong, but he could never have appealed to the Pope and secured their release. I understood well enough that there were horrors in the world. Every day people were broken on the rack in civilized places. The Inquisition went further than most, but in our Italian states people were tormented in ways that made the Crucifixion seem merciful. I had no illusions that we were good. I only hoped, like Rodrigo, that we could be better than the worst we might be.

If today Mois and his sisters were safe, it was because of a concubine and a corrupt churchman. Were I a good young wife, and Rodrigo a chaste and honest priest, Mois would be dead in the streets by now. Chaya and Sincha would be raped and left for anyone to pick over. But because of our sins, we had the power to do good.

I folded my hands across my belly, the child quiescent within. *Mary, Queen of Heaven*, I prayed, *let the good I do outweigh my crimes and be worthy of Your merciful intercession.*

Chapter Six

I dreamed, and in my dream I walked through the halls of a great palace. It was night. There were no lamps lit. Rich, strange furniture and bright hangings were all dimmed. I walked on stone floors, my mother at my side, a baby in her arms.

There was a long gallery that we hurried along, the walls decorated with great gold and turquoise bulls, but all was silent and empty except for us. There was a chamber with chairs strewn about, a little table tipped over lying on its side. The black pool on the floor and the long streaks from it were not spilled wine.

"Quickly," my mother said. "And keep your eyes down."

And yet I did not. I scrambled after her through the doors to a courtyard. As things suddenly turn in dreams, it was day. Alessandro strode across the courtyard before me, red robes like Rodrigo's flaring. "Alessandro, wait!" I called, but he did not. I ran after him, up the steps of a strange temple, its door handles rearing cobras, gilded and glittering.

And into the nave of St. Peter's. It was morning, and light came in the clerestory windows. There were twelve cardinals, each with a candle in hand. The Pope stood in the center, white in red like the center of a rose, his back to me. They were pronouncing anathema. My hair stood on end. *"Et potestate ligandi et solvendi in coelo et in terra nobis divinitus collata...." By the power which is given me to bind and loose all things in Heaven and Earth....*

The floor of St. Peter's was a vast chess board, black and white squares alternating. It went to the horizon, passing through the walls which stood about us like ghosts, ephemeral as glass.

"To bind and to loose," I whispered. The squares each held a letter, like Dr. Treschi's squares. I turned around, back toward the doors. "I don't understand, mother," I said. "And I must!"

She sat on an intricately carved stool, Rodrigo's beautiful statue, Isis with her son in her arms, only like Galatea her skin flushed warm and living, her eyes bright as stars, a statue come to life. "The Dove," she said.

"I am no longer a Dove," I said. "I am no maiden, but a mother to be."

She cradled her son who reached for her breast. "You are what you are, no more and no less, and ever shall be."

"You are saying that a Dove does not have to be virgin?" I asked.

"A child is malleable. A woman is not." She smiled at me as though we shared some joke. "Mystery is not only for men. Nor is magic. Mistress of Magic they named me once, here in this city, calling upon me from the streets beneath your feet."

"And now they fear it, and only let a child touch it," I said. Bracciano and even Dr. Treschi dismissed the Dove, but perhaps it was for fear of what she could do if she knew it. After all, they could not see the future in mirrors themselves. "The book of the Erythraean Sibyl," I said. "The Year of Wonders."

"You cannot stop the flood," she said. "But who will guide it?" She smiled, a slow, sweet smile. I raised my head and opened my eyes.

I looked up at the coffered ceiling above my own bed. Light came in through the slats of the shutters. The beams of the ceiling made a

patchwork of squares. "Squares," I said. A chessboard. The square of Saturn I had made for Dr. Treschi's rite to protect Rodrigo. The square I had sat in as a Dove.

I got up, going to the basin and splashing my face with tepid water. Then I went to the doors and opened them, walking out onto the balcony. The pots of jasmine were in bloom. The sky was white hot over the red roofs of the city. The bells of St. Peter's began ringing Prime. August 4 had begun. Two more days.

The dream faded with the sun, only shreds remaining. Alessandro in a cardinal's robes. A rite of anathema. And a strange palace by night where something terrible had happened. That had all the vividness of a memory, not the odd, morphing possibility of the other. I had been a little girl. We had been fleeing by night—to where? My father was waiting for us? To send us somewhere? So that we would be safe? I shook my head. I had known everything in the dream, but it was gone now.

Squares. I had an idea. I dressed quickly, then hurried downstairs, running into one of the young maids who was going up with a washing pitcher. "Rosalia, is that for Dr. Treschi?"

She bobbed. "Yes, Donna Giulia."

"Will you ask him to join me in the garden? And when you've taken the pitcher up, bring me bread there."

By the time he came down, I was sitting in one of the chairs in the shade, a book in my lap, bread and peaches and watered wine on the table beside me. "Donna Giulia," he said, sketching a bow. "To what do I owe the honor?"

"Is breakfast such an honor? Sit down, Dionisio." I smiled at him. "I have a technical question for you."

He sat in the other chair, helping himself to the bread. "I am at your disposal."

"The squares and circles you chalked when I was scrying for Bracciano," I said, "the protective ones. Could I have done them from inside?"

"Of course." Dionisio popped a piece of bread in his mouth. "If a magus is working alone, it's more usual to ward oneself in rather than out."

I stared at him. "Why didn't you say that before?"

"Why would I?" He shrugged. "You're not a Dove."

"And why does that mean I can't do what you do? Other than the old saw that women can't learn it?"

He looked vaguely embarrassed. "You're a cardinal's concubine. And you said very clearly that you would have no more contact with…things…like the one in the mirror."

"Are there not entities one can call upon besides those?" I asked. I had promised Rodrigo no demons, not ever, not under any circumstances, and I meant to keep that promise. But we had called upon the Archangel Raphael to break the demon's binding, and we had often discussed that neutral spirits existed. I had not promised to avoid those.

"Well, yes." He looked sheepish.

I leaned forward. "Dionisio, I want to enclose the entire house in a protective square. Can that be done?"

He blinked. "I don't know. I've never heard of doing it."

"Fair enough," I said. "I know a building can be permanently protected by consecration. It's the same thing."

"Is it?"

"Yes," I said. My mind was aflame. "It's exactly the same thing. When Cardinal Borgia consecrates a church, he's asking it to be hallowed in the name of God and whoever the patron saint is. He's calling them to pay attention to it and to be present in it and to protect those within it. That's what holy ground is. But I'm not talking about consecration. I'm talking about a temporary protection for the next week or two." I could see it. "You chalk formulae in the four directions and round about. Why can't the edges of the square be the walls of the house?"

"To protect the house from a mob?" Dionisio looked thoughtful.

"I'm not sure it would be strong enough. The squares and circles I've used are for summoning. They keep an incorporeal entity in or out. They wouldn't stop a physical person. If you'd decided to get up and walk out of the square, you'd have broken the binding but it wouldn't have stopped you as it would the entity."

I considered. That was indeed a problem. I bit into one of the peaches. "And yet I wouldn't have done that," I said. "It seemed like a barrier to me. I felt averse." I chewed thoughtfully. "Aversion might do. After all, a mob isn't very intentional. They want to loot something. It's not terribly important what. If this house seemed unattractive, why not simply pass by?"

He nodded slowly, his eyes unfocused as though he were visualizing the operation. "Maybe. That might work. It wouldn't last. And chalk would be very obvious."

"If it lasted a few days, it would be better than nothing, even if we had to renew it," I said. "And not chalk. Holy water. We've got Alessandro in and out all the time. There's no reason he can't bless a bit."

"We can draw power from that too," he said.

I put my head to the side. "What do you mean?"

"All operations require power as well as intention, whether sacred or profane. Remember how, two years ago, Bracciano had his men offer life or service to the demon so that it could manifest?"

And how there had been a blood sacrifice of a dog. I remembered well. "So entities have to be paid, like street bravos."

"It's not just payment." He took another bite of his bread. "Just as we need food to eat, so do the incorporeal. If you hired men to move your furniture, you'd offer them water, wouldn't you?"

"Well, of course," I said. "They'd pass out in this heat otherwise."

"If you want an entity to appear in a mirror and talk to you, you offer it incense or something like that. The ancients made offerings of wine—libations."

"Or sacrificed animals," I said.

"Yes. The water to asperge can also be used. But every operation has to run on something. Bracciano used his men's lives, promising the demon their service. It's possible sometimes to run on the will of the magus, but that's taking it out of yourself."

"So when I see—" I began with some alarm.

He shook his head. "That's different. You're not manifesting something or making something happen. It's perceiving, not doing."

I took a deep breath. "Perception is passive. Manifestation is active. I see the difference. Think about how to do it, Dionisio. We will do this as soon as it's feasible."

When Alessandro came that afternoon, I put the question to him. He sighed and looked at me sideways. "I can certainly bless holy water for you," he said. "Do I want to know what you plan to do with it?"

"Probably not," I said. I smiled. "Do you?"

"I am really trying not to involve myself in anything actively heretical while clerking at the Vatican for a papal election," Alessandro said tiredly. "Do you think you can manage whatever astrological operation this is without me?"

"I expect Cesare will do it," I said. "So you may be excused."

Alessandro shook his head. "Seriously, Giulia?"

"Absolutely," I said. "And if we need another, Cesare will bring Juan."

"Juan is sixteen and doesn't know the first thing about this," Alessandro said. "I can't say I'm an expert but I'm better than Juan!"

"You said you didn't want to do anything."

"What are you doing?"

I explained, ending with, "So we are going to guard the house against violence. I understand if the method is too heretical for you to feel comfortable with, but surely the purpose can cause you no qualm?"

He looked intrigued. That was always the way to Alessandro's participation in anything—curiosity. "Do you think it will work?"

"I think it's worth trying," I said. "Dionisio intends to ask angelic powers for their help, which I cannot see is bad. Surely it is no different than petitioning a saint!"

"And you intend to do this. In your condition." He looked at me skeptically.

"It was my idea," I said.

Alessandro shook his head. "Fine. I'm in."

I jumped up and hugged him. "I knew you would be," I said laughing.

"You're a menace," he said. "I don't know where you'd be without me to take care of you."

"Oh? Where I'd be? I'll tell you where you'd be—in a rural parish somewhere instead of the Vatican!" His face fell and I regretted it immediately. "Alessandro, I'm sorry. You deserve..."

"No, it's true," he said. "These clerkships are about patronage. I wouldn't have it without Cardinal Borgia." He took a deep breath. "And my pride isn't great enough to cut off my nose to spite my face. It's a fantastic opportunity and I'm making the most of it."

"But it's hard," I said.

"Of course it's hard to hear I have my job because my sister earned it on her back." Alessandro sighed. "Not that he says that. Or for that matter Cardinal Sforza, who I work with a lot."

"They know your worth," I said stoutly.

He nodded. "Cardinal Borgia's an exacting master but he's fair. He wants to know where every single soldo has gone and God help you if you can't account for funds! He never skims off the top and he has no patience with anyone else doing it. Every soldo of benefice is accounted for. Mind you, he's generous with them if you support him, but it's not under the table. It's honest graft."

"Well, I suppose that's something," I said.

"I'm not complaining," Alessandro said. "That's how benefices work. I just wonder if there isn't a better way to organize Church funds."

"That's a much bigger job than a clerk's accounting," I said.

He shrugged. "It's a pope's life work," he said. "And the pope had better be a Medici banker to straighten it out. Which I'm not. I'd rather be in law than accounting."

"Well, perhaps," I began.

"Yes, perhaps," Alessandro said. "Perhaps if Cardinal Borgia were pope I'd move to the Courts of Law. Something in it for everyone."

"A small reward for good service," I said. "And why not? You're as qualified as anyone. Just because you happen to be my brother…"

"…and I happen to mention that I'd like to move over to legal to my sister who's expecting the Cardinal's child…."

"Alessandro, if you were a condottiero it would be the same!" I exclaimed. "Or if you'd been born the heir to a great property. The world runs on patronage, whether you're priest or soldier or just a woman. That's how it is. I'm not ashamed of using the rules to my advantage. A woman has few enough advantages and no chance of rising based on her supposed merit as you do. If my lover gives me the means to help my family and those I think deserve it, I will gladly dispense favors. If you don't want Rodrigo's patronage, you'll have to take that up with him."

He shook his head. "Forgive me, Giulia. I don't mean to be ungrateful. Nor do I mean to imply that you shouldn't take his favors. I respect him. If I must attach myself to a faction, the Borgia faction is the best. I suppose I had imagined that the College of Cardinals was better than this, pure spirits inspired by the love of

Christ, not a bunch of quarrelsome nobles and schemers."

"My dear, you may find that in a monastery, but not in Rome," I said quietly. "This is a city-state, not a brotherhood of believers. The pope rules in the world, not in heaven. He is simply a man who may try his best or not."

"As is a priest." Alessandro's face cleared. "Ah, Giulia. I do try my best."

"I know you do," I said, and put my arm around him. "Of course you do."

"It's not that I don't want a family as well," he said. "I do. But it's not fair to sire a child I can't support, and right now I have no way of caring for a woman who entrusted herself to me. And it's not right to do that to her, do you see? So I stick with friends who understand."

"I do see," I said. Alessandro had always appreciated beauty in all its forms, whether male or female. Yet it had not occurred to me that perhaps Alessandro wished he could be a father as I would soon be a mother. "But that may change, my dear."

"Through your patronage," he said. "And here we are all the way around again!"

"I have not asked Rodrigo for anything for you," I said. "If he decides to reward you, it is his decision. Does that make you feel better?"

My brother nodded. "Yes." He gave me a squeeze. "I'm sorry to have said anything."

"You're not going to remark on how much I'm getting out of him, are you?" I said. I was appalled that my voice choked. "Everyone seems to. How clever I am and how much of a fool he is for me! I expect he feels it too. A rich old man wrapped around my avaricious little fingers."

"Giulia, you know I don't think that," Alessandro said. "Cardinal Borgia is nobody's fool." He frowned. "And you're nobody's victim."

"Is it so hard to believe that I love him?" I asked. "If he were cruel and I endured much, or he had nothing but shame to give me, perhaps then my love might be believed. But he is good to me in every way, and so it seems nothing but self-interest to please him, rather than that I desire his happiness."

"If he is good to you and you love him, then I am glad for you," Alessandro said. "There's not so much love in the world that we can afford to throw it away."

"No, never," I said. "But I grow tired of being congratulated on what a fine whore I am or pitied for imagined suffering!" I shook my head. "And when I am angry, I say, *Well enough! I will play at whatever you imagine me to be. You would not believe my truth if I told you.*"

Alessandro gave me a rueful look. "I believe you."

"Do you?"

"Yes." He put his head to the side. "And I believe he loves you, for whatever that belief is worth. And yes, I can see it rankles to be thought your fool, but I put it to you that it is his trial. He's willing to be thought manipulated by a greedy whore, which surely strikes at his pride. He's a proud man, Giulia"

Something made sense to me. "And so he struts and swaggers," I said. "He'd rather be thought a villain than a fool."

Alessandro shrugged, smiling. "And you'd rather be thought a harlot than a victim. So the pair of you put on a show like players and have half Rome talking about how he guards you jealously as a miser and how you have him fetch strawberries and feed them to you like a baby while you lick his fingers."

"Fiammetta's party. You heard about that."

"Giulia, everybody heard about that. Did you think they wouldn't talk? I bet he did."

"I'm sure he did," I said. Well, better a villain than a fool. "Perhaps we could both be villains," I said. "I'd rather be hated than pitied."

"You could work on that," Alessandro said seriously. "So when am I supposed to be here to help with this magical operation? How bad can it be, really? Just because the last time I did this with Dionisio, I nearly got killed in a fight with four Orsini guards?"

"We won't invite the Orsini this time," I promised. "Let us go find Dionisio and ask him."

We found him and went into my sala, closing the door so the whole house wouldn't hear. "I presume you've thought about how to do this," I said.

Dionisio blew out a long breath. "I think it can be done, but I warn you that I've never done this nor heard of anyone doing it this way. You are talking about using a magical circle as a permanent protection."

"What do you mean, plainly?" Alessandro asked.

"There are two kinds of protections," Dionisio said. "Magical circles are intended to protect a small space for a short time, an hour or perhaps two, long enough for the magus to do something specific. Protections like talismans are meant to permanently protect a place." He glanced at me. "Giulia likened it to consecrating a building. This is not an easy or quick process."

"No, it's not," Alessandro said. "How would you do that for a house?"

"Ideally, this would involve creating a protective sigil at an astrologically auspicious time and then tying it to physical features within the house, carvings or painted ceilings or other features that could not be readily or easily changed."

"As one does with a church," I said. "A painting or stained glass window or statue of the saint in whose name the building is consecrated."

Alessandro nodded. "That's clear. Go on."

"There are two problems here. First, changing a physical feature of the house isn't easy."

"What about using a wax sigil, like the one we made before?" I asked. "Surely we can make a wax sigil and keep it in the house relatively easily."

Dionisio sighed. "Yes, but that brings us to the second problem. The curse sigil that was intended to cause Cardinal Borgia harm was created by a specific rite enacted at an astrologically appropriate time. You had no need to know this, but we timed it to the hour. And then it was activated by blood." He had the good grace to look abashed.

"So you're saying this would have to be done at a particular time?" Alessandro asked, and Dionisio nodded.

"So when is an auspicious time?" I asked.

"I don't know."

"You don't know? How do you find out?" I asked.

"Consult an ephemeris, which is a book that shows the position of the five planets, moon and sun at all times, thus allowing an astrologer to look up what their positions will be or have been in the past," he said. "And before you ask, yes, I have such a book, but I had to abandon it in Florence. I couldn't carry everything. Does Cardinal Borgia have one?"

"Not to my knowledge," I said. "Why would he? Is it not a specialized tool for an astrologer?"

"Or a navigator," Dionisio said. "To steer by the stars."

"Surely there is one in Rome," Alessandro said.

"Surely, but we cannot hunt for one at present," Dionisio said. "And even if I had one, we do not have months to choose a date from. If the auspicious time were the ninth hour of Thursday, August 23rd, it would not help us."

"Two and a half weeks from now? I think not," I said. "You're right, Dionisio. That's not going to work."

"So I reluctantly concur that using a magical circle is best, since it does not require the correspondence of a particular planetary position, but rather draws its strength from the angelic powers invoked. I do have two major caveats, however."

"It won't last," I said.

"Yes. They're designed to last hours, not weeks. Even if we don't take it down, it will fade in strength and eventually decay to nothing."

"How long?" Alessandro asked. He sounded fascinated.

Dionisio shrugged. "A few days? A week? Maybe a little more? As I said, I've never done this or seen it done."

"So it's very temporary," I said. "Even so, it's better than nothing. And if we have to do it a second time, we will. What's the other problem?"

"I'm not sure what it will do. Other than have the seeming of a barrier," he said. "This isn't what they're intended for. I don't know what will happen if it's misused."

Alessandro looked at me. I sighed. "Surely angelic powers will intend no ill. If we use holy water to mark the squares and Alessandro blesses everything in sight...."

Dionisio spread his hands. "This is all theoretical, Giulia."

"Then let's do it," I said. "After all, you said it could be taken down. If it is unpleasant, we can take it down." I was, perhaps, overly optimistic.

While Alessandro blessed holy water and Dionisio got together everything he needed, I took Maria aside and explained that Father Alessandro was going to bless the entire house. He was worried about me, of course, and he thought that it couldn't hurt to call upon angels to watch over us.

Maria didn't look disturbed at all, but then she liked Alessandro. "There's nothing wrong with a little extra blessing, is my thought," she said.

"I quite agree," I said, one hand curling over my belly protectively. The baby was moving a lot. "I'm going to help him and hold things for him, but he's going to go around and bless everything. If you don't mind telling everyone else so they won't be worried?"

"Of course, Donna Giulia," she said, and went toward the kitchen.

Alessandro came downstairs then, with Dionisio and a big basin of holy water. "We're ready," he said. "Where do we start?"

"The back of the garden?" I asked. "That's the northernmost wall. That's how you did it before in the squares."

"You were watching!" Dionisio said.

"Yes." The number of times I'd sat there on that three-legged stool with nothing to do but stare back at the men around me, watching him chalk his symbols…. Of course I knew he started at the north and went around sunwards, like a compass.

"Let's go bless the garden," Alessandro said.

We started in the middle of the back wall, Alessandro splashing holy water on it in the shape of one of Dionisio's symbols while Dionisio said something in Greek. I held the basin for Alessandro. When Dionisio finished, he added, "*In nomine Patri et Filii, et Spiritus Sancti,*" as a matter of good measure. Then we moved on, splashing the wall from time to time as we went. When we got to the corner we went inside.

The guardroom was next, and having been duly warned they stood respectfully while Alessandro blessed his way along. "Thank you, Father Alessandro," the captain said.

"Peace be with you, my son," Alessandro added as we moved into the saletta. The captain must be ten years his senior, but things like that didn't matter.

The next sigil got splashed in water in the saletta, then we turned the corner again. Through the stairwell, through the foyer, through the first floor study. I could feel it building, like lightning in the air before a storm. It ran like prickles up my spine. The baby kicked. It could feel it too and didn't particularly like it.

We turned the corner again into the kitchen. Silvia and Tina and Beneo were waiting. Alessandro marked the kitchen wall firmly. "*In nomine Patri et Filii et Spiritus Sancti,*" he said.

"Will it really do anything?" Tina whispered to Beneo.

I didn't hear if he answered or not. It felt like pressure in my ears, like a sound too high for hearing scaling up and up. It was quite uncomfortable.

We did the back of the storeroom and the locked street door, then came out of the storeroom, back through the kitchen, and then the well of the servants' stair. That brought us all the way around to the garden wall, twenty feet or so from where we started.

"Let's close it up," Dionisio said, and Alessandro started splashing his way along the garden. The basin was almost empty. Surely it would feel better when it was finished.

We reached our starting point. Alessandro splashed water over the marks we had already made, now nearly dry in the sun. "*Finis est,*" he said. "*Fiat lux!*"

The world spun and I stumbled, everything going dark.

I fell to my knees beside the bed. It was hot even with the shutters closed, a meridian of white light along the crack. Already the room was close, smelling of illness and the faintest lingering scent of incense. Alessandro put his hand on my arm to raise me. "Giulia, you have to come!" His voice was raw and I looked up at him. He wore plain clothing, a sword at his side, a day's beard on his face.

"No," I said. I laced my fingers with Rodrigo's, though he didn't move. There was still a pulse in his wrist, though his face was already slack, as though he was in a place beyond pain. "No." He lay on the bed as if on a bier, the covers pulled up to his chest.

There were no attendants. There was no one but Burchard, the fussy chronicler, sitting in the corner like a rabbit.

"If we don't go now, we won't be able to!" Alessandro's voice was urgent. "Listen!" I could hear the sound of voices on the floor above. I could hear shouts outside. "You have to come now."

'I can't. He breathes. I can't…." My voice broke. Every detail of his face, every graven line, every hair on the back of his hand was precious to me. How could I leave him? How could I leave him now?

"He would want you to," Alessandro said. "He would tell you to think of the child." Yes, the child. I was pregnant. I could feel the hard roundness of my belly, the faint movement of the baby within. "He would tell you to go if he could." Alessandro put his hand on my shoulder.

I could not see through the tears spilling down as I lifted his limp hand to my lips, kissing it as I had so many times. "Rodrigo. Rodrigo." They say the dying can still hear. They say it is the last of the senses to go. I leaned close to his ear. "You are my love and my heart's breath. I will love you forever. I'll meet you at that symposium with Virgil you used to promise me. In those dark fields by night, among the lilies." I thought his eyelid twitched. It might have. "I will miss you every day until I see you again." I closed my eyes, bending my head against his shoulder. "I can't leave you alone."

"I will stay," Burchard said. I looked up. He stood very straight, his mouth set in a line beneath watery blue eyes. "I do not have a child to think of."

The noise above was louder. "We have to go!" Alessandro said, pulling me to my feet. My hand parted from his. Burchard took his hand and folded it on his breast properly.

I could hardly see. I stumbled through the door into the servants' stair, Alessandro going ahead of me, the sword drawn in his hand. He listened at the bottom. It was silent. We went out, passing through a broad gallery, tables and chairs scattered about on a black and white floor, then through another room. There was a curule chair, a little table turned on its side, broken glass and a smear of wine across the floor….

"I think we can get to the passeto," Alessandro said. "Giulia!"

I staggered suddenly, the world spinning, clutching his arm….

"Giulia? Giulia!" Alessandro's voice came from a long way away, urgent and worried.

"I'm here," I said. My voice was barely more than a whisper.

"Some water?" That was Dionisio.

"You shouldn't have had her out in the hot sun. None of you have any sense." That was Maria.

"I'm all right." I opened my eyes. Above me was the painted ceiling of the saletta. I lay on one of the couches, all three of them bending over me. "What happened?"

"You fainted," Alessandro said. "You were insensible. We carried you in out of the sun."

"And you should know better than to have a breeding woman out in the hot sun on a day like today," Maria snapped. "You're a priest, but you don't know anything!" Alessandro looked sheepish. She put a cool compress on my forehead. "How is your head, Donna Giulia? Are you cramping?"

"No cramping," I said. "I am well enough." My head didn't hurt. But Rodrigo. I gasped as it came flooding back. "Rodrigo!"

"He's not here right now," Alessandro said.

"He was dying. Where is he?" I tried to sit up.

"At the Vice-Chancellor's palazzo this morning," Alessandro said. "And he was perfectly fine. I saw him not three hours ago." He looked at me with concern.

"She needs to go to bed in her own room," Maria said with a sniff. "I'll get it ready."

"It was the rite," Dionisio said in a low voice as soon as Maria left.

"Of course it was the rite!" Alessandro snapped. "Something was wrong in the way you set it up!"

"No, it wasn't," I said, propping up on one elbow. No cramping. The child was fine. And the pressure on my head had eased. I thought I understood. "It was a summoning square designed to allow the Dove to see the future. It did just what it was supposed to."

"You're not a Dove anymore," Dionisio said.

"Obviously I am," I said. I sat up. "The sibyls of old weren't virgin girls, or didn't have to be. The Book of the Erythraean Sibyl—she wasn't a child! They were grown women, mothers and priestesses, old women who had lovers and children. There is absolutely no reason a Dove has to be virgin." I looked at Alessandro. "No more than a priest has to be chaste. You don't stop being a priest if you satisfy a friend."

He had the decency to look embarrassed. "We're not supposed to."

"No, you're not supposed to!" I exclaimed. "And Rodrigo's not supposed to fornicate, is he? But you know what he does when he says Mass is real. Your blessings are real. There's sinning and breaking the rules, but it doesn't change what you are. Nothing changes what you are."

Dionisio looked intrigued. "So you're saying that being a Dove is what you are?"

"That's exactly what I'm saying." I hadn't put it in so many words until now. But it made sense. "I am whatever the sibyls were. Virginity has nothing to do with it. The rites are just a channel for grace."

Alessandro took a deep breath. "Listening and hearing," he said.

"What?"

He shrugged. "We call it listening and hearing. Everyone who seeks ordination can learn to listen for God's voice. We spend a great deal of time learning to listen. Learning to sort out the whisper of the divine amid the noise of everyday life. But hearing…. You can't learn to hear. Some men can and some can't. For some people, the world is a numinous place. Every stone tells a story. The voices of the past, of the future, and of God echo in the ordinary. Learning to listen can help you refine it, but hearing…. Even little children can hear."

"You hear," I said. Alessandro had always had true vocation. He had always yearned for the touch of grace.

He nodded. "And so do you." He sat down next to me, putting his arm around me. "Alike as twins, everybody always said. It's more than being tall. When you told stories when we were children, I could see them. And you could see the angel in a beam of sun."

My eyes overflowed, and I bent my face against his shoulder. "We are of the same blood."

He nodded. "Whatever it is that lets me hear, we're the same."

"Today we call that being a Dove," Dionisio said. "The ancients would have called it being a sibyl."

I closed my eyes. "I saw Rodrigo's death. By poison, by illness, by magic…. I don't know. But I saw him on his deathbed and you were taking me away." A connection knitted. "Dea Peregrina. Pregnant and fleeing from the city, from the hands of Set raised against her, Osiris murdered behind her."

"The manuscript of Plutarch's *Moralia*," Dionisio supplied. "The one that Mois Sarfati is selling. It's part of Isis and Osiris."

I felt Alessandro take a deep breath. "All right."

I lifted my head. "I'm not going to let it happen," I said. "The future can be changed. I'm not going to let him die. Will you help me?"

"You know I will," Alessandro said.

Chapter Seven

Naturally it was easier said than done. It was all very well to vow I would change the future but much more difficult to do it. Alessandro left that evening. Rodrigo sent a note but did not come. I had not really expected him, but I wished he would. I was certain he had a great deal to do tomorrow and could hardly take precious hours to spend with me. And yet it would have reassured me to see him.

I tossed and turned in my bed, the balcony doors open to the sky. It wasn't late yet. I supposed I had never really thought that he might be killed. Yes, I had feared for him two years ago, but it had come out right. And Rodrigo always seemed supremely confident. He never seemed afraid. He was so much the master of his world that to me it seemed that there was nothing he couldn't do, no situation he could not scheme his way out of, no solution he could not contrive. I idolized him.

I got up and paced to the balcony doors, looking out over the city. Of course I did. He was much older. He was protective of me. He faced all dangers with a wink and a nod, or at least an expression of temper which made even mortal perils into nuisances which displeased him. I had seen him angry. I had never seen him frightened. I had certainly never seen him helpless.

I took a deep breath of the night air. Ill, dying…. He had said two years ago that he would die someday, in the course of time. It was to be expected. He was decades my senior. But it was easy to say, *Someday is not today. What will happen far in the future will happen. It does not have to be imagined. I do not need to borrow tomorrow's pain. If death takes him long years from now, I will not think about it. And yet now I must. It might not be long years, but a few days or weeks if this vision were true.* I was still pregnant in the vision. It could not be as long as four months. Twenty-three weeks since I had bled, and seventeen left to run. And it was summer in the vision. Tomorrow was the fifth of August. If this danger were imminent, it was in the next few weeks.

I passed my hand over my eyes, pushing my errant hair back. Warn him? Of what? He already knew that there were rivals who would poison, and he was surely as careful as he was going to be. He already knew Bracciano was his enemy. There was nothing I could tell him that he didn't know. I had run to him in the night two years ago to tell him Bracciano intended to murder him by black magic, but now I did not even know as much as I had known then. At least then I had known the means. Now I knew nothing but the intention. If I related the vision, all I would do was cause him to worry for me and distract him from the contest at hand or, worse, believe that I was not up to my part in it. No, I had to do this myself.

Which meant I had to claim this power. If I was a sibyl, I could no longer afford to be afraid of it as I had been when I was Bracciano's Dove. I had to seek mastery. I had to learn everything I could—to learn to listen, as Alessandro would say. I raised my chin. Well, if learning was required, Rodrigo had given me the tools. I had to use them myself. Just as I was now the mistress of this house, I would have to decide what needed to be done and do it. Closing the house in a square had results I didn't expect, but I had taken no hurt from it, and if I had learned of a threat, it had been beneficial.

I took a deep breath of the night air. Rodrigo often came to my house late and unexpectedly. I was at his house often, but it was always at a time we had planned. And yet I needed to see him, to reassure myself that he was well now. If I were going to seize control, I would do this. I went back inside, closing the doors and dressing in my plainest cotta. I bundled my hair into a simple snood. Then I went downstairs.

There were four guards in the guardroom. Two others were on duty at the door. "Captain," I said, "I need four men to escort me to the Vice-Chancellor's palazzo immediately."

To my surprise, the guard captain didn't ask any questions. He simply stood up, telling off the men to accompany us. "Yes, Donna Giulia." He answered to me as readily as Adriana or Rodrigo, and that was something to know. Directing servants was one thing. It was another to command guardsmen. I thought, as we set off into the night, that I rather liked it.

Needless to say, Rodrigo was surprised to see me. His guards let me in despite the hour, a servant running up the stairs seconds before me. Rodrigo had not retired, but was in shirt and hose in the heat, the windows of his study and camera alike open. He looked alarmed. "Giulia, what has happened?"

"Nothing," I said. "I wanted to see you." The stage was not set. There were no glittering side lamps, no cold supper laid. His robes were a pile on a bench at the end of the bed, his red slippers kicked off beside the fireplace. An empty glass and a plate of crumbs sat on the little table. It was not an enchanted underworld.

"Then come in, sweetness," he said, and the servant closed the doors to the camera and the sala beyond. "I have nothing prepared for your delight."

"I don't need anything but you," I said, and stepped closer, one hand against his cheek. Alive. Warm. Mine. *Blessed goddess*, I thought, *if you have helped me appreciate what I have, for that I thank you.*

I woke at dawn because the baby was kicking me in the bladder. I got up and went into the bathing room, then came back. Rodrigo was still sleeping. He'd thrown the covers off, legs bare against the sheets, and was snoring loudly. I had actually gotten used to it. I sat down on the side of the bed to braid my hair. I couldn't do it properly without help, but I could at least tidy it up.

"Slipping off like a little succubus at daybreak?" His voice was muzzy with sleep, one hand reaching for my hip.

I smiled. "Vanishing into thin air with morning light." I twisted my hair and tied off the end with a ribbon.

"Sadly, I can't stay in bed today," he said. Of course not. He had to be at the Vatican.

"I know." I turned around and kissed him. "I won't keep you. I just want to go in the gallery on my way out."

"I'll come with you. Give me a moment." It didn't take him long to dress. I did up his points and he laced my gown. We might have been any bourgeois married couple, a young second wife and a prosperous merchant. Well, neither of us had been raised like the great families, who would never dream of sharing a bedroom or dressing without a maidservant. I daresay my father had laced my mother most mornings.

The house was airy and cool in the early morning. White marble gleamed, light coming in from high windows. It was very quiet. Presumably Rodrigo's sons weren't up yet. The gallery was filled with sunbeams making a path across the floor. I knew exactly where I wanted to go.

The statue of Isis and Horus sat at the far end, the light from the windows above not quite touching it. I walked around to the front, looking at her serene face. Rodrigo came to stand beside me, silent as I was.

"Do you believe?" I asked quietly.

"In what?"

"Do you believe she's real? I know, *prisca theologia* and the rest. I don't mean intellectual exercises about the nature of the universe. Do you believe?" I looked at him sideways.

He looked at her rather than at me. "I feel," he said, and shrugged. I waited. The light moved on the stone, slow as centuries. She watched us. "When I was a boy, my uncle said 'You have a fine mind and might go far if you don't let your heart interfere.' I do have a fine mind. I say so without false modesty. But I have always let my heart lead." Rodrigo glanced at me. "It gets me into trouble."

"That doesn't answer my question," I said quietly.

"Well then." He took a breath, looking up at her. Such an ordinary face, if one were to paint it, a jowly middle-aged man who hadn't shaved this morning, laugh lines at the corners of his mouth. "I feel her peace. I feel a kind of serene sadness. When she was pulled from the rubble seven years ago at the excavations, I knew I had to have her. To save her. As though my mother lay in the gutter. I don't know if you can understand."

"I think I do," I said.

"And now she is clean and safe, restored to beauty and conserved and appreciated."

"But do you believe she's real?"

The corner of his mouth twitched. "Ah, my sweet, what is real? When we look at a statue or painting of the Virgin, it's not a likeness of Mary. No one knows what Our Lord's mother looked like. Probably she was not peerlessly beautiful and eternally graceful. An artist has a model in which they see the face of the Queen of Heaven, and they add to it the things that they see beyond a real woman's face. Or perhaps, if they're lucky, they see Her reflected in a face that is dear to them. But it's not Her. It's a flickering embodiment."

"The same way that when you say the Mass, for a moment that grace reflects through you," I said, trying to understand.

He nodded. "Very much so." His eyes did not leave the statue. "A painting of Our Lady is an imperfect rendering of Her. So is this statue. Both of them are Her. They have different names, but they're reflections of the same thing. That is what I feel."

I paused, phrasing my question carefully. "And do you think she can also be reflected in a living person, as you do with the Mass?"

"Without a doubt." His mouth twitched again. "And there is the heresy, my love. Adoration of the Virgin is one thing, but to suggest embodiment, as though a woman could be a priest? That is indeed beyond doctrine."

"And yet the Pope is addressed as God's earthly habitation," I said.

"Indeed." Rodrigo took my arm. "Christ's representative."

"Murdered and risen, like Osiris," I said.

He looked at me sharply. "What are you getting at?"

"I don't entirely know," I said. "Turning things round and round in my head, I suppose. I can't quite see the shape of it." Almost, but not quite, a story just out of reach.

"Maybe your mind is getting in the way of your heart." He put his hand over mine on his arm. "But now we must start the day. I have quite a lot of simony and corruption to accomplish today."

I laughed. "I will be waiting for your directions." I kissed his cheek quickly. "I won't fail you."

"I know," he said.

On Sunday at sunset the Vatican went into lockdown. Doors were closed and windows shuttered so that those within could not even look out and see someone who made signs to them. The cardinals within were put into deep isolation. On Monday morning they would meet in consistory in the Sistine Chapel. The ceremonies would begin with prayers for the purity and wisdom of the vote, and for God's aid in selecting His new earthly representative. There would be addresses from various worthies. There would be lengthy benedictions from distinguished visitors. It would take a day or two before they were even ready to vote, eating and sleeping within the Vatican so they might have no influences upon their votes except for one another.

Of course in reality people passed in and out of the Vatican constantly. The cardinals must eat and drink. Beds must be made, slops emptied, clothes washed, baths drawn, doors guarded. An army of clerks, servants and guards was required to keep the conclave working. Each of those men and women needed money. Some were already personal servants or protégés of prelates. Others could simply be given a silver soldo or two to take a message to someone. In theory, anyone carrying messages would be dismissed. In practicality that was nearly impossible.

Alessandro would see Rodrigo constantly. Every cardinal had several aides and clerks, and Rodrigo had chosen Alessandro as one of his. Meanwhile, Alessandro had made arrangements with a senior guard. He would drop messages with the man and one of our men could pick them up, leaving a return message for Alessandro when we had one. It was quite straightforward. No doubt the guard would make a tidy sum if the conclave lasted a week.

I expected that it would. It was clear that no one was close to fifteen votes, and presumably it would take days of wrangling and politicking and bribery and possibly outright threats for someone to reach it. Hopefully there would be few outright threats. The Gonfaloniere had not gotten the extra troops he wanted, though he had plenty of men of his own. However, most of the cardinals had sent their families to the country, and those who had not had made provisions as Rodrigo had. I felt the house could withstand anything short of an actual siege with crossbows and rams. A mob would be hard-pressed to break in, and surely even in the heated climate of a papal election an all-out military assault was unlikely.

Alessandro's first letter arrived that night as I rose from dinner with Dionisio and the Sarfati family. *Dearest Sister*, it read, *we are closing the doors in a few minutes, so a letter to you first. Tomorrow we will begin with the Mass of the Holy Spirit, followed by a speech on the solemn duties of the electors. It is to be given by the Spanish ambassador. This is greatly to His Eminence's advantage, as it will make clear to the other cardinals what the position of their majesties is in regards to the election.*

"Well, obviously they want a Spaniard and there is only one Spanish cardinal," I said. "Is that news to anyone?"

Chaya Sarfati had been following her brother and sister out of the room. Now she halted. "It seems very complicated. How does one elect a ruler? It seems counterintuitive to think that an election could choose a man to be anointed."

"I suppose it does," I said. "Certainly most rulers are born to the throne. However, that's not always the case in Italy as it is in other places. The Florentine Republic has been governed by election, even if in practice a few families control it. I guess that here we have never entirely forgotten the democracies of the ancients, even if we fall far short of the ideal." I came around the table, the candles on it casting a warm glow over the red and gold cloth. "But if you read Plutarch, it is clear that the ideal was always a goal rather than a given. I am not sure Rome has changed so much since the days of Pompey and Caesar. Perhaps it is simply who we are."

Chaya nodded slowly. "And you are Roman?"

"My family is from Tuscany the last six hundred years. But we were here before that." I leaned over to blow out one of the candles. "There are tombs near Montalto that were made by the Etruscans. Maybe my ancestors were buried there. This land is in my bones."

"And I am of no land," Chaya said. She shrugged, slight in her worn dress. "Castile, Aragon, al-Andalus…. Now Rome. I am lucky to be here with my family. I don't know what the conversos will do."

"Surely if they have converted and been baptized, they will be safe in Spain?" I asked.

Chaya's eyes filled with tears. "No. Never. Not with the Inquisition. Even people whose parents or grandparents converted are not safe. They could be denounced and tried at any time."

"And where are your parents?" I asked gently. I hesitated to, but it seemed the time.

"I don't know," Chaya said. "My father said we should separate into three groups so that each of us would have a better chance of escape. My mother and my oldest sister and her husband and baby were going to Valencia. My father and my youngest brother hoped to get a ship to Oran. I don't know if they did."

"I will pray that they did," I said solemnly. I had never given a great deal of thought to the Inquisition before. It was away in Spain where I had never been, and when Rodrigo spoke of it, it was in the same breath as he spoke of Savonarola in Florence. Now it seemed real. Of course Savonarola was real too, or Dionisio would not have fled Florence.

"Thank you, Donna Giulia," Chaya said, and hurried out. I had been no help, I thought. But what could I do besides what I did—give them temporary refuge?

The next morning the conclave met. We could hear the bells calling them to order for the first time. I tried to pay them no heed. There would be no news today. As Alessandro had said, they would spend the entire day in formalities. We could expect the first vote no earlier than late tomorrow or perhaps Wednesday.

Of course it was likely Rodrigo would have work for me before then, but since right now he was in an endless series of services and meetings, he would not have the opportunity to send word, or indeed to do much of the politicking that he needed to. I expected much of that would happen after hours this evening, when the official functions broke out into smaller groups to socialize. Thus,

I tried to occupy myself and not think about it more than I could help.

I had a note from Alessandro that evening. *Dear Giulia*, he said, *It was all speeches today. Tomorrow every cardinal who wishes will be able to speak in consistory about the qualities required of the next pope and will make their positions and recommendations clear. Right now the first ballot will be taken early on Wednesday. So far all is well.*

By which he meant everything was as expected. Tomorrow they would get a better idea of exactly who was in what position. Presumably Rodrigo was certain of his starting five votes, but beyond that…. There was no point in speculating, I told myself firmly. We would know soon enough. There was no note from Rodrigo.

Wednesday morning was overcast and cool. There had been noise in the street the night before, but morning showed no evidence of what it had been. Shuttered windows and closed doors were all I could see from my balcony. I stood upon it looking out like a ship's captain overlooking hostile seas, scanning for a sign of danger and seeing only rolling waves that concealed all malice beneath the surface. Fanciful, I thought. And perhaps overwrought. We had guards aplenty. The front doors were stout and barred. The kitchen door was also barred and in any event led into a storeroom with a heavy door to the street which locked with an iron lock. Even if a mob broke down the street door, they'd be in a storeroom with stone walls and a barred door ahead of them. I was simply on edge because of the vision of Rodrigo's death and making too much of everything.

I cupped my hand around my belly, the baby shifting. Thursday would be twenty-four weeks. "There now, little one," I said. "What shall we do today? Perhaps we should read some Plutarch. One is never too young to read Plutarch."

It occurred to me that I could take another look at the pages from Plutarch's *Moralia* that Mois Sarfati was selling. That was where the vision of Rodrigo's death had begun—the story of the murder of Osiris. Yes, I had felt faint before, but this time I was prepared. If I intended to master this ability rather than have it master me, I had to challenge it. I had to deliberately cause a vision and remain calm.

Mois was happy to show me the pages again, though Dionisio was nervous. "Are you sure this is a good idea?" he asked as Mois brought the manuscript to the table in my sala, the table near the window but not in direct sun so that it would not harm it. Chaya came in with him.

"I am ready for it this time," I said. I took a deep breath. *It is a manuscript. A book is a door. And that is all it is. It is not a living thing and cannot master me.* I glanced up at Mois. "Are the pages in order?"

"There are eleven pages," he said. "I have put them in order as best I can, but there are many pages missing." He frowned. "Though the illumination is beautiful, I hesitate to offer this for sale because it is incomplete."

"If Cardinal Borgia won't buy it, I will," I said. I could afford an incomplete copy of *Moralia* without recourse to his funds, and I wanted this if only for that one page of illustration. Chaya's eyebrows rose. "So let us see what we can." I sat down at the table, the first page before me.

Or rather the first page there was. "The opening is missing," Mois said. Presumably that had been the most lavishly illuminated. And also it would have carried the title, the initials of the copyist, and perhaps where and for whom this copy had been made.

Still, there were clues in the text. I looked at it carefully. The script was not difficult at all. It was recent in style, the same neat hand that Rodrigo used for all his correspondence that showed he'd been trained as a clerk. It had the same perfect squaring, the same margins. "From Valencia?" I guessed.

"It's possible," Mois said. "Certainly in Aragon. It would be reasonable that it was copied in Valencia before 1390. That's when many of us came to al-Andalus, after the riots then."

I nodded. So fifty years or so older than Rodrigo's boyhood. That followed. I could sight-read easily enough. "The effort to arrive at the truth, especially the truth about the gods, comes from longing for the divine. The search for truth requires for its study the consideration of sacred subjects, and it is more hallowed than any form of holy living or temple service. Not least of all, it is pleasing to that goddess whom you worship, a goddess exceptionally wise and a lover of wisdom. Isis is a Greek word, as is the name of Typhon, her enemy, who is conceited in his ignorance and self-deception. He tears to pieces and scatters to the winds sacred writings and beautiful things, which Isis collects and puts together in the care of those who are initiated into holy rites."

That seemed rather on point. And yet it was completely true. For decades Rodrigo had collected ancient and beautiful things, some of them great works of art and others simply fragments of life, a box of little objects on his desk that he played with idly or used for page weights—a stone bobbin, a leaf-shaped arrowhead, a blue faience scarab, a tiny bull of black stone, a piece of pottery with a brilliant border. He kept these fragments as well as statues and manuscripts. Of course that was pleasing to her.

I turned the page. The next passage did not continue the idea. "And there are pages missing next?"

Mois nodded. "Yes. It picks up with an explanation of why priests should abstain from eating fish." I glanced over the page. It seemed much less germane. Also I had no strange feelings at all about which kinds of fish were forbidden to priests at the Temple of Isis.

"And the next page?" I laid this one carefully aside.

There was the illumination I remembered, pregnant Isis fleeing, her scarf over her head, her eyes cast back to look behind her. I took a deep breath. For a moment the world swam, but I could focus. I could steady it. I could read the text aloud. "Typhon secretly measured Osiris' body and had a beautiful chest of corresponding size made and ornamented, which he caused to be brought to the procession where it was in progress and gave it to Osiris. When the holy king laid down in it, the cover was put on and nails driven through from outside, and then through the holes was poured molten lead until he was dead. When Typhon had done the dreadful deed, he dishonored the body in all ways, cutting it into pieces and scattering them as offal. Therefore the Wandering Goddess fled in fear of her life, for she carried his child, and it was no longer safe in the city."

I shivered. Dionisio looked alarmed. "Giulia?"

"That is dreadful," Chaya said. "What a terrible way to kill someone! Why not just stab him?"

"Cruelty is the point," I said. I could control it. I could control vision just as I had lied to the demon in the mirror two years ago. I could almost feel an encouraging hand on my shoulder. I turned the page.

"There is a great deal missing," Mois said. "It picks up in the second book. You see?"

The illumination showed a ship under sail, a statue upon its deck. "Ptolemy Soter saw the colossal statue in a dream," I read, "and in his dream the statue bade him to bring it to Alexandria. Thus he spoke to his friends, and one said to him, 'I will fetch this if it is your will and bring you a god as I brought you a king.' So they set forth and came to Sinope, and with great difficulty brought the statue away. When it had been conveyed to Alexandria, it took to itself the name that Pluto bears among the Egyptians, that of Serapis, which is to say Osiris who rules in the underworld, having been dead and restored to life. For this reason Serapis is a god of all peoples in common, even as Osiris is, as those who have participated in his rites know well."

"That's very..." Dionisio began, then stopped.

"*Prisca theologia*," I said. "The golden thread of truth that runs through all." I took a deep breath. I could see the connections clearly enough, the ways this story tied to the more familiar one of the Resurrection. Mary came to the tomb as Isis sought Osiris.

There was a knock at the sala door. "I beg your pardon, Donna Giulia," Beneo said. "But a man is here with a note for you."

I jumped to my feet, excusing myself quickly, and ran down to the foyer. One of our guardsmen had brought it from the Vatican, and it was clearly Alessandro's hand. I opened it quickly. It was the count from the first vote. *Carafa 5 Borgia 4 della Rovere 4 Sforza 3 da Costa 3 Orsini 2 Piccolomini 1 Colonna 1.*

"What a mess," I said to myself. Well, at least nobody else was far ahead. I frowned at the rest of the note. *Eight thousand to Piccolomini.* That was plain enough. Cardinal Piccolomini set the price for his vote at eight thousand ducats, or not quite three times my original dowry—a handsome sum but not more than a noble bride. Rodrigo would make a lovely noble bride!

I turned to the guard captain. "Would you send a man to the Vice-Chancellor's palazzo? I will write out a note for the Archbishop of Valencia."

"Of course, Madonna."

I went back up to my sala. "I am sorry to cut this short, my friends," I said. "Unfortunately, I have work that I must do for the Cardinal. Signore Sarfati, thank you for your time and the look at the manuscript."

He made agreeable chat while gathering up the pages, Dionisio helping. Chaya looked at me. "What kind of work?" she asked curiously.

"I need to have money conveyed to a certain gentleman," I said. I got out pen and ink.

"He trusts you with his money?"

"Yes." She followed her brother out and I wrote a note to Cesare. *Your father needs eight thousand ducats delivered to Piccolomini.* I also gave him the vote count. *I will tell him it will be done.*

Chapter Eight

Cesare arrived just after Compline. We were sitting down to dinner so he joined us. Because the Sarfati and Dionisio were present, he said nothing of his father's business. Rather, he made small talk with Mois about Spain while Chaya and Sincha both made eyes at him. He was handsome, and I suppose made a great impression on girls of fourteen and twelve. Fortunately for them, he paid them all the attention he would have Lucrezia's school friends, which is to say brief replies when one interrupted him.

After dinner Cesare came into my camera and we walked out onto the balcony together while the maids cleared the table in my sala. Chaya watched us go with interest. I suppose taking a beautiful young man through my bedchamber wasn't done in the seraglios of Grenada! It was very strange to imagine that my relations with Rodrigo should be respectable and yet a conversation with his son compromising.

"I've delivered the funds to Piccolomini's household," Cesare said. "All in cash with no way to trace it. If Papa doesn't get his money's worth, Piccolomini can say it never happened." He shook his head.

"And face your father's wrath as Vice-Chancellor even if not as pope," I said. "He'd be wise to stay bought."

"Undoubtedly." Cesare looked out across the city in the dark, his elbows on the railing. Somewhere to the north there was the glow of a fire. A building was burning. On the other side of the river, I thought, and well upriver from the Vatican, toward the northern city gates. It was a good distance from here.

"The Gonfaloniere's troops aren't doing much of a job of preventing violence," I said.

He shrugged. "They don't mean to. The more chaos, the better. It covers anything they want to happen." Cesare glanced east. "Della Rovere arranged an omen for himself. Mysteriously, a light appeared in the highest window of his house. Mysterious."

I laughed. "Very." Obviously one could arrange such an omen easily. "Why does he hate your father so much? What's the bad blood between them?"

"Other than disagreeing on almost every issue?" Cesare asked.

"Other than that," I said.

He leaned against the railing. "It goes back to the last election, ten years ago when Sixtus died. Sixtus was born Francesco della Rovere; Raffaele Riario and Giuliano della Rovere are both his nephews. He made them cardinals on the same day. He also did a lot of things that Papa didn't approve of, like founding the Inquisition in Spain. Anyway, when Sixtus died both Papa and della Rovere wanted to be elected. Della Rovere was too new, and Papa wasn't quite there. He knew he wouldn't get a two-thirds majority. So he made a deal with della Rovere for them to back Cardinal Cybo, who became Pope Innocent. The theory was that they'd be the powers behind the throne."

"Together?" I asked. Rodrigo and della Rovere couldn't agree that the sky was blue.

"That worked as well as you think." Cesare gave me a sideways glance. "They've jerked Innocent first one way and then the other like a dog on two leashes for ten years. The last straw for Papa was della Rovere interfering in Spain." He shook his head. "Papa got Pope Innocent to issue a directive that anyone convicted of a capital offense by the Inquisition had the right to appeal to the Papal Legate for Spain. Guess who that is?"

I knew that. "Rodrigo," I said. "So he was supposed to review all capital cases on appeal? And presumably could reverse a lower court?"

"Got it," Cesare said. "The Spanish Crown screamed murder but they'd have had to live with it if della Rovere hadn't gotten Innocent to reverse his own directive four months later. So the Inquisition started burning people again and Papa was furious. Then della Rovere worked out a treaty with France, and the moment he left for Paris as Papal Legate to France, Papa had Innocent disavow the treaty. Which basically left della Rovere standing in a snowstorm in his underclothes looking like an idiot. It's been more of that ever since."

"Heresy charges," I guessed.

Cesare nodded. "Della Rovere wants the Church to crack down on the universities. Papa doesn't. Somebody brings a heresy charge against a scholar, and della Rovere and Papa take opposite sides. Innocent went whichever way was easiest, or whichever one was standing there."

"In other words, no coherent policy," I said, thinking of Dionisio and his former maestro, Pico della Mirandola. "Nobody knows what they can say or do without charges."

"In a word." Cesare shrugged. "There's been enough of this nonsense. We need a strong pope who knows what he's doing. That's Papa. We can't take ten more years of indecision on every issue."

"No," I said. "Not now." There was a hint of strangeness, like a hand at my back, a whisper behind me. "The next decade is critical. The world will change. It matters whose hand is on the tiller."

"So Papa says." He straightened up. "Bracciano's not the only one who'd like to kill him. Though della Rovere is more likely to use poison than bravos. Easier to pass off as the hand of God," he said with a cynical twist of the lips.

I shivered though the night wasn't cold. "Do you want to stay here tonight? There's plenty of room."

Cesare nodded. "If it's not trouble."

"None at all," I said. We went back in the sala and I sent one of the little maids to tell Maria that Cesare would be staying in Lucrezia's room tonight so that there was no need to open another and get linens out.

I meant to retire early and rest, as everyone kept telling me to. Easier said than done. A few hours after Compline was often when I sat down to a late supper with Rodrigo if we were not at a play or dinner together. I was used to discourse, if not an evening's entertainment in the world. We would linger an hour over dinner before retiring together to a play of our own. It was difficult to simply go to sleep.

After turning round and round like a restless cat, I got up and lit the candles near my bed to read my current book. *The City of Ladies* by Christine de Pizan had been delivered and was proving tough reading. The allegory was quite thick, and I wished she had spent more time showing the deeds of the great women rather than telling me of their virtue. Still, I had not quite imagined there were so many worthy ladies to take as examples, though I had thought myself reasonably well-read. I did not know of Artemisia of Caria, who commanded naval vessels, or Semiramis who led troops into battle like Jeanne d'Arc. I supposed the point she was building to was that such events were not as far beyond the ordinary as they at first seemed. Perhaps the ability to command men in battle was not a unique gift of saints or viragos! Perhaps Lucrezia should be Gonfaloniere, as she'd said.

This book was my own purchase, not borrowed from Rodrigo, and I had skipped ahead to the beginning of volume two to read the section on Herophile and the other sibyls. I had not realized that the name sibyl itself meant one who knows the mind of God, or at least can see some of the greater purpose. However, it seemed that simply stating what one knew was out, and that prophecies had to be hidden for some purpose or other, Herophile writing hers on leaves so that the first letter of each utterance carried its true meaning when put in the correct order.

I was musing that this seemed undesirably obtuse when I heard a sound. At least I presume I heard a sound. It felt like a scratching at the door, or perhaps like a sound in the next room, the sound of a lute string breaking.

Who should be in the sala with a lute? I got up, putting on a robe over my camisa and taking a candlestick in my hand, and went into the sala. It was quiet as it should be. There was no one there. The windows were open and a little moonlight came in, shifting clouds revealing and then concealing.

And yet something was not right. I knew it. Something was very wrong. I knew it as I had known that night two years ago when I had killed an assassin in this room. I blew the candle out. I opened the door to the hall. The stairwell was empty, the house silent. It was late. The candles on the landing had been snuffed. I hesitated. Up or down? The problem was down, but Cesare was on the floor above, sleeping in Lucrezia's room. I felt danger like a horse scenting smoke from a brush fire. Yes, there were guards, but it would be better to have Cesare. I went up. I knocked on the door very softly. "Cesare?"

He answered almost immediately. Cesare must not have retired either, for he was still in shirt and hose, a candle burning on Lucrezia's desk behind him. "What's wrong?" he asked in a low voice.

"Something is wrong," I said. "There is someone in the house who shouldn't be." I knew it only as I said it. What felt like a lute string snapping had been the protective square breaking. "Downstairs."

For a wonder he didn't question it. He simply turned and picked up his crossed belts, buckling them on quickly, sword to the left and dagger to the right. He followed me into the hall. I went ahead of him down the stairs, our feet quiet on the marble.

We reached the ground floor. It was very late. The saletta was dark and quiet. The front doors were still closed, the bar secure across them. If there were guards outside in the portico, we'd have to open the doors to get to them. Cesare raised an eyebrow at me and I shook my head. Opening the door when we didn't know what was on the other side seemed like a mistake.

There should be six men in the guardroom down the side of the house, but that wasn't where the problem was. Whatever sense it was led me toward the kitchen. I leaned close to Cesare. "The kitchen door," I whispered. He nodded.

I let him go first through the ground floor. There was light from the kitchen, more than there should be. The fire should be banked if Silvia and her assistants were finished cleaning up and had gone to bed.

Cesare stopped. I could hear it too. Someone was moving around. He stepped forward quietly and I followed.

Silvia lay in a pool of blood, one hand outflung, one of our guards bending over her, fumbling at her waist. I couldn't see her face. It was behind him. But the blood.... I think I froze in horror.

Cesare didn't. The scrape of his draw seemed loud in the dark. The man turned, the heavy iron keys to the back door in his left hand. He drew sword with his right as Cesare charged. He barely got his sword up in time. The blades clanged off each other and Cesare sprung back into guard like a cat, circling. The other man circled too, the keys in his hand.

"I hope whatever they paid you is worth dying for," Cesare said. He struck on the last word, a vicious right to left slash. The man dodged, but he couldn't counterattack because Cesare had the end of the table in the way. "Bracciano or some other?" Cesare asked conversationally. My father had always said that the cooler man wins. He'd never seen coldness like Cesare's. He seemed as cool as if he sat in the sala.

"Bracciano." Sweat stood out on his brow. "He paid me to open the door. It's just money. Maybe we can make a deal."

"I don't think so." Cesare lunged. The man caught it high on his blade and they locked together, straining, each trying to push the other down on the floor slick with blood. The man got his left hand up and hit Cesare in the side of the head with the keys.

They broke apart, Cesare shaking his head. "Now you've upset me," he said quietly.

They circled again, leaving bloody footprints on Silvia's nice clean floor. *She will be so upset when she sees it*, I thought, and then the realization broke the hold of the horror on me into grief. I ran back to the door to the wing. "Help! Help!" I shouted. "Murder! Help! Danger! Help!" The guards could surely hear that. "Help!"

I missed the next passage of arms. They were struggling breast to breast again, sword to sword. It was almost too fast to see. Cesare did something, some sort of twist, forcing the man's arm back as his left hand came up. I heard the crack as the long bone in the man's arm broke, and then he fell to his knees screaming. Cesare was behind him in an instant, sword against his throat. "Bracciano paid you to open the door."

"Yes," the man said through gritted teeth.

Cesare looked at me. I looked at Silvia. "Kill him," I said. Cesare drew the blade across his throat as the first of the guards pelted in. He let him fall forward on his face and stood up.

I went to my knees beside Silvia, heedless of the blood. Her throat was cut, her head lolling back, mouth open and eyes wide as though surprised. "I'm sorry," I said. "I'm so sorry. I am so, so sorry." I pressed her lifeless hand in mine. "Silvia. I never thought this would happen." But she had. Of course she had. It almost had happened three elections ago. God help the pawns.

The guardsmen were clattering around. Cesare was explaining. I knelt beside Silvia. The guard captain was asking questions.

"Here are the keys," Cesare said. "He said that Bracciano paid him to open the door. As you can see, the door to the storeroom is open. He must have killed the cook, opened the door to the storeroom, and then realized the street door also required a key. He was looking for it and had just found it when Donna Giulia and I came in."

"Silvia," I said. She must have heard a noise. Or perhaps she'd been in the kitchen when he came in and he'd simply eliminated her. He could have waited for her to leave. It wasn't necessary. I closed my eyes.

"Your Eminence," the guard captain said. "Have you checked the street door?"

"If he'd unlocked it, we'd be knee deep in the Gonfaloniere's men already," Cesare said. "But I expect they've fled by now."

"Beneo," I murmured. He was Silvia's husband. Someone should get him, but he shouldn't see her like this. I took off my velvet robe and put it over her, touching her face to compose her a little more. There was blood on my hands from the floor. My camisa was soaked from the knees down. "Someone needs to get Beneo and tell him there's been an accident."

"Madonna," one of the men said. They knew Beneo, of course. Most of them had been here for weeks if not months. "I'll get him."

I looked up at Cesare, my voice choking. He was, after all, an archbishop. "Will you pray for her soul?"

"Of course," Cesare said, and knelt beside me. It was best if Beneo found us thus.

The rest of the night and the next morning were terrible. The entire household was numb with grief. Silvia's husband had loved her and so had everyone else, even Maria who had often been annoyed by her complaining. I kept the Sarfati girls well clear of the kitchen, but the little maids had to clean it up with Maria's help and the kitchen assistants.

Cesare took care of the guardsman's body. I had no idea what he'd done with it and didn't ask. The man had taken his thirty pieces of silver, and if he had paid for it with his life, so be it.

Dionisio was grim. "At least the square worked," he said about a dozen times.

"If it had not, we would all be dead," I snapped. Which was true. I understood exactly what was supposed to happen. He would have let a dozen men in and they'd have killed us all. Our guards would have been taken by surprise. It would have passed as one of those things that happened in the city at this time. Worse did. And it would have worked, if not for the warding and Cesare.

"Do you think he was after the Prophecies of the Erythraean Sibyl?" Dionisio asked quietly.

"Perhaps," I said. "It may have been only to hurt Rodrigo." And yet killing me would not prevent Rodrigo's election. Knowing Rodrigo, it was more likely to cause him to enact swift and terrible revenge on Bracciano if he was elected. I had seen Bracciano's machinations for three years now. He did not act without a clear goal that would accomplish something. He was ruthless but not particularly cruel. Killing me would not get him anything he wanted. However, if the goal had been the book.... "I did not consider that, Dionisio. Do you think so?"

Dionisio shook his head. "I told no one, but you know Mois said that he had inquired after Pico della Mirandola and other people in Florence. He told them what he had to sell. Whether they believed him or thought he was peddling to the credulous, I can't say. Nor whether anyone would pass it on to Bracciano."

That was a new thing to worry about. "It could be," I said. "We will have to be very careful."

We spoke no more because I was called away to see about the funeral arrangements. In this heat, it would be best if we could do it today. Silvia and Beneo had usually attended the church of San Salvatore in Lauro, which was not too far away, just down the hill and across the square from the back door. I went out with four guardsmen to arrange the funeral mass and interment since Beneo was lying down. Their grown daughter was in service, but she was at Vasanello with Orsino and Adriana. I sent a messenger but if she was able to come given the chaos in the city, she would be several days. We could not wait several days.

Fortunately, Maria knew everyone Silvia knew, and sent word to her friends. The funeral Mass was an hour after noon and was surprisingly well attended, considering events. I sat in the front as I was the only noble present, across the aisle from Beneo, and so I could not see people coming in, but it seemed that the little church was nearly full. It made tears start. Silvia had been well-loved.

I closed my eyes when the choirboy began to sing. *Heavenly Father*, I thought. *This is my fault. If I had considered the danger more closely, I would have sent her to the country. If I had not insisted on staying….* I felt the tears creep from beneath my eyelids. She had been so kind, in her no-nonsense way. She hadn't wanted the Sarfati to stay, but once they did she had been good to the girls. She got cross with Lucrezia, but someone had to be. *I will miss you so much*, I thought. *I will not forget you.*

I came from the funeral to find a boy with a note for me. It was Alessandro's hand, and exceedingly brief. *We must hold Riario*, it said.

I put my hand to my brow. I had to concentrate now, whatever had happened. "How, Rodrigo?" I mused aloud. Cardinal Raffaele Riario was one of Carafa's adherents, only thirty years old and a great lover of the arts. He liked Rodrigo and supported some of the same humanist writers. He hated the Orsini because they had killed a friend of his several years ago. He was a close friend of Franceschetto Cybo, the son of the old pope, who had reputedly lost vast sums of money to him at the gaming table. If it were simply a matter of being a younger man who engaged in high living, money should suffice, but he was related to della Rovere. He supported Carafa but backing a Borgia against his powerful cousin would be difficult. Giuliano della Rovere was not a terribly forgiving man.

A large and prestigious benefice was all I could think of, plus the fact that Rodrigo was of the Humanist faction. Maybe both together would be enough? But how to make the offer? Who would he communicate with outside who wasn't his della Rovere kin? Of course he was communicating with somebody. Everybody was. Thankfully, despite her possessiveness at Fiammetta's idyll, he was not involved with Elissa. He had a mistress that he kept in style, Emanuela Alberini, but I'd only met her twice. I couldn't say I knew her well.

Still, I thought, pacing around my camera, Fiammetta knew her. I could ask Fiammetta to talk to her. I went out on the balcony, looking toward the Vatican. Rodrigo trusted me to find a way to do it. He couldn't deliver bribes within the conclave itself. What was the worst Fiammetta would do? Refuse to help? It was certainly worth asking.

I sat down at my table and wrote her a cheerful little note reminiscent of those days not three weeks ago when we didn't all sit breathlessly waiting. It seemed an aeon ago. I asked if she would care to join me for First Meal, and that if so, my guards would wait to escort her here safely. Three weeks ago there would have been no talk of guards. She would know that I wanted something. But perhaps the opportunity to socialize would win—I doubted she dared the streets herself, and she didn't have a cardinal's guards at her beck and call.

For what that was worth. I shivered and applied the seal firmly. I went down and gave it to one of the guards, sending a pair to deliver it. Two guards in broad daylight. Well, it would be better once they elected someone. There would be the initial uproar and then it would settle down.

The guards had not been gone half an hour when there was a knock at the street door. I went down immediately. Had she come straight back with them?

It was Cesare. He wore brown leather over his doublet, no badge upon it, looking less like a bishop and more like a bravo, sword at his side. I drew him in. "I'm glad to see you."

His stance changed, alert, like a hunting dog's ears pricking. "What happened?"

"Nothing like that." I did not ask him what he'd done with the body. Probably the river. "Your father sent a note this morning that we have to hold Riario. Any ideas?"

Cesare followed me into the garden where there was still shade at this hour. "If he's going to piss on his own cousin, a big benefice."

"That's what I thought." I sat down in one of the chairs at the little table. "Which one?"

"The Bishopric of Cartagena," Cesare said. "Papa's had it ten years. It's the best one in Spain, saving my own. Papa would kill me if I gave away Valencia. If I could give away the ring with it...." He shrugged self-depreciatingly.

"You'd rather not be an archbishop?" I asked. The youngest of the maids was bringing out wine and water, her eyes red. They would make the meal appear. To do less would be to let Silvia down.

"Got it in one," Cesare said, pouring for himself unwatered. "But can you see Juan in the Church?"

"Not easily," I allowed.

He took a drink, gesturing to my middle with the glass. "Papa's had me for the Church since I was a baby. Your lucky one there doesn't have to."

"It's much too soon to think about that," I said. "Besides, it will legally be an Orsini."

"I forgot you're married," Cesare said.

He could. "Cartagena then. If you can write a letter to that effect, I think I have someone who can make the offer."

Maria came into the garden then, like a player making a cue. "Donna Fiammetta de Michelis, Donna Giulia." Fiammetta was right on her heels.

"Fiammetta!" I flew to her and embraced her as though we hadn't seen each other in a year. It seemed a year since her party in June. "I'm so glad you came."

She wore peach over white, a summer flower with her red hair braided up to show a few delightful freckles on her neck. Other women avoided them. On Fiammetta they gave her a mischievous charm, as though she were still a young girl rather than ten years my senior. "Darling Giulia!" She kissed me on both cheeks. "It was so good of you to invite me to your little intrigue." She looked over my shoulder. "And who is this gentleman?"

Cesare did not look like a gentleman. He looked like an assassin, standing with one knee bent, his hand cocked as if for the draw. "This is His Excellency the Archbishop of Valencia, Cesare Borgia. Your Excellency, may I present Donna Fiammetta de Michelis?"

He bent deeply over her hand. "Donna Fiammetta, the honor is entirely mine. I heard that you were beautiful, but I was not prepared because even the most complimentary rumors fall far short of the truth."

Fiammetta looked at me, her brows rising. "And I have heard of the young bishop, but once again rumors lie."

"Well," I said. Cesare was looking at her as though someone had hit him on the head with a rock. "Let us sit and talk. Maria, will you see that First Meal is served for us here?" I gave Maria a pleading look behind Fiammetta's back. If the assistants could manage even a simple lunch, it would be not much short of a miracle. "It's so warm. Perhaps just some light odds and ends." They could at least put some cold meat and fruit on a platter.

Cesare showed her to her chair as though it were a formal dinner. "May I pour for you, Donna Fiammetta?"

"Half and half, please," she said. "And just Fiammetta. I feel we are friends already."

"Then you must call me Cesare."

"If Your Excellency insists." She took the glass from him with a little smile.

"Unlike my father, I don't stand on ceremony." Cesare sat down without even glancing at me.

I sat down. "Fiammetta, I hate to be so crass, but you know they are taking the second vote today. I need to get word to Emanuela Alberini and I don't know her. If you could help…." I let my voice trail off.

"You would have my eternal gratitude," Cesare said. He fixed black eyes like Rodrigo's on her, an all too familiar expression on his face. I had never thought I'd hear the words eternal gratitude come out of his mouth! So he could be smooth. Usually he simply didn't bother.

"How long is eternal?" Fiammetta asked with a little pout.

"At least until the middle of next week," Cesare said with a smile. It was not at all what Rodrigo would have said. Rodrigo would have said something like *Until the stars fall into the sea.*

Fiammetta laughed. "And all I need to do to earn this mutable grace is to take an offer to Emanuela Alberini? I presume Cardinal Borgia has a gift for Cardinal Riario."

"I would be honored to offer him the Bishopric of Cartagena," Cesare said. "As a mark of my father's esteem."

"And time is of the essence," I said. "Even if Emanuela has a way to contact him, it will hardly be instant."

"Doesn't everyone?" Fiammetta asked. "Obviously you do."

"Of course," I said. "Will you help?" I considered reminding her of Rodrigo's words—that sooner or later she would have to pick a horse to bet on.

She looked at me, then turned her head to Cesare with a little smile. "Since His Excellency asks so nicely."

"His Excellency has no choice," Cesare said. "I don't generally ask nicely."

I was beginning to feel superfluous. Fiammetta got to her feet. "Then let's go. Soonest done, soonest finished."

Cesare jumped up. "I will escort you personally. For your safety."

"Very gallant," she said. "Giulia, dear, I'd love to chat but as you say time is of the essence."

"Our meal will only be a few moments," I said.

"I can feed His Excellency at my house," Fiammetta said. "If he is hungry."

I think my eyes were wide. And yet Cesare positioned himself at her back like a cobra on a leash. "As you wish," he said. He looked at me. "Tell Papa I'm offering Cartagena."

"I will do that," I said, and watched them hurry out just as the young maid arrived with a tray. "I'm sorry, Rosalia," I said. "There they go. It's only me now." I sat down again, breaking bread and smearing it with soft cheese. A note for Alessandro, I thought. One word would suffice. "Cartagena." Rodrigo would know what I meant.

Chapter Nine

Unfortunately, the messenger came straight back. "Donna Giulia, the guard I was supposed to meet was not there," he said. He handed my own note back to me..

"Not there? You mean off duty?" I asked. "Did you find out when he would be on again?" We had a man in our pay who would take a note from one of our guards and give it to Alessandro, and vice versa. He was being well compensated for his trouble.

"He's been dismissed, Madonna," the messenger replied. "He was passing messages for six different cardinals."

"Lovely," I said. Why couldn't the man have made do with two or three? Greed was always the downfall of mankind. "Did you offer the guard you talked to a bribe to take the note?"

"Of course, Madonna!" he said, looking offended that I thought he might not have. "But he said it was too dangerous right now and he couldn't afford to lose his job."

"Very well. Thank you." I shook my head and let him go. I paced out into the garden. The clipped rosemary bushes were fragrant in the warm day. I brushed my hand over them, enjoying the scent. How was I going to reestablish communication with Alessandro? I could only hope that Riario's mistress, Emanuela, wasn't using the same guard we were.

Beneo came to the entrance of the garden, walking stiffly. "Donna Fiammetta de Michelis," he said.

"Please send her in," I said. What was she doing back? I had expected Cesare. Fiammetta came in more sedately than she had the last time, though she had a smirk like the cat who's gotten in the cream. "Fiammetta! I didn't expect you. What's happened?"

"I wanted to let you know that Emanuela was very helpful," Fiammetta said. "She said Riario would definitely be interested. She's breeding too, so he's about to have more expenses. Also she said that Franceschetto Cybo lost an enormous amount of money at cards to Riario and hasn't paid his debts. Emanuela is worried that he won't be able to now, since his father is dead, and he's going to default on the entire amount. It's close to thirty thousand ducats."

I pursed my lips. "I don't even know how you lose such an amount at cards."

"Nor do I," Fiammetta said. "How could anyone be that unlucky?"

I laughed. I had meant caution and she meant luck. Rodrigo never played for money. I asked him why once and he'd laughed and said that women were a surer pleasure. He certainly spent enough money on women if I was any example. I had beautiful clothing and some very expensive pieces of jewelry in addition to the cost of an entire household suitable for a noble lady.

Fiammetta glanced down at my belly. "I take it Rodrigo has made provision for the baby?"

"Oh yes," I said, thinking of Vasanello, the castle he'd traded to my husband. "It will inherit a good property."

Her brows grew a tiny wrinkle. "And you? You know it's lovely that your child will inherit someday, but what's going to keep you in the meantime? Cesare said his mother had four rental properties in town and a vineyard." She looked at me critically. "You haven't even asked for property, have you? Sugar, you have to take care of yourself!"

"No, I haven't," I said. I felt my life was quite full without managing real estate. And I hated to be mercenary. Rodrigo was generous. I already felt somewhat guilty about the amount of money he spent on me. Asking for investment properties seemed crass. Also it was worth pointing out to her that Cesare wasn't independently wealthy, if that's what she was looking for. "And just so you know, Cesare doesn't have property in his own name. Rodrigo gives him an allowance and he has several benefices, including Valencia, but he has no estates."

Fiammetta laughed. "Dear Giulia, I don't need a man to give me property at this point! I tied that up twelve years ago. I'm my own woman and I can support myself in the style to which I have become accustomed. A friend's contributions are icing on the cake."

"Is he your friend?" That was fast.

"Maybe he will be in the future. I've left it at that," Fiammetta said with a smirk. "He's going to have to work for it. I'd like to see him in a sweat."

"I'm sure that will be entertaining," I said. Who Cesare was sweating with was the least of my worries. I took a deep breath. "My problem at the moment is that I've lost my way of communicating with Rodrigo. The man we were bribing has been dismissed. My brother, Alessandro, is locked in as a clerk, but I can't reach him except by hoping that one of my men can bribe a different guard to take a message to Alessandro. But then how Alessandro is going to get one back to me...." I shook my head.

Fiammetta looked thoughtful. "I do know of a way into the Vatican."

"A way that isn't locked down?"

"How about a secret passage?" she said with a mischievous smile.

"A secret passage?" That seemed incredible, the stuff of romantic tales.

Fiammetta sat down in one of the chairs at the little garden table. "I used it once, when I was with—let's say an old friend.

It goes from one of the houses in the street that backs up beside St. Peter's. The palazzo has a private chapel and there's a passage from there into a robing room. And then a door from the robing room into the Choir Chapel at St. Peter's."

I boggled at her. "Truly? What was it for?"

"Cardinal Zeno's convenience. He had it built thirty years ago when he was Cardinal-Deacon of Santa Maria in Portico. It's the palazzo next to the church. He owns the house but he doesn't live there anymore. He rents it out."

"Zeno supports della Rovere," I said. "He's a staunch Traditionalist. He's never going to let me use a secret passage in his house to get messages to Rodrigo."

"Ah, but he rents the house through someone who manages property, and he rented it to a friend of mine, Antonia Camporesi. And she's seeing Ascanio Sforza at the moment."

I spread my hands to the heavens. So that was how Sforza was getting his information in and out. Much simpler than bribing guards to just have his mistress bring a note! "And would Antonia let me use it?"

"I don't see why not," Fiammetta said. "It's not opposite to her interests. And you could pay her."

"True," I said. "Could I impose on you to write to her and ask if I can use it? I would be happy to pay her for her trouble. I just need to slip in and give Alessandro a message."

"It's no imposition," Fiammetta said, and I sent for ink and paper.

Fiammetta left soon after, and I sent her note off with one of my men. It was dusk when the messenger returned. Antonia's reply was brief. "Yes, come before it's late and be discreet." I put on my plainest gown and a dark cloak, and for good measure added a small purse with five gold ducats in it. It was a generous sum but it was a generous favor, and I suspected Ascanio was parsimonious. I doubted her ready cash was as great as mine. Normally I had ten or twenty ducats in the house all the time to pay this and that; but right now, knowing that I might need cash bribes or to pay household expenses if he was shut in for a week or more, Rodrigo had made certain that I had ninety, divided between three different strongboxes and my desk.

I dithered between two and four guards. Four was safer but conspicuous. Two was more discreet. That decided me. Two would be enough given that the city was relatively quiet. We set out as Compline was ringing. The streets were nearly deserted, and those few people we saw afoot avoided us entirely. All the tavernas were closed. I supposed the chances of being torn up seemed too great to open, despite the custom they would surely have had. Or not. Perhaps there were no customers either.

We hurried across the Ponte St. Angelo. There were two men lurking at the far end, but seeing me tightly guarded by two men with conspicuous swords, they simply watched us appraisingly as we passed. "They'd have gone after us if there hadn't been two of us," one of the guards said.

"I will send you in pairs from now on," I said, and he nodded. Whether they were footpads or someone's agents was impossible to tell. After all, the Borgia guards with me weren't in livery either.

Palazzo Santa Maria in Portico was a pretty little palazzo built in the style of the last century, not large but certainly conveniently located to the Vatican, practically in the shadow of the tower of St. Peter's. This entire street backed up to the Vatican walls along the side of the basilica. It was easy to see why a cardinal would choose it for his residence. It was ten minutes from the Vatican, if that. However, as the city had prospered in the years since the Pope had returned from France and the Avignon Captivity, grander houses had been built across the river. If this one had a garden it was small, and with the houses abutting each other there was no room to expand.

The gates across the portico were wrought iron, good and sturdy and also graceful, twisted into lilies for beauty as well as strength. Perhaps it was a good omen, I thought. Lilies were the Farnese device. Beyond a little portico with a single door there were heavy oak doors to the house beyond. I stepped up to the guard inside, the space well lit by two hanging lanterns so there could be no doubt as to a caller's identity. "Giulia Farnese," I said. "To see Donna Antonia Camporesi."

"You are expected," the guard said, and opened the gate. After it was opened and closed he knocked on the inner door, which was opened for us by another guard. I was impressed. It was very secure. Providing that the other door went only into a guard room with no other egress, it was the model of safety.

I was led upstairs to a pleasant sala. Somewhere, on the floor above, a baby was crying. Two little girls, perhaps three and five, looked up from a game as a petite woman with dark hair and a curvaceous figure stood up from her chair. "Donna Antonia," I said. "I am so pleased to see you."

"It's good to see you as well," she said, coming and taking my hands. "I'm afraid I missed you at parties this spring. My youngest was born at Easter, so I haven't been about as much as usual."

"Congratulations," I said. "That's wonderful! A boy or a girl?"

"Another girl," she said. "Three girls." She glanced down at the two looking up from their play.

"What lovely children," I said, smiling at them. "I did not know Ascanio had such beautiful daughters."

"Yes," she said. I wondered if Ascanio Sforza was as generous with daughters as Rodrigo. Probably not. Most men weren't, whether the daughters were legitimate or not. A son would be different. Three illegitimate daughters might or might not be much of a claim. Certainly the Sforza family as a whole would make little of them.

"I'm not a Sforza!" the oldest one exclaimed. "I'm a Cavalcanti!"

"It is a fine thing to be a Cavalcanti as well," I said. She had traded up between the first and second, I thought, a banker for a cardinal from one of the most powerful families.

Antonia shrugged. "So. Business."

"Yes," I said, and gave her the purse.

She weighed it in her hand. "I presume you'll want to use it more than once."

"If I can," I said. "It seems that it would be easiest."

"More discreet if you simply send a man in the future," she said.

"I will do that," I said. "But this time my brother does not know to expect me, so I must find him."

She nodded. "I'll show you," she said. I followed Antonia downstairs and through a neat little saletta. It was darkened, all the plate and treasures put away. Through it was a door to a private chapel. It was small, with room for only about ten worshippers, though there was a very nice painting of the Annunciation above the altar. Only the lamp of the Presence was lit. "Here," she said, stopping halfway along the left wall. The paneling was in sections, and one crack between them was wider than the others. There was also a keyhole lost in the elaborate carving of the frame.

"Nice," I said. Unless I were examining the chapel for it, I would not have noticed it was there.

She produced a key from her skirts, inserting it and turning it soundlessly. Then she handed me the key. "Lock it from the other side so people can't wander in. Bring me the key back when you're done."

"Antonia, I don't know how to thank you enough!"

She shrugged. "Money does nicely."

"Absolutely," I said. I wondered if she worried about being put aside after another daughter and a time in which she wasn't going about with Ascanio, or if in general she was making a nest egg. Either way, if this was a side job I could certainly provide money for the use of the secret door. She held the door open and I slipped through, closing the door behind me. It was hard to lock it in the nearly complete darkness, but I heard the tumblers turn.

With the door shut behind me there was no light at all and my eyes strained to see in the dark. I took a deep breath and reached out carefully. My hands touched stone to either side, smooth and even as though blocks had simply been removed. Which of course they had been. This was not a cave in the depths of the earth or even an ancient tomb. It was merely a passage through the Vatican walls. It could not be very long. Perhaps I should have been terrified, but I was not. I have never been afraid of the dark.

My hands on each wall, I stepped forward into the dark. One, two, three—ten paces before I reached another door. Twenty feet or so, no more than the depth of the walls and the wall of St. Peter's beyond. Well enough. I found the keyhole by feel and opened it carefully, though no light came through. The hinges were well oiled and it opened soundlessly. Beyond it, I touched cloth.

There was a rack with clothing on it, soft and smelling of incense and sweat. This was no doubt where robes and vestments were stored. Perhaps it was also used as a changing room when the Choir Chapel was in use. Well, I thought, no one would be using it between Compline and Vigil. There wasn't a sung office between an hour after sunset and two hours after midnight, and certainly there would be no choir practice. I had learned the Church hours in detail in the last two years. It was, I supposed, no different from the draper's wife knowing cloth.

I stood still, letting my eyes adjust to the dim light. There was a slightly lighter area beyond the clothing rack. Presumably the door into the Choir Chapel? Carefully I made my way around the clothes. Yes, there was the door. I listened. It wouldn't do to have a strange woman popping out of the robing room. It would make people wonder where she'd come from.

There was no sound nearby. I opened the door carefully. It was a chapel off the nave of St. Peter's, a few candles burning here and there. I could hear the echo of footsteps in the nave, a quiet voice. The basilica was not entirely deserted, even at this time, but there was no one in the chapel. I shut the door behind me, tiptoeing toward the entrance to the basilica. I stopped a moment, looking out into the nave, trying to get my bearings.

Where in the world would Alessandro be at this hour? With Rodrigo? Probably not. The cardinals would be expected to attend both Vespers and Compline, so they'd be having Second Meal after Compline. One could imagine this to be a lengthy affair. The clerks would not eat in this state. Alessandro had probably finished eating by now, but even if Rodrigo wanted him to attend on him, it would not be until the cardinals parted for the evening. In all likelihood, Rodrigo would be at dinner and Alessandro would be…somewhere. I had no idea where.

I was going to have to find someone to fetch him, I thought. Wandering around the Vatican would be conspicuous. A random woman would be noticeable at ordinary times, and now, when supposedly the cardinals were in complete isolation, I would be lucky not to just be thrown out. Perhaps if I were simply looking for a clerk? And did so in a direct manner?

I squared my shoulders and walked out into the basilica, making no attempt to hide. I bobbed a curtsy to the high altar, then proceeded down the nave as though I knew where I was going.

There were guards at the doors off the aisle, of course, halberds at the ready. I walked straight up to one of them. "Excuse me," I said softly, "do you know Father Alessandro Farnese?" I didn't wait for him to answer but tumbled on, looking up at him with big eyes and my most innocent expression. "I'm his little sister. My mother needs me to get a message to him. Our brother is very sick! Mother wants to know if he can come."

The guard looked at the other guard on the same door. "We can't let anyone in."

"Oh, please!" I said with tears in my voice. "I know you can't break a rule and let me in, but can you tell him to come here? Surely I could talk to my brother for a few minutes, right here in front of you in St. Peter's? We need his prayers. Our brother is so sick. If he dies...." I choked off.

The other guard, older and with a kind face, shrugged. "I could get him," he said. "He's a junior clerk, yes?"

"In finance," I said. "He's very junior." Both true, though Alessandro wasn't as unimportant as that sounded, not when he'd been chosen by the Vice-Chancellor.

"Wait here," the guard said.

I stood there with the other guard while one went in. I fidgeted for a bit then asked quietly, "Would you mind if I went in the St. Catherine Chapel right there to pray? My brother can join me when he comes."

"Of course," he said.

I went into the chapel and made my obeisance, but I could not actually pray. I was too nervous. It seemed I waited forever before I heard a step behind. I sprang to my feet and ran to Alessandro, who stood in front of the guard. "Giulia!" he said. "What's wrong?"

"Alessandro," I said, burying my face in his chest.

The guard backed off, going back to his post, apparently satisfied.

"What's the matter?" Alessandro demanded.

"Nothing," I said in a furious whisper, "except that the guard we bribed has been dismissed." I drew him into the chapel further from the door, where we could not be seen.

"You'replay acting?" he whispered. "Giulia, you nearly gave me a fit. I thought something terrible had happened. How did you get in here?"

"Would you believe a secret passage?" I said.

I thought he would laugh. Instead he shook his head. "I do not even know how you do these things."

"I had to come up with an alternative," I said. "So here's the plan. In the future, when you have something you need to say, leave a note behind the clothes rack in the robing room off the Choir Chapel. We'll leave notes there for you."

"In the robing room of the Choir Chapel?" Alessandro looked utterly confused.

"It's a long story," I said. "But it's the best solution I have. Surely you can come into St. Peter's without drawing undue attention."

He nodded. "I have information for you now but I couldn't find the man to take the note."

"And I for you. Cesare is offering Riario the Bishopric of Cartagena, and he'll take it," I said. I considered telling him about the attack at the house, but it would only worry him. Alessandro could do nothing, and everything that Rodrigo could do, he'd already done. I had his guards. No good could come of telling Alessandro things that would only distract them.

"I'll tell His Eminence," Alessandro said. "Here's what I have for you." He presented me with a note he'd had tucked in his sleeve and opened it. "Carafa 6 da Costa 6 Borgia 6 della Rovere 5. Almost dead even."

The sides were clear, first ballot posturing gone, twelve for the Humanists, eleven for the Traditionalists. Della Rovere would get da Costa's and Rodrigo would get Carafa's, if he held Riario. We needed to move three. They needed to move four. Were della Rovere's chances of picking off four of Carafa's greater than Rodrigo's chance of picking off three of da Costa's?

"Sforza voted for Carafa to show he could," Alessandro said. "He was letting della Rovere know not to take him for granted."

"Telling him to bid," I said.

Alessandro's brows twitched. "Is that the game? If I were a cardinal, I wouldn't be bought and sold."

"You wouldn't have to be," I said. "You'd be loyal."

"To Cardinal Borgia? I'd vote for him because I agree with him. Not because he owns me," Alessandro said. "It's an important distinction. Do you know what they call me? The other clerks?"

"No," I said.

"The Borgia brother-in-law."

I shrugged. "That's how it is, isn't it? They're jealous. But you know he wouldn't give you responsibility if he thought you weren't capable, even if I asked him to, and I haven't," I assured him. It was true, and I hoped it salved Alessandro's pride.

"True," Alessandro said. "He expects obedience. He requires competence."

"Well then," I said. "We're competent."

"Colonna's switched his vote," Alessandro said. "We got him. That's how the Cardinal went from 5 to 6. Now he needs Orsini. That's his message for you."

I took a deep breath. This was the point where it would have been very useful to have Adriana, since I didn't know the Orsini as well as she did. Who was the proper person in the family to approach who wouldn't run straight to Bracciano? His mistress, Lucia, was not in town. She had been sent with their four children to one of the Orsini strongholds in the country. Who would he be communicating with besides the Gonfaloniere? His mother? She was still living and had a spacious palazzo in town. I had never met her, but Adriana had spoken of her. If she would see me, that was a possibility. How much did Clarice Orsini hate the Sforza?

They'd want lands, not bishoprics. Rodrigo had traded Vasanello to the Orsini for me. There must be other properties on their lists. "I'm going to have to work on that," I said. "Tell him I'll do my best."

"He knows you will," Alessandro said.

"He expects obedience but requires competence?" I said with a smile.

Alessandro gave me a hug. "Be careful. For you and the little one."

"I'll be careful," I assured him.

I made my way home, though it was growing late by the time I arrived. I went up to my camera and wrote a note for Cesare at the Vice-Chancellor's palazzo: *Properties the Orsini want. Lands in Church hands. Revenue? G.* I had no idea which Church-owned properties could be signed over. Cesare would know. Then I wrote another note, a long and formal one this time, requesting the honor of visiting with Donna Clarice Orsini on the morrow, the kind of note my mother had taught me to write. I sent it off before midnight. The fourth day of the conclave was ending.

Chapter Ten

At dawn on the 10th I had a message from Cesare: *Monticello and Soranio. 5,000 ducats annually between them.* Not the largest, I thought, but I knew Monticello at least. It overlooked the Via Appia leading south from Rome as Montalto did the Via Aurelia to the north and was likewise a strategic position. I presumed Soranio had equal value.

I dressed exceedingly carefully. I did not wear red, which was both Orsini and Borgia colors, but Farnese blue, a bright medium shade. It was a new gown I had not worn before because I'd gotten it just before Innocent died. I wore it with the plainer sleeves for day, not the ones with silver brocade and silver ribbons. I had Maria do my hair carefully, rolls on the side and in the back beneath a small net with pearls on it. I wore pearl drops at my ears and the matching pearl cross Rodrigo had given me not quite two years ago. I hoped I was communicating prosperous and tasteful. It was still early morning when I set out with four guards.

The streets were quiet. Here and there were signs of disturbance from the previous days, windows which had been boarded up and tavernas that remained closed. With two guards before and two after, I was a very obvious presence. I looked like a great Roman lady.

Now if only she would admit me. We were stopped at her closed gates, as I expected. Everyone's gates were closed. The guard was very polite, however. "Who shall I tell Madonna is calling?"

"Giulia Farnese," I said.

He bowed. "A moment, Madonna."

I stood absolutely still under the portico, not fidgeting, my hands cupped at my waist. It must have been ten minutes until the guard returned and began opening the gate. A tall majordomo stood within. "If you will follow me, Donna Giulia?"

"Of course," I said, and turned to my guards. "You will wait here for me." I followed him serenely. Her sala was on the second floor, broad windows down the side opening over a garden. Clarice Orsini herself was seventy-something, her white hair braided up in an elaborate style, one dark streak in it remaining like an accent. She sat utterly straight in her high-backed chair, and I curtsied before her as to a queen. "I am pleased to meet you at last, Donna Clarice."

The majordomo likewise bowed himself out, closing the door behind him. One of her beringed hands gestured to the smaller chair opposite. "So you are Giulia Farnese, concubine to the Spanish cardinal."

"I am Giulia Farnese, who has returned Vasanello to the Orsini," I said. "It seems to me my efforts on behalf of the Orsini have borne more fruit than others."

The corner of her mouth twitched. "And you hold the good of the Orsini so close to your heart?"

I chose my words carefully. "Fascinations do not last. Castles do." I put my fingertips together. "One may hold lands for decades or generations. My youth is a few short years."

At that she lifted her chin. "So it is, and you are wise to remember that. The enemies one makes in youth follow one into old age, to one's regret."

"I have no desire to make enemies among my husband's kin," I said. "And he is the one who has derived the most good from my actions, has he not? What does it matter if people talk for a few years when he has Vasanello?"

"True enough." She met my eyes. It could be worse, I thought, though she had not offered me refreshment. "And you are easily put aside, much more easily than a castle can be taken back with the deed duly transferred."

"I should hope my good service would preclude that," I said. I put my hand to my belly. "And an acknowledged heir is not easily put aside."

Her lip curled. "The child of that marrano to inherit the Orsini name."

"Is that not a worthwhile price for several properties?" I asked.

Clarice's eyebrow twitched. "Several?"

"Monticello, on the Via Appia," I said. "And Soranio. To be made over to your son or whomever you prefer."

"Those are not such great properties," she sniffed.

"And yet strategic," I said. "But that is not the reason in your greatest interest."

"What reason would that be?" She regarded me steadily, her arched brows risen, her forehead plucked in the old style. She must have been reckoned a great beauty fifty years ago.

I had bluffed a demon, but this was harder. "Ascanio Sforza," I said, "has voted for Cardinal Carafa as a sign of their alliance. He will take his votes from da Costa and Carafa both. That will make him one vote short of the papal throne, and he has a large sum of money that della Rovere has given him from the King of France. He will get one more vote. Ascanio Sforza will be Pope." I dropped my voice. "We both know Cardinal Orsini doesn't have the votes, nor the money to buy them when France plays the table. Would you not rather have Borgia than Sforza?"

She snorted, looking away from me. "I would rather the devil than a Sforza."

"Then vote for the devil," I said. "You know him. He is carnal and corrupt, but he has no love for the Sforza or their interests. He is not tied to them or the Colonna." She said nothing, so I continued. "Properties lost are not easily regained. The Sforza will swallow up generations of work and who knows when you will recover them? And heirs killed are not so easily replaced either." I blackened Ascanio's name, as he did not have the reputation of a murderer, but some of his kin certainly did. "Cardinal Orsini can't win. Isn't it wise to make the best bargain possible?"

Clarice pursed her lips. "As you have?"

"Yes, Madonna," I said. "I play the long game, as I expect you do. I want my child acknowledged. The Orsini name is worth more than ephemeral favors."

"You are playing for yourself," she said.

"What woman can afford not to?" I asked, "Tossed about by the currents as we are?"

At that she smiled. "Very well. My son's vote to Borgia. The towns and castles of Monticello and Soranio. I will see the deeds today."

"I will have them executed and brought to you after the vote," I said.

Her smile broadened. "So trusting."

"It is wise, Madonna."

Clarice laughed. "Then I will see the deeds the day after the vote."

I inclined my head. "It shall be done."

When I got home I sent a note to Alessandro. *Have Orsini. Monticello and Soranio.*

Alessandro's reply arrived in the middle of the afternoon. *Vote just taken. Carafa 5 da Costa 4 Borgia 7 della Rovere 7. Sforza to della Rovere. Orsini to Borgia.*

I blew out a long breath. So Clarice had swayed her son. But Sforza had gone from Carafa to della Rovere. That was the French king's money in play. Rodrigo was going to have to deal with Sforza. There wasn't anything I could do there. And we were still at twelve to their eleven. Della Rovere and Rodrigo were consolidating. And yet neither was in striking distance of the fifteen votes required for a two-thirds majority.

There were also two words added at the end in Rodrigo's hand: *Everyone—Gherardi!* I passed my hand over my eyes. The Patriarch of Venice? An eighty-four-year-old man I had never met who didn't reside in Rome? He was already rich. His family connections were miles from Rome. Surely if honors would move him, those had to be offered by Rodrigo rather than me or Cesare. I didn't even know any of the Venetians. What was Rodrigo thinking? Did Cesare know someone? I shook my head and wrote a note for Cesare, telling him the vote count and passing on that he should go after Gherardi. I sent the note to him at the Vice-Chancellor's palazzo, but of course he probably wouldn't be there in the middle of the afternoon. He'd get it when he returned from whatever business he was on. Maybe I should send a note to Fiammetta's house as well. It couldn't hurt. If he wasn't there, she'd just hold it. I wrote out a more discreet version and sent that off too.

Dusk was just falling when a note from her came by return messenger. *Darling*, it read, *I'd love the pleasure of your company for an informal meal at Compline with Giani de Bastian.* It took me a minute to remember who that was. He was the aide to the Venetian ambassador and I had met him very briefly at Fiammetta's party in June. At least he was Venetian, I thought, and Fiammetta was trying to help. Surely if there was any offer Cesare or I could make to Gherardi, the Venetian ambassador would be the most likely to reach him with it.

I dressed hurriedly. Not the Farnese blue this time, but Borgia red, a scarlet gown for a scarlet woman. What else would he expect at Fiammetta's house? Besides, my position had been adequately clear at the party.

I took four guards in Borgia livery to escort me the short distance to Fiammetta's house with two torchbearers. We made a striking party in the streets. A few people who were out and about stopped to watch. Everyone in the neighborhood knew me, of course. Near Fiammetta's there were some who didn't. I heard one young woman telling another who I was, "…a great concubine…" She was my age or so, and what I heard in her voice was envy. Envy cuts two ways—admiration and the desire to drag down the object of admiration, to prove that she isn't as good as she thinks she is. Every woman with wit or skill knows the danger of that.

We were four at dinner in Fiammetta's garden, a table arranged under the bestarred sky. Cesare and de Bastian stood as I arrived, Cesare dressed in a doublet of Borgia red slashed with black. He was taller than his father by several fingers' width, and I remembered what Rodrigo had said about siring tall sons on tall women.

De Bastian bowed deeply over my hand. "Donna Giulia, I'm delighted to see you again."

"And I you, Ambassador," I said, giving him a little promotion. He was the ambassador's aide, not an ambassador himself.

Cesare handed me into my chair very properly. He did have nice manners when he bothered to use them, and apparently showing off for Fiammetta was a good reason. We made small talk. The first course had been served when I caught Cesare's eye and got to the point. "Ambassador, you asked me at Donna Fiammetta's party in June who Cardinal Borgia intended to support. Who does Cardinal Gherardi support?"

De Bastian knew it was coming, of course. He put his fork down. "Cardinal da Costa. However, it's becoming increasingly clear that august as he is, da Costa does not have the votes."

"As you may recall, Cardinal Borgia supported waiting for Cardinal Gherardi before beginning the conclave. And it is certainly true that da Costa does not have the votes." There was no point in any pretense that the counts were confidential. Everyone had bribed somebody to get them, or was getting the counts directly from the college themselves. Theoretically everyone was locked and could not communicate, but the Vatican leaked like a sieve.

De Bastian nodded. "And I'm certain you know that Cardinal Gherardi is quite elderly. He referred to Cardinal Borgia as 'a dangerous young man'."

"Are you sure he didn't mean His Excellency the Archbishop of Valencia?" I said. Rodrigo might be dangerous, but he was only a young man to someone who was eighty-four.

Cesare said nothing, only leaned back in his chair, his long legs stretched out. Clearly he was going to let me carry this one. De Bastian met my gaze candidly. "His Eminence is forgetful. And he does not embrace new thoughts easily. He is…disturbed…by some of Cardinal Borgia's positions."

That was no surprise. "And to put it bluntly, Venice would rather have a French alliance than a Spanish one."

"True." He lifted his glass. "So when da Costa drops out, Cardinal Gherardi will give his vote to della Rovere."

"Unless?" Cesare asked.

De Bastian shrugged. "Unless nothing. Della Rovere is the candidate France supports. His Eminence doesn't need money. He knows he has only a few months to live. He wanted the honor of this convocation—to end his long career in the Church as a cardinal voting in the Sistine Chapel. He has that. Money's no use to him. He will not live to hold further offices. There's nothing you can offer him."

"Then what's the point of this?" Cesare said. Fiammetta gave him a quelling look.

"Not even the interests of Venice?" I asked. Not money. Not honors. Not ideals. That left one argument.

"France is our ally."

"But is it in Venice's best interest for France to dominate the

Papal States?" I asked. "Right now, France needs Venice. Their relations with Milan and Genoa are shaky and their relations with Naples hostile. You are their best friend. If you were replaced with a better, newer, perhaps richer friend, would that be in your interest?" I leaned forward, putting my elbow on the table and meeting his eyes. "Della Rovere will lead Rome into the arms of France. He owes King Charles two hundred thousand ducats. As Pope, he would recognize French claims to Naples, putting Naples in their hands as well. Venice will seem little compared to all of that. You can't imagine that France will work in Venice's best interests when there is no longer any incentive to do so. They won't need you anymore."

De Bastian blinked. "There is something to that," he said. "And what would Cardinal Borgia do?"

"He respects King Ferrante's sovereignty over Naples as an independent state," Cesare said.

"That he is Spanish is no secret," I said. "Perhaps it would best serve Venice's interests to remain France's most important friend in Italy."

"Perhaps these are thoughts I should convey," de Bastian said.

"At the very least, you will be thought astute for raising the point," I said, and let the topic change.

As the dinner ended, I let Fiammetta draw me away under the portico. "Thank you so very much," I said. "Fiammetta, this has done me extraordinary good. I owe you."

"Maybe I owed you," she said with a glance toward Cesare, deep in conversation with de Bastian at the table in the garden. "I think I'll keep this one a while."

I looked at Fiammetta incredulously. "Just like that?"

"I'm tired of wrinkled old men," she said, "with their lagging appetites that have to be piqued with filthy games and who paw at you half the day. I want a man who just wants a good fuck. No offense intended."

"None taken," I said, though I felt my face heat. I knew my tastes were not ordinary. I had heard as much in the conversations of women these past two years, even if I volunteered little.

"If I can choose, why not a young man who's handsome, rich, and ready? He'll be a cardinal in no time if his father is Pope. And he's ten years younger than I am. He's not going to tell me what to do." Fiammetta looked at me with something like sympathy. "I'm too old to put up with the father. I'll take the son."

"To whom shall we give the Holy Spirit?" I wondered, and we both leaned over laughing.

"You're naughty," Fiammetta said. "And quick-witted. You'll do all right even when Borgia is through with you. And he makes lavish provision for his children." She looked at my middle. "So you're lucky he managed to do the job."

"There's not really a problem with that," I said. "I'm glad Cesare is to your taste." Inwardly, I shook my head. If I had ever wondered why not Rodrigo and Fiammetta, the reason was clear now. He said he didn't want a financial transaction, but to be loved. He said I was rare and wonderful, and I had thought it was an idle compliment. Now I knew just how rare I was. I was a strange creature indeed.

"He's beautiful," Fiammetta said. "Intense. Hot as a furnace and easy to satisfy. What's not to like?"

What indeed? And yet I could muster no more enthusiasm for Cesare than she could for Rodrigo. If I told Fiammetta that I found Rodrigo beautiful, or that I had never imagined pleasures like our games, she would not believe me. She thought I put up with him and that I was well-paid for my pains.

Needless to say, Cesare stayed at Fiammetta's when I left after the dinner. We had gotten nearly home through the dark streets when my luck ran out. Six men, young and rough looking, though not poor from their weapons, ran out from a sidestreet into the square we crossed. The first I saw was when one of our torchbearers shouted, and then they were upon us.

"Rich pickings!" someone yelled. I heard the guards draw steel and I stopped in the center, letting them make a close ring about me and the other torchbearer. The one on the edge backed toward us, sweeping ahead of him with his torch as they closed.

"I get the whore!" another yelled.

"Don't move, Madonna," the guard captain said.

"Yes, Captain," I said. I understood. They could defend in a ring, but if I moved I'd throw them all off. I had to stand still, not panic and try to flee. I stood while the assailants circled, no one willing to rush forward for all their bravado. The Cardinal's guards were steady. They didn't attack either, just waited in guard covering each other while the assailants hurled insults. Professional, I thought. I stood perfectly still. It was four on six if you didn't count our torchbearers, but the defenders had the advantage. They'd have to run at us.

A few feints failed to draw the guards out. They stood disciplined, me in the center of the ring in my scarlet dress. It wasn't worth it. Still shouting invectives, the bravos retreated down a side street, looking for an easier target.

The captain didn't put his sword away. "Now," he said. "a brisk pace but in good order. Back to the palazzo." It was not far. My heart pounded, though I kept pace and did not run. We turned into Via dei Coronari, and the guards closed behind me rather than to the side. The street was too narrow for anyone to come upon us except from the front or rear. I confess that I was relieved to see our back door. It opened, and we went inside, the guards locking the door behind us.

The captain turned to me. "Well done, Madonna." He must be used to ladies who screamed or fainted.

"I should say that to you," I said, "as I am well and safe and no harm done to any."

He took the praise with a nod. "That rabble wasn't a problem. It's trained men who are."

"I will keep that in mind," I said. Like Orsini guards.

I went up to my camera where the candles were already lit and wrote a note to Alessandro telling him what we'd done. I had no idea if it would help or not. I didn't know how much influence de Bastian had, but he was the only entrée I had. Then I came back down to send two guards with the message to the Vatican.

The captain was still on duty at the doors. He saw the messengers off and came back to me. "Thank you again," I said. "Your professionalism is impressive. What is your name?"

"Giovanni Rizzoli," he said. "I've been in His Eminence's service for five years." He was perhaps thirty, clearly an expert at his work of guarding a target.

"I hope he pays you well," I said.

At that he grinned, white teeth under a dark mustache. "That he does! And fine quarters with room for my family." He glanced at my middle. "We have six."

"Six children?" It seemed a lot at his age, but perhaps he and his wife were enthusiastic.

"Six," he said. "The youngest is seven weeks tomorrow. So I can use the extra pay."

"You certainly deserve it," I said. "I hope His Eminence is a fair master?"

"Always." Rizzoli seemed amused. "He trots us all over town in the middle of the night and there's guarding his lady," he nodded to me, "and there's always someone who wants to kill him, but he pays well for it." He looked at me more seriously. "That Bagnoli was trouble from the start."

It took me a moment to realize that Bagnoli was the dead man. I hadn't known his name. "I see," I said.

"You can rest easy with us," Rizzoli said. "Good night, Madonna." I went upstairs feeling considerably more confidence. Of course Rodrigo trusted his men. He had to.

Maria helped me undress, putting the scarlet gown away carefully. "I hope it went well, Donna Giulia?"

"I think so," I said honestly. My back hurt.

"Will His Eminence be pope?" she asked.

"I don't know." It was going to be close. "One vote either way."

"I will pray for him," Maria said seriously.

"Please do." I reached out and embraced her quickly. I had never told Silvia *Thank you* enough. "Either way, he will need your prayers."

Maria woke me up just at daybreak. "Donna Giulia, you want to come. They have just seen white smoke." There was black smoke from the burning of each inconclusive ballot. White smoke meant they had elected a pope.

"Who is it?" I said, leaping from my bed and reaching for the cotta she held out for me, pale blue and one of my newer ones.

"We don't know yet."

"No messenger?" I asked. Of course if there had been she would have told me first, but I asked anyway.

"No, Donna Giulia."

I threw my balcony doors open and ran out, Maria following me. It was the best place to see in the house. I could see the tower of St. Peter's well, and the streets and the bridge. I could not see the smoke. Below, people were pouring into the street. Everyone had heard.

I put my hands together. "Please," I whispered. "Please." There was a sound in the camera, and I looked around. Dionisio and Chaya stood there, one of the young maids behind them. "Come out on the balcony," I said. "Come on." I beckoned. "You should all see this if you want to."

"Thank you, Madonna," the young maid said. Dionisio let her stand in front of him since she was much shorter.

I let Chaya in beside me. "Is it your cardinal?" she asked.

"I don't know yet," I said. Something had new had happened because the crowds building across the river suddenly moved, shouting. It was impossible to hear what they said, just that something was a cause for jubilation. Perhaps the doors to the balcony had opened. Perhaps someone had stepped out. "Please," I whispered again.

Someone would be making the announcement, *"Habemus Papem!" We have a Pope.* But who?

It moved like a wave. You could see the news sweeping across the bridge, hats thrown in the air, people shouting. It was someone popular. "Not della Rovere," I said. "Please not della Rovere."

It came like the rushing wind of a storm, the news flowing over the city. I caught the first whisper like a wind off the sea growing to fill a sail. "Borgia! Borgia!"

I would have fallen to my knees if I hadn't been up against the railing. So much anticipation, so much fear and now joy. "Borgia!" someone shouted in the street below, and Dionisio whooped.

"Borgia!" he shouted.

"Blessed Mother, thank you! Thank you!" I said, looking skyward, Maria's arm unexpectedly around my waist. She had been afraid I would fall, I thought. I tilted my head back. "Borgia!" I screamed, my voice one with the crowd.

Chapter Eleven

It was two hours before a messenger came, a boy in Borgia livery who looked somewhat the worse for the crowd. There was a neat, formally written letter in Alessandro's hand. *Last night the College heard Vigil in Consistory at two hours past midnight. Having thus asked for God's guidance in this manner, they proceeded to a fourth vote. The final count was Borgia 15 and della Rovere 8.*

"One vote," I said. "One vote."

Cardinals Gherardi, Sforza and Sanseverino cast the deciding votes, it read. Sanseverino was Sforza's seventeen-year-old nephew.

"He got Sforza," I said aloud, though nobody was listening except Maria, who had brought the message up. I wondered how much Ascanio Sforza had cost. A great deal, I was sure. And somehow, whether through our efforts or his own, he had gotten Gherardi.

They then allowed accessus, which permitted the eight remaining cardinals to change their vote, thus making the vote unanimous for the record, Alessandro wrote. *It was quite a moment, Giulia. I hope I will see such again, for it filled me with awe. The vote being concluded, His Eminence Cardinal Borgia accepted the results. The coronation will take place two weeks from tomorrow. He will take the regnal name of Alexander the Sixth.*

I nearly laughed with delight. "Of course he will!" I said aloud. Of course he would be Alexander.

He says to tell you that he knows and appreciates your efforts and your prayers on his behalf, Alessandro wrote. Considerably more than prayers, I thought. But he knew that, and letters might go astray. *He hopes you remain in good health and looks forward to receiving you as soon as is practicable. He sends his fondest regards, as do I, dear sister. Alessandro.*

As soon as is practicable. Well, that wasn't soon, I thought. They'd have every moment of his time scheduled, possibly until after the coronation. Alessandro might be able to escort me to the Vatican next week so that I could slip into some private apartment. Otherwise I would have to wait patiently. Rodrigo was not simply my lover anymore. He could not go about the city or visit as he had. It was, for me at least, a high price. And yet I had known from the first that he intended to be Pope. Now he was. He had said he had no intention of giving me up, so he must contrive. I smiled at that. I was starting to sound like him. *He will contrive,* I said to myself.

Lucrezia arrived three days later, escorted by her brother, Juan, who had also brought her mother and Gioffre back from the vineyard. She flew to me with kisses and demands that I tell her everything since she had missed all the good parts! I hardly thought some of the things she had missed were good. Her face fell when I told her about Silvia. "And where is Adriana?" she asked.

"She went to the country as well," I said, "to stay with Orsino at Vasanello. She isn't back yet, so it's just us."

"Juan is staying with Mother and Gioffre," Lucrezia said. "Can I stay here with you? Please?"

"Of course," I said. "Your father sent for you, so he no doubt meant for you to be here. We will manage ourselves until Adriana returns."

The next two days were full. Rodrigo was receiving torchlit processions of worthies while I received other kinds of processions. Everyone who had ever met me sent their felicitations. A good many people I had never met but who knew someone I knew wrote asking for introductions, favors, or simply to drop in. I set up shop in the sala downstairs with two guards at the door and greeted people for three hours in the morning and two in the afternoon. It was amazing how many people were eager to be my dear friends now that Rodrigo was Pope. I even had a very friendly letter from Clarice Orsini.

In the fourth hour of the third day of this, I reflected that I had wanted to be a patron. Now I was about to greet a gentleman who was apparently my mother's second cousin and completely unknown to me before now, but who had a daughter of marriageable age—all the while maintaining the fiction that I was a respectable wife to Orsino when obviously he would not have been here if I were!

Beneo was back on his feet and announcing visitors. "Father Alessandro Farnese," he said.

I jumped to my feet as he entered. "Alessandro!"

He came and embraced me. He looked well-groomed and cheerful. "Giulia," he said, kissing my forehead. "I finally escaped! I haven't left the Vatican in eleven days. But he said I could clear out until tomorrow, so I thought I would come see you."

"Hold the other visitors," I instructed Beneo, and he closed the door. "How are you, Alessandro? How is he?"

"I'm worn ragged," my brother said, sitting down in the chair opposite mine as I poured wine for him. "It was literally day and night for nearly a week. But it's better now that the vote is done. There's a lot to do, but it's not all night. We do get to sleep now." He took a quick sip as I handed him the glass. "He's fine. Happy as a puppy. You'd think he'd get tired, but no. He runs the clerks around in circles. Burchard is nearly hysterical. I'm hiding from him."

"From Rodrigo or Burchard?"

"Both of them," Alessandro said. "Burchard and the Holy Father."

"It is going to be very strange to think of him that way," I said.

"I imagine so." Alessandro looked at me keenly. "You mean to keep on?"

"Of course I do," I said. "And so does he. The logistics may be a bit challenging."

"I should think," he said. "Given that there are a half a dozen pages and guards in his rooms all the time. He doesn't even have bed curtains for privacy."

"Oh dear." Rodrigo clearly wouldn't like that. But then he was pope. "Well, surely he can tell them to leave."

Alessandro looked skeptical. "He's not supposed to."

"He's the pope. Anyone who thinks he won't rearrange everything doesn't know him."

"He's certainly rearranging things," my brother said. "He's creating a force of watchmen for the city to patrol the bridges at night. He's also planning to hold open public audiences on Tuesdays and allow anyone to come before him. Burchard's about to faint because he said anyone included women. Women! Putting issues before the pope!"

"Heaven forfend," I said dryly. "The next thing you know, women will be representing themselves in court. Or being appointed governors. I'd like to be a governor. What's the difference between running a town for a husband or for an overlord? Women do the former all the time."

"True enough," Alessandro said. "Do you mind if I stay here tonight? I'm exhausted."

"Of course not!" I exclaimed. "I'd be delighted. You and I will have a cozy dinner and catch up on everything and then you can sleep in the plushest guest chamber I have. It will be wonderful."

The next morning Alessandro departed, and I settled in for another day of seeing people. Our seamstress, Signora Corsi, came to measure Lucrezia for a gown for her father's coronation. She was at an age where she was growing so fast that her measurements were constantly changing. Normally I would have joined her in the sitting, but de Bastian was announced just as the seamstress arrived, so I left Lucrezia to handle it herself, with some trepidation.

I offered him watered wine and we sat together in my sala. "I trust that Cardinal Gherardi is well?" I asked.

"Not really," de Bastian said. "It's taken a lot out of him. But he wanted to do this." He sipped his wine. "Cardinal della Rovere came to see him after the vote."

"I expect he wasn't happy," I said.

"Livid. Screaming, in fact." De Bastian met my eyes. "He wouldn't have won even if Cardinal Gherardi hadn't changed his vote. Della Rovere would never have made it to fifteen. There would have had to be a compromise candidate. That was clear to Cardinal Gherardi."

"I see that," I said. I lifted my glass. "Screaming?"

"Cardinal della Rovere says there will be consequences. French consequences." De Bastian sighed. "Maybe it's bluster. Maybe it isn't. But I thought you should know, under the circumstances, that della Rovere doesn't accept losing. He says the election will be invalidated."

"I appreciate the warning," I said. That was all we needed— another problem. But at least della Rovere disliked Bracciano as much as Rodrigo did. They might both be enemies, but they weren't playing the same side of the board at all. It is best to try to understand one's enemy as much as one can. After all, how could you guess what someone might do or how they might proceed if you didn't try to stand in their place? "Tell me something, ambassador," I said, "if you know the answer. Why does Cardinal della Rovere support France's interests so strongly? He is not French."

De Bastian looked thoughtful. "I think he sees the French as his tool, not himself as theirs. And he is an idealist of sorts. He believes that the temporal power of the Church rests on orthodoxy, and that any lapse from orthodoxy, whether to asceticism or heterodoxy, must be sharply curtailed. Hence Savonarola and the universities are both suspect. One leads to heretical purification and the other to heterodoxy."

I nodded slowly. It was easy to comprehend how that was completely incompatible with the way that Rodrigo saw the world. He had been formed in the Valencia of his boyhood, where three disparate groups of people lived in one city. Insatiably curious, he had decided there was no such thing as too much knowledge.

"And so we should remain forever in the status quo, balanced between extremes," de Bastian said. "But that's never been true. Everything is in flux and always has been. If he brings France into the game to maintain the status quo, that is the last thing France will want to do."

"Is that what he wants to do?" I said. The prospect was alarming. France was a much greater kingdom than any in Italy, and their claim on the Kingdom of Naples was already a problem.

"He does not accept the results of the election," de Bastian said. "How far will he go? Your guess is as good as mine."

"I don't know," I said. I did not know della Rovere. I had met him on a few occasions, socially and politely. We had exchanged pleasantries. I knew the mother of his daughter, Lucrezia Normanni, slightly. She was perfectly nice, but much older than I and in a different social set. Her daughter, Felice, must be nearly Lucrezia's age. Vannozza knew her better, I thought. I could ask her once things calmed down.

De Bastian looked concerned. "Needless to say, the prospect

of instability is bad for business. That is Venice's interest."

"I believe that Pope Alexander will seek stability," I said. "Perhaps della Rovere can be politically isolated. At which point, being a sore loser is of little account."

"Hopefully so," de Bastian said, and we spoke of other things. Nevertheless, I was troubled. And yet what was the answer? To have simply given the Traditionalists what they wanted? That would harm so many people immediately, including Dionisio's master, Pico della Mirandola, but other scholars and artists consequently. No, I thought. Della Rovere had taken two hundred thousand ducats from the King of France and lost anyway. He would have to live with it.

That night I woke to loud knocking on the doors of my sala and leapt out of bed. What had happened? The room was dark. It must be around midnight. "Donna Giulia?" a voice called. It was Captain Rizzoli. Surely he wouldn't wake me unless it was important. I had gotten as far as the sala when the door at the far end opened, several men silhouetted against the lamp in the hall. "Donna Giulia? You have a visitor."

A visitor that they let in at midnight? I had formed that thought when one of them crossed the room to me. "Rodrigo?" I said incredulously, and threw myself into his arms.

"Giulia, sweetness," he said, gathering me up.

"What are you doing here? You can't be here!" I said, kissing any part of his head I could find in the dark.

"I am here." We bumped noses, but that gave us both our bearings, and the next kiss hit the target.

I pried myself away as I heard the sala door close. "How did you get here? What are you doing?" He was wearing his plainest brown doublet, not anything remotely papal.

"I sneaked out." Rodrigo sounded enormously pleased with himself. "With Cesare. We're inconspicuous. Just two ordinary men."

"No guards?" I boggled at him.

"Much more visible. Who would notice just me and Cesare?" He kissed me again, smugly.

"You're running around Rome with no guards?" I said as I came up for air. He felt so good against me, and yet common sense hadn't entirely fled.

"There are guards here. And as I said, it's much less conspicuous. I need to go to my house and pack some things."

"Pack? Can't you send Cesare to do that?"

He laughed, bending his face to my neck. "I do have some things I'd rather not have Cesare pack."

"Your books," I said. I gasped as he kissed his way down my collarbone.

"I wasn't thinking of the books." I laughed, and he raised his head, lifting a hand to play with a strand of my hair. "And I wanted to see you."

"I have missed you so much," I said. "I don't know how we're going to do this." Obviously the Pope couldn't have a grand procession to Adriana's house. Nor could he sneak around town like a bravo.

"I'll have to think of something," he said. "I'm going to see you. And Lucrezia. I have to see Lucrezia too. And you can't move into the Vatican."

"Clearly not," I said. "Lucrezia is here, by the way. She's back from the country. Juan brought her. Though I'm sure she's asleep now."

"I won't wake her," he said. He waved a hand around, infinitely certain in his ability to arrange matters to his own satisfaction. And mine. "May I come into your camera?"

"You may come into my bed," I said, and led the way.

We settled down in shirt and camisa, him on his back with me on his shoulder, my bump comfortably arranged between us, his arm around me. He sighed. "Ah, Giulia."

"I was worried about you," I said.

"And I was worried about you. But you're all right."

"Not really," I said, and for the first time thought that I wasn't. "Silvia—you remember our cook—is dead." I controlled my voice with effort. "Cesare killed the man who killed her."

"My dear." He tightened his arm around me. "Cesare told me what happened."

"God help the pawns," I said, and closed my eyes. Tears leaked out the corners. I had not let myself cry. Now I did.

He simply held onto me, murmuring comforting nothings, while I cried. "There, sweet," he said. I cried myself out, ending in hiccoughing sobs. Rodrigo stroked my hair. "There, my Giulia."

"I'm sorry," I managed at last.

"Don't be sorry." He shifted to hold me better.

I took a deep breath. "I told Cesare to do it."

"Well." He censured neither of us, though he should.

"And I am not sorry for that." One pawn for another. Pawn takes pawn and threatens the queen, bishop takes pawn. That is the game.

"He killed an unarmed woman with premeditation," Rodrigo said. "Execution is just."

I craned my neck to see his face. "So says the Pope?"

"He would if it ever came before courts of law, which it would not," he said. "Nearly two hundred people have been killed so far in the city since Innocent died, and I will be surprised if any of the murderers are ever caught. If Cesare provided rough justice, and if you avenged your own, who is to say that is wrong?"

I took a deep breath. "It doesn't help much," I said.

"It never does." He stroked my hair. "Vengeance is never as sweet as it seems it will be. But the next man will think twice."

I nodded. "I hope so," I said. "I confess the guards make me nervous."

"But they will consider when anyone tries to bribe them again," Rodrigo said. "Money is nice, but is it worth their life? That's what they must think. Remember, these are men at arms, hired soldiers, not fanatics. It's not worth giving their lives for. It's not personal."

That did make sense. "It's personal to their masters."

"To Bracciano? Maybe." He looked thoughtful. "But you don't see him risking his own life, do you? I'm not sure he'd play that card. He gives every indication of being the kind of man who is happy to risk others instead of himself. He maintains deniability. It's a weakness of his."

"I suppose," I said. I closed my eyes. It was very late. He kissed me, warm and tender, and I leaned into him. Like a dream, like deep waters moving in the sea. How could this be even sweeter after two years? His hand on my back beneath my camisa was gentle, tracing meridians on my flesh, maps of our world. And yet sleep beckoned. "I'm so tired."

"Little one," he said, resting his chin against my forehead. "I am, too."

"Then sleep," I said. "Stay with me."

"For a little while," he said. "Cesare and I need to be at the Vice-Chancellor's palazzo by dawn. By the way, I'm giving it to Ascanio Sforza."

I opened my eyes again. "What?"

"Or rather, I'm giving it to the Church to be the official residence of the Vice-Chancellor, which he will be. If I didn't win, he wouldn't get it." Rodrigo sounded amused. "A lovely house, but just a house. A small price. He did say to leave the plate."

"Your books, your clothes, your statues…" I began.

"All that is mine. But I need to pack up some things I'll need in the next weeks. So a few hours, and then we'll go."

"I should have made certain Cesare had a bed," I began.

He tightened his arm around me. "Cesare is perfectly capable of finding a bed."

"Good," I said. He stroked my back under the camisa, and I relaxed into his hand. "Then stay a few hours."

"Yes, love." I curled up on his beating heart and slept.

I woke, or thought I did. Bright daylight came in around the closed curtains to the balcony. It was hot and stuffy. How had I slept so long? And then I turned. Rodrigo lay beside me on the bed, his hands clasped across him, his eyes shut. His chest did not move. His skin was waxy and sunken. A fly crawled across his hand..

I screamed. I jumped to my feet, screaming and screaming. He lay on my bed as if on a bier, the summer heat already touching him. The palazzo was entirely silent. Nothing stirred, still in the heat. Nothing moved but me, looking at him, my throat raw as I stumbled to my knees beside the bed.

"Will you raise him up from the dead to get a son on you, Mistress of Magic?" a woman said. I looked around. She was there, his statue come to life, only instead of her child on her shoulder she was pregnant like me, her belly rounding six months gone. "I did."

"Dea Peregrina," I said. My heart was in my throat, but I stood up. "Isis. This is a dream."

"Yes," she said, "it is a dream."

"Not the future."

"I cannot see the future," she said, "for humans make it. You see shadows, parts of fears and hopes, and yes, what may be or what once was. Your Rodrigo stirs the currents. He invokes legends deliberately, in all their darkness and brightness. He cannot invoke Alexander without the dream of Babylon."

I shivered, though the room was hot. "A few bright years of glory and then the bier, the swords around his deathbed." I knew my Plutarch. He had given me the book with the life of Alexander.

"Is that not what he wants? Is that not what he has wanted since he read it himself and dreamed as a boy in far Valencia?" Her face was compassionate. "He is not young. Not for him to die young and beautiful, praised for the ages. But you cannot invoke a story and not get all of it."

"Babylon," I said, and the room changed. It was not my room at the palazzo. It was an echoing palace by night, images of bulls vast on the wall in tile, the floor echoing under my feet. The halls were empty. Here and there, from some distant place, came shouts and the sound of arms. It echoed strangely on the richly decorated walls.

She stood beside me, her son in her arms. She looked down at me. "Come, Chloë," she said. "Your father is waiting." Her long scarf covered her hair, and she reached for my hand.

The bastard child of a general, a little girl like Lucrezia—and the King was dead. Alexander was dead. Alexander, not Rodrigo.

"What is this place?" I asked.

"A memory," she said. "Your memory of another place and another time. Is this not your story as well? Have you not yearned for it as much as your Rodrigo?"

I had, of course. I had read Plutarch and imagined myself part of the events I studied. "Why am I dreaming this now?"

"He wakes the echoes," my mother said. She looked away through the darkened halls as though looking for someone. "There was a boy page, new to his king's service, twelve years old when he defended his lord's bier, moments he kept in his heart in all the long years that followed, through all the days of his life. He wakes the echoes now, not with a child's dreams, but a man's desires to change the world. But you cannot have the bright without the dark. You can choose whether you want to be part of it or not, but you cannot change who he is or what fate he courts."

"I understand," I said. In that moment my fear left me. He

would die. "Tomorrow or two years from now or ten." The story would end as he wanted it to. I could walk away, or I could accept the pain of the ending in the beginning. I could love in spring knowing that autumn would come.

Her eyes were kind. "The difference is what he may do in that time. It matters whether it is tomorrow or ten years from now." She looked toward some horizon I could not see. "It matters who makes decisions. It matters what the Pope does, to you and to the people of Rome and to people you cannot even imagine yet. It matters if it is your Rodrigo or some other man."

"But why does it matter to you?"

She smiled. "You need to ask me that? Mother of the World you have named me, and Mother of the World I am."

I met her eyes. "Everyone dies," I said. I heard my voice harden. "But he will not die soon if I can help it."

She smiled. "That's my girl." She let go of my hand, still my mother in this dream of Babylon. "Giulia, wake up now."

I jerked awake. Rodrigo was snoring loudly beside me, one arm flung over me, his face buried in my shoulder. *Not dead*, I thought. Snorting against my skin, too hot and too tight in this closed, over-warm room.

I slipped out from under his arm and went to the balcony doors. The glass doors were open, the shutters closed. I needed some air. I opened one of the shutters quietly and stepped out onto the balcony, looking out over the quiet city. It was hours until dawn, the stars not fading yet. I put my hands on the rail, taking deep breaths, dreams fading to shreds as dreams do. Cooler. Quiet. Rome slept.

Except for a group of men making their way down the street toward the house. There were ten or more of them in dark leathers, and I caught the glitter of swords. They walked in good order, disciplined men though they dressed like bravos. The Gonfaloniere's men.

"Thank you," I whispered to the goddess who had awakened me. "Thank you." And then I ran back in the room. I shook Rodrigo hard but quietly. "Rodrigo! You have to get up. The Gonfaloniere's men are coming!"

Chapter Twelve

He woke quickly for all that he'd been deeply asleep. "What?" He half sat up.

"There are men coming. They're dressed like a mob but they walk like guards," I said in a low voice. "They're Bracciano's men. You must have been followed."

Rodrigo was on his feet in an instant, pulling on hose. "We couldn't have been," he protested.

"You're not nearly as subtle as you think you are," I said, drawing on my cotta over my camisa and reaching for my slippers.

"Cesare and I didn't see anyone."

"How conspicuous is one man?" I asked. "Obviously you were followed and he reported to his master. If the house is attacked by the mob and you happen to be here and happen to be killed...."

Rodrigo was fastening his points. His clothes were more cumbersome than mine. "Yes, yes. I see the idea." I ran back to the balcony again. The men had torches. They were definitely coming this way, quietly and without the shouting one would expect from a mob. Rodrigo joined me, still tying on his left side. "How many?"

"I count fifteen."

If the pope swore, he would have sworn a streak. Rodrigo half-turned. Behind him I saw a movement. A man in black was slipping along the tile roof. He tried to freeze, but a corner of tile was loose and skittered away, rattling against other tiles. I screamed at the top of my voice. A second man was behind him. Assassins. The men at the door were a distraction for our guards. The men on the roof were sent to kill the pope.

Rodrigo grasped it at the same moment. He shoved me ahead of him through the balcony doors, then spun around to close the shutters. It was just a latch. The doors were glass and wood. They wouldn't hold. He shut the doors too, then yanked the heavy curtains across them. It would at least confuse things for a moment.

I dashed out of the dark camera ahead of him and he slammed the door shut behind him. "Where's the bar?"

"On the inside," I said. "It's meant to keep people out, not people in."

We heard the glass break. Rodrigo spread his hands, and we both turned and ran through the sala. At the doors I turned back. "Come on!" he yelled.

I ran back in and grabbed the bow and quiver beside the credenza, hearing the wood of the balcony doors splinter. I ran into the hall, Rodrigo slamming the sala doors behind me. "Let me guess," he said. "Bar is on the inside."

I nodded. He pushed me ahead of him to the stairwell, flights going up and down. We hesitated. Down were our guards, two at least awake and on the front door, stout oak and barred on the inside, as well as Captain Rizzoli and the other guards in the guardroom. Up was Lucrezia, sleeping in the room above mine. And Cesare.

"Up," Rodrigo said.

We took the flight swiftly. Dr. Treschi was in the hall. "I heard someone scream?" he asked.

"There are assassins in the house and men attacking the front door," I said. At that moment we heard a thud against the street doors and our guardsmen called out, shouting for reinforcements.

Cesare's door opened, one down from Lucrezia's. He was in his leather doublet, sword and dagger on crossed belts. "Every damn time I stay here," he said. "I told you this was a terrible idea, Papa." Captain Rizzoli's voice echoed up the stairwell, shouting something to the guards.

"Two men came over the roof," Rodrigo said to Cesare. "They're in Giulia's room."

"Not for long," Cesare said grimly.

From the other side of the stairwell there was a clatter, Mois Sarfati coming down the other hall with his sisters behind him. He had his sword in his hand. "An attack?" he said.

"That's two of us armed," Cesare said. "We can hold them at the stair."

Lucrezia popped out of her room wearing just her camisa. "What's going on?"

"I have a knife," Dionisio said. He did indeed have a dagger. He put himself in front of Lucrezia.

"Lucrezia, stay in your room," Rodrigo snapped. As though that would have any effect!

"Take the Sarfati girls in your room," I said. I dropped my voice, putting my hand on her shoulder. "You have to take care of our guests. Their safety is our responsibility."

Her eyes widened. She nodded sharply. "Come on then. We'll go in my camera and bar the door."

"An excellent plan," I said. "Dionisio, can you guard the door?"

"Yes." He stationed himself in front of Lucrezia's door, a last defense if they got past everyone else. Cesare and Mois Sarfati had started down the stair, stopping at the turn of the landing, side by side with drawn blades. There was room for both of them; anyone coming up would be in plain view on the flight below and would have to rush them going up. I saw their postures change, Cesare going to low guard. They must have seen them, though I could not from the landing above. Rodrigo took a few steps down.

"Papa, will you get back?" Cesare said. "You're distracting me."

"We can negotiate," Rodrigo said to the men.

One of them lunged at Mois, clearly testing him. He caught the blade neatly in a parry, shoving so that the man was forced back. Cesare lunged, a dangerous slash at the other man's head. But these were professionals. The man ducked instead of backing off, coming up under Cesare's guard, dagger in his off hand.

Cesare caught it with his left-hand dagger and for a moment they swayed thus, in close, chest against chest. Then with a heave, Cesare threw him off. The man's foot slipped on the step and Cesare slashed at him, the blade scoring across the man's leather sleeve but not drawing blood.

"Papa, get back!" Cesare yelled. Rodrigo wasn't far behind him. The other man rushed Mois, hitting him body to body and sword to sword, forcing him against the rail.

I remembered I had the bow and quiver in my hands. I slung it across my body, the strap between my breasts, and pulled out an arrow. I'd been good once, five years ago. The body remembers. The draw thus, feet a shoulderspan apart, the left foot pointed at the target, left arm extending along the line of the foot. Thus. The string sang. I put an arrow into the thigh of the man fighting Mois. He yelled. Mois shoved him, and he stumbled back down the flight.

Cesare sprung after, out of sight now beneath the landing above. I put another arrow to the string. Rodrigo looked around. "Giulia, what?"

My second arrow bounced off the wall near the other man's head. He ducked, backing down the stairs from Mois. I followed a few steps, a third arrow aimed over the railing, trying to get a shot.

One of the assassins lunged past Cesare, scrambling low on the stairs, trying to get to Rodrigo, who threw himself in front of me. Fortunately I didn't release yet, so he didn't get the arrow in his back. He covered me, which also completely blocked my shot.

The assassin slipped on the marble step where it was worn, and Cesare was on his back. The pair of them rolled, each with a dagger, each trying for a blow. They rolled two steps down to the landing, Cesare beneath. I aimed over Rodrigo's shoulder, but the arrow turned on the man's leather doublet. And then Cesare had his point in the man's neck at the side. Blood spurted, soaking Cesare and the white marble. Cesare shoved him off, the man's eyes rolling up and his body shaking. He picked up his sword and dashed down the stairs after Mois and the other assassin.

I took a heaving breath. Rodrigo hurried down the stairs, kneeling next to the dying man, making the sign of the cross over him. "He just tried to kill you!" I said.

"I'm still a priest!" There was no point in arguing with Rodrigo over that. I picked my way down carefully. My slippers had smooth soles and the marble steps were spattered with blood. I kept the bow at full draw, an arrow at the string as I looked down the second flight. I saw no one, though I heard the fight below. They must be at the foot of the stairs on the first floor. Further from Lucrezia and Rodrigo was better. There were shouts of guardsmen and then a crash. The front door had finally given way.

I turned the corner, starting down the flight to the first floor, looking over the rail. Our guards and the supposed mob were locked in a struggle in the foyer. The door to the saletta was open, and Captain Rizzoli was holding off two men on the bottom step of the stairs. At least one of our men was down by the doors, lying in a heap against the wall.

It made me so angry. I knew them all. He was hurt or dead to defend me and mine. I went to the landing, lining up a clean shot. I only had eight arrows. This was the fifth. It needed to count. That one. I released, the arrow straight and true into the right upper arm of one of Rizzoli's opponents. The man spun around from the impact. I drew another arrow from the quiver, putting it to the string.

Cesare was in the middle of the melee, ducking beneath a halberd that someone swung at him, closing graceful as a dancer, a spin of steel and leather. The sixth arrow slid past the man he fought by a fingerswidth, hitting the tapestry on the wall behind. Cesare didn't flinch, but the man did, and that gave him an opening. He went down before Cesare's sword.

"Giulia!" Rodrigo was at my elbow. "Get back upstairs!"

Rizzoli saw him there and swore. His job was to defend the target. He disengaged, fighting his way back to put himself squarely in front of Rodrigo, who stood halfway down the last flight. "To the Pope!" he yelled to the other guardsmen.

I saw the instant that they recognized him, and so did Rodrigo. The supposed mob were Orsini guards, not assassins. They'd probably been told they were going to loot the house of a rival, not that they were going to assassinate the pope. I saw one's expression of horror as two of our men managed to disengage, one with a sword and one with a halberd, dropping back to the foot of the steps to guard as they did in the street.

Rodrigo's face was red with fury. "In the name of God and on pain of eternal damnation!" he shouted, "This mayhem and lawlessness must cease!" Hands on hips, he strode down the steps, Rizzoli staying resolutely ahead of him. "You raise your hand to Christ's representative?"

That did it. The young one near the door turned and fled. The man next to him, bearded and older, hesitated a second and then followed, one hand up as though he thought God couldn't recognize him if Rodrigo couldn't.

Cesare lunged at one. "Let them go!" Rodrigo shouted. "Enough blood has been shed! This criminal behavior must stop!" He reached the bottom of the steps, the guard with the halberd keeping it across him. "It's disgraceful. Get out! Now!"

They broke and ran, all who could, one of them limping with his arm over the shoulder of another. Four men lay on the floor, one of ours, two of theirs, and the second assassin. Mois Sarfati was holding his left shoulder, blood seeping through his fingers from a cut across his upper arm.

I lowered the bow. Rizzoli looked back at me. "Are you all right, Donna Giulia?"

"Yes, Captain," I said. My voice didn't shake at all. I was still angry. I wished I could pursue them into the night.

Clearly Cesare did too. "Papa...."

"Your holy office, Cesare," Rodrigo said. "Let them go." Cesare shook his head.

"Get the doors," Rizzoli said. I could see where they were damaged, but it was the bar that had splintered. The doors should close and a new bar wasn't that hard to get. "You two, sweep the house. Make certain nobody got past us. Donna Giulia, could you see if your housekeeper could help? There are wounded men and she has a deft hand." As he'd seen before, no doubt.

"Of course," I said, and went with one of the guards to find Maria. No doubt all the maids were hiding in their rooms, terrified. It was the smartest thing to do. Nobody was after them in particular, and being overlooked was the best plan. I thought with a pang of Silvia's story of hiding in the barrel of beans when Cardinal de Mila's house was looted three elections ago.

Maria had barricaded herself in her room with two of the young maids and one of the kitchen boys who was only ten years old. "I told you our men could handle it," she said as she opened the door for me and the guard. "You see?"

"His Holiness is here," I said. "And your help is needed. Several of our men are wounded."

One of the maids crossed herself. "His Holiness?" Maria said. She was only fazed for a moment. "Of course." She gave me a look that said louder than any words that she couldn't believe Rodrigo had chanced it. Well, neither could I.

When we got back to the foyer, Cesare was clearly in the midst of expressing the same thing. He and Rodrigo stood on the stairs, the saletta door open and the dead attackers laid out inside. I went to join them.

"I don't see that," Rodrigo said.

"I do," Cesare said. "I told you. You put Lucrezia in danger. You nearly got Giulia killed. This is not going to work. You can't leave the Vatican and wander around town! You're the Pope! You have to stay there, under guard, like you're supposed to!" Cesare shook his head like a beleaguered bull himself. "What would you be saying right now if I'd been killed? I could have been!"

Rodrigo looked pale. "What would you have me do?"

"This is a house, not a fortress." Cesare wiped his face with his hand. "You have a fortress, the castle at Nepi. You need to send Lucrezia and Giulia to Nepi. Out of Rome, out of reach. If you keep this up, they're going to get killed. It's selfish to put your pleasure in seeing them before their lives!" He turned and walked away.

"Where are you going?" Rodrigo called after him.

"To tell Lucrezia what happened and reassure her," he shouted back.

Rodrigo took a deep breath. His hands were shaking, whether with rage or belated fear I couldn't guess. "Are you all right, Giulia?" he asked quietly.

"Yes," I said. Truly, it was easier to fight than to wait. I still felt the fighting rush in my veins. I was clear as cool water. Perhaps later I'd be frightened.

"I'll help you upstairs," he said, and I let him, his hand at my elbow. The stairs were ornamented with bloody footprints, the dead man still lying on the landing. My sala doors were open but not broken. They'd just been closed, not barred. The same was true of the door to camera. The shutters had been forced, the wood broken where they'd been kicked in. Broken glass from the doors glittered all across the floor.

"I will need the doors repaired," I said, going to them and looking out. The city was quiet before dawn. He didn't answer, and I looked back.

Rodrigo was standing by the bed amid the broken glass, his eyes closed, his face twisted. "I said I would hold nothing back. I said you could have it all. All of me." He wasn't talking to me. His chin tilted up. "I can't do it," he said, anguish in his voice. "I can't give up my family!"

The pope is supposed to have no family. He is one. He is sole. He is alone. Those things went through my mind. Rodrigo knew that. Maybe this wasn't a rule that would bend for him.

My family. We were his heart. Me, his children, this child who leapt inside me at his voice. He needed us. "Is this what I have to do?" he asked. He was not talking to me.

"I won't go to Nepi," I said calmly. "I will not be stashed at a country estate far from Rome where I will never see you. That is not what I have worked so hard for."

He opened his eyes. "Giulia...."

"I won't," I said. "And I will not be hidden somewhere under guard to be smuggled into the Vatican for an hour to get it done like a streetwalker. I am not a dirty secret and I will not be treated like one." He was speechless. "I am your lady. I was won, not bought!" My voice broke.

His arms were around me and mine around him, the fighting rush that had carried me leaving me like water down a drain, and I buried my face against his shoulder. "I won't go to Nepi. I won't. I am staying here."

"Giulia, you can't," he said, and I could hear the tears in his voice. "I can't protect you here. Even with guards, the house isn't safe. You can't have any kind of life. The baby...."

"There are other houses," I said. I held onto him. He was the one they wanted to kill. He was the one they might kill.

"Cesare's right. I can't run around town with only him. I can't visit you with forty guards and a procession. If you won't be smuggled into the Vatican..." He stopped, then went on. "Giulia, you can't live in the Vatican. Lucrezia can't."

"Not in the Vatican, no." The idea came to me complete and perfect. "But what about a defensible house with a secret passage?"

"A what?" He leaned back to arms' length, trying to see my face.

"A secret passage," I said. "That's how I was getting messages to Alessandro after our guard was dismissed. There's a house that backs up to the Vatican walls, to the Choir Chapel in St. Peter's. You can get through a secret door from the chapel into the house."

Rodrigo looked at me incredulously. "Who does it belong to?"

"Cardinal Zeno," I said, "but he rents it to Ascanio Sforza's mistress, Antonia. That's how I used it. She was using it too, to coordinate Ascanio's dealings." I took a deep breath. "It's smaller than this house, but I remarked to myself when I saw it how defensible it is. I'm certain it could be perfectly comfortable. Then you wouldn't need to leave the Vatican with a procession. You could just duck into St. Peter's and…"

"…disappear?" He almost laughed. "Go into the chapel and vanish?"

"Why not?" I asked. "Surely you can use a chapel if you wish. And there are already guards in St. Peter's. There are guards on the entrances to the Vatican from the basilica. It's the same guards that you have now. And I could come through into the basilica and then just go to the doors to your apartments and be passed through. No sneaking required."

"A house that backs up to the Vatican walls."

"Palazzo Santa Maria in Portico," I said. "You could rent it or buy it from Zeno. Lucrezia could live with me. You could see us and the baby all the time."

He bent his head against my shoulder. "I need you."

"I will contrive," I said, and felt him smile. It was what he always said, after all.

Chapter Thirteen

Adriana returned from Vasanello three days later. She had not brought a letter for me from my husband, Orsino, but I didn't expect one. He'd written to me twice in two years, stilted greetings on Eastertide that could have been to a mere acquaintance. Well, that was what we more or less were. I had no idea if he was happy in his role as lord of a country estate, but it was at least an honorable position that gave him a comfortable income to pursue…something. I'd never quite worked out what it was that Orsino actually wanted to do.

Adriana had brought Silvia and Beneo's daughter with her, and there was a long and painful conversation in which I related to her what had happened to her mother. I stressed that it had been exceedingly quick and that Silvia had neither lingered nor suffered. "She probably did not even have time to realize what had happened," I said. "The Archbishop of Valencia prayed for her. He was holding her hand." Well, after he killed the man who killed her, but entirely true. Cesare might not like being a bishop, but he was one legitimately.

She cried, of course. She cried in Adriana's arms, Beneo coming to join in their embrace, and I went away awkwardly. No one had said it, but I was to blame. Adriana had told me that if I played Rodrigo's game, people would die. All I could do was light a candle for Silvia and ask for her forgiveness.

It was Lucrezia who found me in my camera, a piece of embroidery in my lap on which tears fell unheeded. She sat down at the foot of my bed. "The house might have been attacked anyway," she said without preamble. "It was when the last pope died. You had nothing to do with it then. Maria told me all about it when I was sent to the country."

"Maria said something like that," I said. I vaguely remembered that she had, when Silvia had told me what happened when Rodrigo's uncle had died thirty-four years ago.

"And last week during the conclave a house was burned near the market and three women raped," Lucrezia said. "Their father was killed." Her voice was very matter-of-fact. "Maria says there have been murders every day since Innocent died. It happens every time. It happens whenever there isn't a pope strong enough to put a stop to it. She says that when she was my age it was all warring families and Rome was a charnel house, the laughingstock of Italy, with cows grazing in the middle of town and bands of bravos taking whatever they wanted. She said a woman had to scuttle from one house to another like a crab in daylight."

I looked at Lucrezia in surprise. But then, why should I be surprised? She had spent a lot of time with Maria and Silvia. Of course she'd heard history from them that I hadn't.

"And then came the power," she said. "Popes who made them behave. Earthly princes who had courts of law and prisons and broke the backs of the great families. They hated that, so they elected my great-uncle Callixtus because they thought he was weak, but he wasn't." Lucrezia looked at me seriously. "And Papa isn't either. Which is what they want. It happens in every country. Lords and barons want a weak king but the commons don't. The commons want laws and justice and the waterworks fixed and reasonable taxes instead of extortion and to be able to get to the market without risking dying."

I stared at her. "You are very right."

"Of course I am." Lucrezia shrugged. "My mother is as common as dirt. That's what she says, and she says that my father's not much better. What do you think I learn at her knee? Not refinements. That's for Donna Adriana. I learn how to be a prince." She pushed her long hair back. "I'm going to rule people. I need to understand what they want."

"I think you understand very well," I said.

"You're not so noble that you don't care about people," she said.

"I should hope not." I put my embroidery down. "Lucrezia, blood has nothing to do with it. My family has old blood, but we never acted like these nobles do. We had responsibilities. We worked. I was raised to work. It's not about who your ancestors are. It's about being spoiled."

Lucrezia snorted. "Like Juan. He thinks he ought to have everything he wants."

"And yet he is the child of the same parents that you are."

"Mother says Papa should have beaten it out of him when he was young enough to beat," Lucrezia said. "But Papa never beats any of us. He's too soft-hearted."

"I am not sure that a beating would improve Juan," I said. "It might only make him angry. Perhaps it is just that he is very young."

She rolled her eyes. "You sound like Papa. Juan could get away with murder. Papa would just say that he didn't really mean it."

"So could you, but you don't," I pointed out. "At some point responsibility for one's actions rests in oneself, not one's parents."

"Then maybe I'm just a better person than Juan," she said.

"Don't you think you're being a little hard on him?" I asked. From what I had seen, Juan was prone to bad language, occasionally rude to his elders, and drank too much at parties. None of these seemed to me like capital crimes in a young man of sixteen.

"No," Lucrezia said darkly. "He wants them to like him. The rich boys his age he spends time with. I'm younger than he is and

I know who my real friends are."

"I think girls are more mature about things like that than boys are," I said. At twelve, girls had already learned vicious politics from one another. I expected her schoolmates were no different than the girls I had known and had no desire to see again, no matter how nicely they wrote to me now. It had made me reserved in the company of women my age. I hesitated to confide, knowing that confidences are a weapon.

Lucrezia looked at my middle. "I hope the baby is a girl," she said. "We have enough boys. I need a sister."

"It will be as God wills," I said.

"Maybe if Papa asks nicely," Lucrezia said.

Cesare showed up at dusk on Tuesday. It had been nearly twenty-six weeks since I had bled, and I was starting to feel a bit ungainly. Not precisely enormous, but I was definitely reaching rotund. "I didn't expect you!" I said, greeting the young archbishop with genuine enthusiasm.

We stood in the garden and no one could overhear us. "Papa wants me to bring you to him after Compline. He thinks the streets are safe enough. Do you want to?"

"With great good will!" I said. Peace was somewhat restored in the city. Rodrigo had ordered patrols in the streets at night, and during the day shops and tavernas were open again. There were even two men who had been arrested for murder, which was a wonder. "Let me dress. I'll have them bring you refreshments while I do."

Vespers rang while I was dressing. I thought the dark blue, perhaps. It was a color that suited me and while it was rich and lovely it was not too ostentatious for going through the streets with Cesare, though there would be guards with us. I looked at myself in the mirror. Whatever I wore, it would be scandalous. The Pope's pregnant concubine? Slipped into the Vatican itself by his son to spend the night with him?

I had not seen him since the battle last week. He had sent me several notes—that he was buying the books from the Sarfati, that he planned to talk to Zeno about the house—but nothing deep or personal. The minutes couldn't fly fast enough.

I was dressed well before Compline. I went down to join Cesare in the garden to wait. He was sitting at the little table, his long legs stretched out before him, talking to Mois Sarfati, who jumped up when I approached. "I beg your pardon, Donna Giulia."

"You are very welcome to stay, Mois," I said. "You are both my guests."

"The archbishop and I were discussing swordmaking," he said. He looked a little sheepish. "The techniques of the Toledo blade."

"They are not really tempered in blood, he says," Cesare said, reaching for his wine glass. "Disappointing."

I sat down in the third chair. "Do you find it so?"

"A bit." He gave me a glance, looking up like a wolf puppy from his glass. "It's an appealing story. Great swords take a man's life at their inception and carry his soul within it, plunged into a beating heart straight from the forge."

"In reality they use a special mixture of oils on the blade," Mois said. "Not as good a story, but true." He bowed. "If you will excuse me, Donna Giulia, Your Excellency."

"Of course," I said and settled back in the chair. It was too early to go quite yet.

"He's all right," Cesare said. No doubt he was thinking of the fight last week. "Is Adriana over her fit?

"She does not like them here, no. Your father is buying the valuable books from them, so now they will have the means to stay in Rome, even if it is illegally," I said. "I can't imagine he'll enforce the laws against Jews with much vigor."

Cesare took another sip, then reached for the decanter. "I hear della Rovere's sending men to Valencia to hunt down the marrano rumor. He'll have no luck with that. Papa destroyed all the evidence years ago."

I think my face showed nothing. Or at least Cesare noticed nothing. "He is very thorough," I said.

"It's not so hard to get rid of a baptismal record when you're the bishop," Cesare said.

"And it was several generations back," I guessed, speaking as though I knew.

"My great-grandmother," Cesare said. He offered to pour for me and I accepted. "My great-grandfather was a landless knight who got granted a farm. They were legally married after she converted. But that was nearly a hundred years ago. Nobody younger than Papa knew her, and they certainly weren't around when my great-grandparents were married. Della Rovere's men might find some people who've heard rumors, but there aren't any witnesses or documents. We're all fine. Even a little nameless." He looked at my belly. "Does it have a name?"

"Alessandro for a boy, Laura for a girl," I said. Of course Cesare thought Rodrigo had told me. And of course he hadn't. Which was what Adriana was talking about. She thought I had a right to know when I carried his child, and he'd played as though he had no idea what Adriana objected to. *Weasel*, I thought. I was going to have a word with Rodrigo.

It was full night when we arrived, going in through St. Peter's. The basilica was still well-lit though it was after Compline and many hours until Vigil, though there were not many people there, and most were passing through. Cesare led me to a side door on the right side and through a passage into a hall. There was a guard there. "His Holiness is expecting us," Cesare said, and we were let through.

Another hallway, another turn, another set of guards, and then into a very stuffy sala. There were two pages, one putting covered plates on a table, and a taster standing ready. I supposed Rodrigo did need a taster now. He was wearing a dark red gown that suited his coloring, and he got to his feet when Cesare and I were announced, his eyes lighting when he saw me. I refrained from running to him in front of all the servants. Rodrigo had no such compunction. He came straight to me, lifting my hand to his lips and meeting my eyes over it. "My sweetest."

At that Cesare made a little bow with a sardonic smile. "I'm not really needed further, am I, Papa? Shall I return for her at Prime?"

"Yes, thank you." Rodrigo didn't let go of my hand as he gestured to the table. "A little light supper for us?"

The taster and the pages were staring at me with expressions ranging from horror to fascination. Cesare had just made it perfectly clear I was spending the night, if Rodrigo hadn't. Previous popes had certainly had concubines. However, I doubted they'd entertained them thus, as though it were perfectly respectable and normal. They'd had shame or at least a sense of propriety. Rodrigo had neither. I had asked for this. I had said that I would not wait for him in some secret place to be visited occasionally, or hustled in and out of his bedchamber, an hour and done, like a whore.

"I would be delighted," I said with my head high, and let him escort me to the table and seat me like his lady.

The pages served with due ceremony. The taster poured a little of the wine from the decanter into a small glass and drank before we were served in goblets of ruby Venetian glass which had just been wiped out by the pages with clean cloths so that nothing could have been placed in the glasses before the wine. Each dish was put before the taster, who ate a little. We waited to see if he showed any ill effects, attempting to make small talk while waiting to see if the man went into convulsions or keeled over across the table. It did impress on one a sense of jeopardy.

At last it was deemed long enough, and Rodrigo waved away the taster and pages. "We need you no more," he said regally, and they departed. The door closed behind them. Rodrigo picked up his glass. "I've made an offer on the house, Palazzo Santa Maria in Portico," he said.

"I thought Cardinal Zeno disliked you," I said. "Will he sell it?"

"He does dislike me," Rodrigo said genially. "But now he's stuck with me. I'm pope. He would be silly to antagonize me rather than take a fair offer on a house he's renting out." He took a sip. "Ascanio is getting ready to move into my house, so his Antonia and their children are going to move into his old house. Everyone's happy."

I shook my head, smiling. And that was Rodrigo. He simply moved everyone around to suit himself, and somehow everyone came out the better for it. "And I will move into Santa Maria in Portico?"

"With Lucrezia and Adriana, of course. Adriana still has her own house, but I hope she'll continue to chaperone Lucrezia until her marriage. Whenever that is." He lifted a golden fork. "I have eleven offers on the table at present. It's going to require careful consideration."

I sighed. "She's not yet thirteen."

"There's an old betrothal that needs to be removed," he said, digging into his dinner with gusto. "And of course there would be a proxy marriage first, and an agreement not to consummate it until she's ready. But it's best to come to an arrangement while I'm still popular." His eyes were laughing. "That won't last long."

"You think?"

Rodrigo shrugged. "The commons like me and hopefully will continue to do so. The usual enemies hate me and always have. But it's the middle—they'll cheer for me now. Let's see if they will in two years."

"You may win them over," I said. I put my glass down. "Presuming della Rovere's agents in Valencia do not uncover the truth." His expression told me everything I needed to know. "Cesare said it," I said. "He presumed you'd already told me. As you should have."

"Giulia." For once Rodrigo seemed at a loss for words.

"Did you think I would be disgusted?" My voice was even. "I am not like the Orsini, as you well know."

He huffed, a rueful expression on his face. "Never that."

"Then why?"

He took a deep breath. "I suppose I'm not a very trusting man."

That was an understatement. "And I am very young and we haven't been together very long in your reckoning, et cetera, et cetera," I said. I reached across the table and took his hand. "I cannot work in your interest if I do not know your secrets. Have I not proved myself at least as discreet and competent as Juan?"

"You think Juan knows that?" There was a touch of amusement in his voice.

I ran my thumb lightly over his fingers. "You should have told me, Rodrigo."

"I should have." He glanced down. "For the sake of the child at least, as Adriana said." He closed his hand around mine. "She was right that it was the one thing that would surely prevent my election. The stakes were too high."

"You must trust me, Rodrigo. I understand what the stakes are. I know that even grandchildren of conversos are subject to arrest by the Inquisition. That was the case in Valencia, was it not? Mois Sarfati told me how you intervened." Even great-grandchildren, like the baby I carried. If he thought I would not defend our child with all my strength, he did not know me.

Rodrigo sighed. "I had to intervene in Valencia. I was as guilty as they were. How could I let them burn for no more than was true of me?"

"You couldn't, of course." But he could have. Most men would have. They would have never dared to call the attention of the Inquisition to their own antecedents.

"Things were different in Valencia in my grandparents' day. There were mixed marriages. My grandfather wasn't noble. He was a good soldier, the kind of reliable retainer who gets granted a small piece of land. He loved her. And they were both very stubborn. My grandmother knew what she wanted and she got it," Rodrigo said. "I come to it honestly. We won't be denied."

"I know, my love," I said. I squeezed his hand in mine on the table. "And perhaps this was what was supposed to happen."

Rodrigo looked at me sideways. "A marrano pope?"

I took a deep breath. "If God had wanted to refuse you the papacy on the basis of your blood, surely He would have. And since He did not, perhaps you are God's instrument to bring mercy to His Chosen People. Thousands like the Sarfati girls have been driven from their homes with no refuge. And at this moment, no one in the world can rescue them except Rodrigo Borgia. Do you not see God's hand in that?"

I watched his face change, raw at the gift of inexplicable grace.

After dinner we went into his camera. I thought it was rather small and cheerless. The windows were tiny and high, both on the same side so that there was no cross-breeze. He had managed by now to get his bed from the Vice-Chancellor's palazzo, but it sat by itself in the middle of the room like a ship at sea looking distinctly out of place.

Rodrigo saw my expression. "It's terrible," he said bluntly. "These rooms won't do at all. I'm going to have to move to a different suite."

"Well, surely you can," I said. "You're the pope." I stood in the middle of the floor with a curious reluctance. Simply undressing and getting into bed seemed terribly wrong. I had shared a bed with him many times, but in the Vatican it seemed worse.

"I can. I will." He went over to the window and closed the shutter and the curtains. "They're stuffy."

So no one would hear us, I thought. So many people, all of them watching Rodrigo attentively. Listening for his every sound. No wonder he slipped out and wanted to visit me elsewhere. He wanted privacy and peace. Well, I would make Palazzo Santa Maria in Portico into an enchanted oasis, but it would be several weeks before the sale was accomplished and I was moved. Hopefully I could get settled in and things arranged before the baby came. I took a deep breath and sat down on the side of the bed.

"Perhaps some paintings?" I said. I supposed the hangings in here had belonged to Innocent. They were not Rodrigo's taste at all. They made the rooms seem dark and close.

"I'm going to hire a good painter to do an entire suite," he said, sitting down behind me. "Something lively and beautiful."

"That sounds like a good plan." I leaned back against his shoulder. Warm. Solid. He didn't feel different, but then the coronation hadn't happened yet. Or maybe he did, but if so it was subtle, a faint shift beneath the surface. He was still Rodrigo.

He rested his chin on my shoulder. "A mythological theme, perhaps."

"Not Europa and the bull," I said.

He laughed, slipping his arm around me so his hand rested on my bump. "Why not?"

"I'd like a more dignified epithet than the Borgia Heifer!" I laced my fingers with his. "Though I feel a bit like a cow at the moment."

"You are beautiful." He raised my hand to his lips, and I smiled as he kissed my fingertips, then the back of my hand. "Always."

I closed my eyes. We would manage. Love would carry us through. I rested on him, his arms around me. It was like soundless music, this connection. Like dancing to something only we could hear, strange and precious. I took his right hand in my left, raising it palm to palm, as though we danced indeed, passing in the turns of a figure. My fingers were long, exactly the length of his, though his palm was broader. We raised them in unison, watching them together, hands circling each other, twining and parting, then coming together again, palm to palm.

"As though they were folded in prayer," I said. "Only one is yours and one is mine." There was something there below the surface, or perhaps it was like the ocean itself, too vast to see, incomprehensibly deep. One could not see, only feel. Rodrigo always followed the compass of his heart.

"Let me adore you," he said.

I nodded, bending my head as he carefully undid my caul and crown of braids, mindful of the pins and the delicate net. His fingers brushed the back of my neck. I sat still. Perhaps it was that we had done our play of Galatea and Pygmalion, but I could see myself as statue and woman both. His statue. His Isis. The one he had seen raised from the rubble of a temple long fallen. Behind my closed eyelids I could imagine him vividly, climbing over the workmen's debris, animated and excited and reverent at once, kneeling on the stones to see, to caress my face with his long fingers.

And there was the touch, as though he had known what I saw or felt what I felt. I did not open my eyes. I just tilted my face up into his touch, lids closed beneath his tentative hands, as though he could bruise marble with a touch.

But I was not marble. Marble can be marred or stained, but it endures better than too willing flesh, a woman's brief youth, a moment of perfection. And yet eternal. This might be two thousand years gone or a thousand years to come, timeless and out of time. Ten years was nothing to his Isis. And yet a moment was everything.

I drew breath, my lips against his, taking the breath from his mouth and melting together. He was Rodrigo. And he was more.

He was every lover, every son, every priest, every man who had raised his face to me, had sought me, had courted me, had loved me. Who had known my love. Who had lain beside me in bright perfection or across my lap like a Pietá, who had nursed at my breast or been raised from a gilded sarcophagus to stand at my side.

"Living, and yet dead," I whispered against his lips.

"Dead and yet living," he replied, and kissed my eyelids where the tears welled beneath them.

Adoration. He knelt beside the bed, taking off my slippers, untying my garters and rolling down my hose. I had seen him wash the feet of the poor on Maundy Thursday. This was like that, and not like it at once. He kissed the top of my foot, his hand on the arch where he elevated it, graceful as a boy. I touched his hair, smiling. He looked up. I do not know what he saw in my face, but he tilted his head back, mouth drawing a little to one side, as though it were perfection.

Adoration. My full and aching breasts, my rounded belly where the child moved in mirror to his touch, as though it too joined in the dance. He laid his cheek against the curve of it, stubble rough against my skin, and I leaned back on my arms, head back as though pulled by the heavy fall of my hair. "My love," I said.

"My lady." Leaning back further yet so that he could get to the pathway of life, his mouth on my sensitive flesh, transporting and transported. Slow and dreamlike as though underwater. Urgent as my pulse. My breath caught at the peak, the ripples clenching deep, on and on, dark as waves beneath the sea.

And then out the other side, breathless and pure. "My turn," I said, and drew him up beside me.

I watched the planes of his face as he lay back on the pillows, me beside him. I watched his eyes close as I opened his gown and untied his shirt, kissing his chest where his heart waited trembling beneath my hand. "Dazzling brightness," he whispered, his eyes moving beneath the lids.

"Always," I said. Dark rooms lit by torches, this room with its still candles, a couch beneath the stars with the sound of the waves against the breakwater.... All these things passed through my head, memories and dreams.

On his back with me astride him, plenty of room for the baby, my long hair falling around us both, taking him so slowly, his hands clenching on the covers. He opened his eyes then. I could not look away from them, nor he from me. He was my own, my familiar Rodrigo, and yet not. I did not have words for the things that pressed to be spoken. I could only speak with my eyes. It was so vast.

He broke beneath me, not looking away even at the height. And then I lay beside him, both of us in the tangles of the bed covers, dizzy with the plunge. My head spun and I held tight to him, his breathing quieting, his hand stroking my hair. "There, my sweet. There, my love."

"So much," I whispered. The world still seemed to spin, and not entirely in a good way. *You have not prepared for it all your life,* something whispered inside me. And it withdrew, water running out of a vessel, out of a shell on the beach, leaving it empty on the sand.

Rodrigo was a rock beneath the sand. "Rest, my darling. I have you." He gathered the covers over me, settling me on his shoulder. "There."

So easy to slide into sleep, to slip beneath the waves, dark and cool and welcoming. "What just happened?" I whispered.

"Don't ask so many questions, my love." His voice was gentle and amused, wonder in it still. "Mysteries aren't meant to be dissected."

"I know," I said, and spread my fingers on his chest and slept.

Chapter fourteen

Morning, of course, was a farce. It began with being awakened by a fourteen-year-old page who took a look at me, yelped, and literally ran out of the room. Rodrigo stretched in annoyance. "I told the pages to stay out until I called them." He did look scandalous, curled up naked with his pregnant mistress.

"Why do we have to deal with people?" I murmured.

"Because dogs don't have thumbs." He sat up on the side of the bed, perfectly unselfconscious, and then ambled off to what I supposed was the bathing chamber. I needed that after he was done.

I sat up, wincing as I sat on a stray hairpin. My hairpins were probably scattered all over the room. The pages were going to have to get used to me. Also to staying out until he called them, as he'd told them to.

Fortunately, I had put on my camisa before I went into the bathing room, because when I came out Cesare was there. "Is it Prime already?" I said, retreating behind the door. I didn't need Cesare to see me in my underclothes.

"Sadly," Rodrigo said. He was dressing with perfect equanimity. "Cesare is here to take you home."

"Can I have my clothes?"

Rodrigo bundled them up and brought them to me at the door. "Here, my sweet." I dressed in the bathing room, shaking my head. This would not do at all. But surely Cardinal Zeno would sell Rodrigo the house and we could refrain from future silliness and discomfort. As for the rest....

I took a deep breath, washing my hands in the tepid water at the basin. What could one say? I felt no ill effects. In fact, I felt uncommonly good, if terribly hungry. This was going to result in sending me off without so much as a piece of bread. I looked at my face in Rodrigo's shaving mirror. Nothing was strange, nothing different. I felt entirely myself. And yet open. In some ways, it reminded me of the first night I'd spent in Rodrigo's bed, two years ago now. I supposed that awakened was the word I was looking for. Myself, only taller and brighter.

I put my hand to my belly, the baby turning slow somersaults. It wanted breakfast. "Come on, my darling," I said. "Home and food. Papa has to be Papa today."

"...he doesn't want me to dismiss him, of course," Rodrigo was saying to Cesare as I came out dressed. "And it's abundantly clear to him that even if I hadn't been elected, it wouldn't have been his kinsman."

"Who?" I asked, taking the bundle of hairpins Rodrigo had hunted up for me.

"Bracciano," Cesare said. "I was saying to Papa that I don't like the way he's kissing ass. It's suspicious."

"Of course it's suspicious," Rodrigo said. "He just tried to kill me! But once again he didn't succeed, and if he does anything that I can pin on him, he'll be relieved of his command at the very least. It makes sense for him to make nice now. The coronation is in two days. As it stands, I have no pretext to appoint someone else Gonfaloniere, though I'd love to. His best move is to wait."

Cesare sighed. "Unless it couldn't be blamed on him. Poison."

"I am extremely careful."

I frowned. "What would happen if you died before the coronation?"

Rodrigo presented my caul, which had been in the bedcovers. "The same thing that would happen if I died anytime afterwards—there would be a new election. But it's abundantly clear that Cardinal Orsini does not have the votes, even if I were dead. It would probably be Ascanio Sforza, and the Sforza hate the Orsini."

"Or della Rovere," I said.

"Della Rovere doesn't like him either." Rodrigo kissed me on the forehead. "I will be careful. To both of you—I promise I will be careful."

I left with Cesare, four pages in the hall scattering and then standing behind half-closed doors to whisper as we went past. Some of them looked about twelve. I suppose at twelve a naked pregnant woman was a new experience and the one who'd walked in had plenty to relate. They'd gossip all over the Vatican. Well, so be it.

Cesare and I emerged into the street with two guards. The day was going to be beautiful, and there was not a hint of rain. "I'm sorry to put you to trouble," I said, aware that he probably had better things to do than escort me around town an hour after dawn.

Cesare shrugged. Once again he wasn't dressed like an archbishop, and he wore sword and dagger as usual. "I don't mind. I'll break my fast with Lucrezia."

"You are very welcome to," I said. It was the least I could offer for his trouble. I knew he had wanted us to go to Nepi, but I had refused. I hoped that I had not tarnished my relations with him forever as a result. "We will soon move into Palazzo Santa Maria in Portico, which will be much safer and will not inconvenience you."

He looked at me sideways. "You're a sensible woman," he said. "That's good. You know Lucrezia isn't, and Papa's not much better than Lucrezia."

"I will do my best to take care of both of them," I promised, and he nodded.

"I don't think Bracciano's done," he said. "I think he's got one more thing up his sleeve. If he can get Papa before he's actually pope…."

I nodded. No, it wouldn't be assassins. Or poison. Those things could be guarded against. But magic? Bracciano had tried that before, unsuccessfully. And Rodrigo had said that Bracciano's demonic summonings wouldn't work on holy ground. Rodrigo was spending all of his time on holy ground at present. It would have to be something else. "I agree," I said to Cesare. "But I don't expect I will see him again until the coronation, and that from among the spectators."

"It's on me," Cesare said. He shrugged. "Not that I mind. But a 'Thank you, Cesare, that was well done' would be nice."

I stopped, taking both his hands and looking into his face. "Thank you, Cesare. You saved our lives the other night. You are a peerless warrior, and I have nothing but respect and gratitude for your skills."

For a moment he looked younger than his years, dark eyes meeting mine above three days of beard. Then he smiled, a sardonic twist full of self-mockery. "Thank you, Giulia," he said. In spite of everything that came after, we always understood one another, Cesare and I.

When I got home, I went back to bed and slept until noon. I woke when Maria looked in to make certain I was well, opening my eyes to see her leaning over me anxiously. "You don't usually sleep so, Madonna," she said.

"I did not sleep much last night," I said, sitting up. The room was warmer than usual. The glass in the balcony doors hadn't been replaced yet and they were still boarded shut. "His Eminence…" I stopped. First, it was inappropriate. Second, I'd used the title I was accustomed to.

"He's a lusty man," Maria said, opening the curtains to at least let some light in around the boards. "And he hasn't seen you in a week." She frowned at the doors as though they personally offended her. "And the glazier is finally coming this afternoon."

"So you thought I'd best get up and dressed," I said, swinging my legs out of bed. "Yes, I want the doors fixed too! I really didn't mean to sleep half the day. What is everyone doing?"

"Dr. Treschi is teaching geometry to Donna Lucrezia and the Sarfati girls," Maria said with a sniff that suggested she thought geometry deeply suspect. "It was Donna Lucrezia's idea. She said he might make himself useful."

"He might at that," I said. Lucrezia's school was not in session due to the instability, and she missed her friends and her usual activities. The presence of two girls her age and a tutor no doubt suggested that they could have school. Something like a tutor, at least.

"Donna Adriana is going over accounts in her study," Maria continued. "And Signore Sarfati is in the library."

The library sounded nice and cool, and also not somewhere the glazier would be sawing and hammering. "If you would, send First Meal in there for me. I will join him."

My stomach was rumbling and the baby making it clear that it had been a long time since supper when I went into the library, feeling a bit confused as to what time of day it was. I was usually an early riser. Mois jumped to his feet when he saw me. "Don't disturb yourself," I said, settling down at the reading table. One of the little maids brought the tray in behind me. "You are welcome to join me if you'd like. There are workmen in my room fixing the door, and I am taking myself somewhere else."

"If it isn't trouble," he said politely, sitting back down. "The other evening…."

I met his eyes candidly. "I told you that Rome was dangerous at this time. I am sorry that such violence occurred. It should be better soon, when Cardinal Borgia—I mean His Holiness—has the city more firmly in hand."

Mois shook his head. "If that is what it is like, I have no doubt we would have been killed by now if we had not stayed here." He looked around the room with its shelves and its latticed window on the garden. "It is like an island at sea or a castle under siege, is it not? A beautiful and comfortable prison."

"It isn't always this way," I said. "Of course it is hard for you not to go about and do things as you usually do. I am sorry it is like a prison to you. But it will be different once we are through the coronation. His Holiness will buy the books and the streets will be safer. They are already safer than they were. His Holiness has put guards on the bridges and there are patrols again." He nodded. "And what will you do then?" I asked. "What do you hope to do when you have sold the books?"

"I hope that we can stay here in Rome. There are Jews who live here. There is even a place of worship by long agreement. If those seeking refuge were allowed to stay, there would be many Jews who would come here." Mois glanced at me. "Perhaps even my family would make their way here."

"I hope so," I said. How to put this? "I feel that His Holiness is sympathetic to your plight. I have every confidence that your situation may be resolved well." I could hardly say that he shared their blood. That was something I must never speak of, except perhaps in time to the child.

"You know his mind better than any," Mois said. "And yet it's clear he has many enemies."

"That is also true," I said. Bracciano had been thwarted again, but like Cesare I was not sanguine. Did he know about the book? "Tell me," I said, "have you read much of the book that purports to be the prophecies of the Erythraean Sibyl? The parts which may be about present events?"

He leaned back in his chair. "I've read them with my father several years ago. To be frank, Donna Giulia, I do not put much stock in it. They read like ramblings. You can see anything in them. As you pointed out before, 'the keeper of the keys shall die' might mean Pope Innocent's death, or any pope in five hundred years or nothing of the kind! And some of it is simply fantasy. 'New worlds shall rise from the seas' is ridiculous. That is not a thing that happens."

"No," I said. "I do not see how it could. These are not the times of myth, but the Year of Our Lord 1492. There are no new worlds and no lost Atlantis to discover." And yet I felt a chill on my spine. I reached for the bread and fresh cheese that Maria had sent. It was just that I was hungry.

"I think the book is valuable because of its historical context," Mois said. "Not because it holds mystical secrets."

"You are probably right," I said. I took a bite.

Dionisio had come to the door. "Do I see First Meal?"

"Come and join us," I said through the bread, and he came around to sit beside me.

"We were speaking of the book of the Erythraean Sibyl," Mois said. "That the prophecies are fanciful. As we discussed before, many of them are simply not realistic."

"Well," Dionisio began.

"New worlds rising from the sea?" Mois said. "You know as well as I do that is impossible."

I put my hand on the edge of the table. My vision swam for a moment. "Three ships," I said. I could see them cutting through the green ocean, sails spread to a following wind, a nau and a pair of caravels. I saw them as if I stood on the wind above, a sea bird following their course. "They bring great harm and return with great harm."

"Giulia?" Dionisio's hand was on my shoulder. "What are you talking about?"

I blinked. "I don't know," I said. I shook my head, shaking the strangeness off. "Dionisio, I have to learn to control this." Mois was looking at me with some alarm. I did not want to be thought mad.

Dionisio nodded slowly. He at least believed me. "There are supposed to be rituals that open the doors, like those we practiced before. Surely there are doors that can also be shut."

"Ah," I said. "We left the door open!" He put his head to the side. "We did the asperging and opened the door but we left the summoning circle to decay. We never dismissed it."

"Of course!" He slapped his forehead. "We never closed it. It must be still active on some level. That's good. I mean, if that's all it is, we can close it. I can close it now."

Mois looked nervous. "I think I had better…."

"Naturally," I said. "This is not your practice, and I understand completely that you wish no part of it. I am sorry to have disturbed you with it."

"Not at all, Donna Giulia." Mois stood and bowed neatly. "I shall take my leave."

"Until later," I said. He thought it some strange Christian magic, and I could not blame him. I waited until he had gone out. "Do you think that will do it?"

Dionisio shrugged. "Giulia, I have no idea! Are you happy with that? I have admitted I have absolutely no idea. I was taught that a Dove's abilities end with her virginity. Obviously that wasn't true. I don't know what rules govern abilities I have been told don't exist!"

I helped myself to more cheese. "We'll just have to find out. Someone has written something about it somewhere."

"Not necessarily," he said. "The ancients guarded the secrets of the sibyls closely. I've never seen anything more than a general visitor's description of the workings of the oracles. Temple mysteries weren't written down. And today…." He spread his hands. "Women can't be mages any more than they can be priests. A Dove is a tool for a magus. She's a receptive principle."

"I am not a receptive principle," I said. The memory of last night was strong. Was that what it was to share in grace? Was that what the ancient priestesses had felt? I had no words to describe it, and I suspected that Rodrigo didn't either, at least not ones he'd readily apply. To even begin to construct such words was utter heresy.

"No, obviously not." Dionisio met my eyes frankly. "I can only surmise you have whatever the raw ability is. Possibly other women do as well but are never chosen as Doves and therefore never know."

"Or it is channeled differently," I said slowly. My grandmother, my father's mother, had told me about the old Etruscan tombs near Montalto when I was a child. She had told me about how the Queen of the World Below would grant a glimpse of a future husband's face. What else had she known? What might she have told me when I was older if she had not died of the summer sickness? I was the only girl in my generation except my baby sister, who had not been born yet when my grandmother died. Was this my birthright, its transmission interrupted?

"Maybe." Dionisio took a bite of his bread. "I wouldn't know that, would I?"

"No," I said slowly. "I'm going to have to find out. Otherwise I will not understand." And that would be intolerable. Rodrigo of all people would know that. Not pursuing knowledge was impossible, as impossible as rejecting mystery. "I hope that if you are staying in Rome, you will continue to work with me. We will take down the summoning circle today, but I want to experiment with this further in the months to come." I put my hand over my belly. "There is a lot happening just now, with the baby and the coronation and I think I will be moving to a different house in the next weeks, but I do not mean to let this go. If this is real and part of me, I will understand it." I smiled at him. "And of course I will grant a stipend to my tutor, if he will work with me."

"I will indeed, Donna Giulia," Dionisio said formally. "We will learn together."

"Then we have a bargain," I said. "And as soon as we have finished eating, we'll take down the summoning circle. I'm starving." I bit into my cheese with great gusto.

Lucrezia was to have a new dress for the coronation. She and her mother and her youngest brother, Gioffre, would be riding in a carriage in the procession, and she was absolutely ecstatic. The older boys had their own parts, Cesare with the bishops and Juan somewhere or other, but this was the first time she'd been allowed to be in something official. I would not be riding. The procession would take hours and jolting along in the hot sun for half the day would not be good for me. Instead, I would watch the coronation and the beginning of the procession from the square outside St. Peter's, and if I felt up to it, I could rejoin the spectators at the end at the Archbasilica of St. John Lateran, where the ceremonies would conclude.

Her father had promised that Lucrezia would also be allowed to attend her first masque, a Celestial Masque the night of the day after coronation day, provided I promised to keep an eye on her and that Adriana took her home early. He had also nixed her dressing as the planet Venus on the grounds that she was too young. "You may be a star," he had said. "And you will be the most beautiful girl there." Lucrezia pouted, but not too much. If she provoked him into a temper, she might not be allowed to go at all.

The morning of the next day her seamstress came for her final fitting, bringing nine boxes and four assistants, which did seem rather a lot. Her camera was too small for all this, so we did it in mine, Adriana sighing with satisfaction over her own gown, which was the first out of the box. It was red, appropriate to both Orsini and Borgia, in a very expensive lampasso with a pattern of twining vines. Since it was silk with only the sleeves pieced with velvet, it would not be excessive in the heat. Lucrezia's gown for the coronation was of the same material, but with more lavish gold trim and a camisa with gold embroidery around the neck where it would show. Red was not particularly Lucrezia's color, but one can't pick one's family devices. Farnese colors were blue and yellow, but I always stuck with blue after one gown as a child had made me look like a giant duckling.

"This one is for you, Donna Giulia," Signora Corsi said, drawing out the third box.

"I did not order one," I said. "I have the lovely blue and silver gamurra that I have only worn once." It had been delivered just before Innocent died, and other than wearing it to visit Clarice Orsini, I had not been anywhere yet where it was appropriate. I intended to wear it with the day sleeves to watch the procession and with the silver sleeves for the celestial masque.

"His Holiness ordered it yesterday," she said.

"Yesterday?" What in the world could she have done since yesterday? And what was Rodrigo thinking?

One of the assistants smiled at me a little shyly. "We worked on it all night."

Signora Corsi drew it out of the box and I gasped. It was a gamurra of cloth of silver, utterly stunning. It was pale blue silk lampasso brocaded in silver gilt, a subtle pattern of feathers and leaves that twined back on itself. It fastened beneath the breasts and flowed from the high waist, so that it would show an underdress and accommodate my baby bump and could be simply laced tighter in the future. I could wear the light blue gown beneath that went with the Farnese blue gown I'd only worn once and it would match perfectly.

"The material came from Venice," Signora Corsi said. "Twenty ducats to the bolt. Only His Holiness, I said. Only His Holiness would have the taste for it."

Only Rodrigo would have the money, I thought. The gown and sleeves would pay one of her assistants for a year. I was stunned.

"It's beautiful!" Lucrezia clapped. And that was her good heart. She wasn't jealous. She was happy I had something so wonderful.

I hugged Lucrezia. "It's amazing, Signora."

"And this for the masque," Signora Corsi said, producing a mask. It was a half mask of silver tissue in the shape of the moon.

I laughed aloud with delight. "It's perfect," I said.

Adriana shook her head, but she was smiling. "Well, nobody will mistake you for anything but what you are."

"She's the Lady of the Vatican," Lucrezia said cheerfully. "Papa means for people to know it."

The morning of the coronation dawned hot and dry. It had not rained in most of a week. Lucrezia had spent the previous night at her mother's house so that they could all leave for the procession together, a wise choice given that even at dawn people were starting to gather in the streets and lay claim to choice places to watch along the parade route. Dionisio and the Sarfati left as the sun was rising to find a good place.

I had longer to get ready. Adriana and I were being escorted to the Vatican in a litter and would be seated in the area for honored guests. The baby gave an excited little bounce, twenty-seven weeks and counting. Perhaps it caught my excitement. Rodrigo's triumph—our triumph—was something to savor.

Admittedly, I was surprised when I came downstairs and found Captain Rizzoli with the guards who were to go with us. His mustache and beard were neatly trimmed, and he wore a new doublet of Borgia red beneath a steel breastplate ornamented with the bull. "Captain," I said with a smile. "I am delighted to see you. But I expected you would be with His Holiness today."

He bowed. "His Holiness has given me charge of your comfort and safety, Madonna."

I supposed Rodrigo had all the official Vatican guards now, and certainly he would be surrounded by prelates all day, but there was also Vannozza and her children who would need guards, and I thought that Rodrigo would want some trusted men with him. Rizzoli was both loyal and competent. I dropped my voice. "Does he fear some particular threat to me?"

Rizzoli's voice was also low. "Not that I know of, and he would tell me if he did so that I might better guard against it. But there will be a great press of people, and you and Donna Adriana will be in a litter in the midst of it. And your condition...."

"Yes," I said. It was good that there was no specific threat. I did, however, see that he feared that some 'accident' might befall me in the streets were I not adequately guarded, wearing a small fortune as I was.

"Don't worry, Madonna," Rizzoli said. "I have nine good men with me and four litter bearers."

Fourteen men ought to adequately protect two women in a litter, I thought. It was rather a lot, but would look like Rodrigo being excessive rather than cautious. "I am sure I am in good hands," I said, and let him help me into the litter beside Adriana.

Even early, the streets were full of celebration. It looked like nothing so much as I imagined an ancient Roman triumph must have, with awnings and banners decking the streets, and throngs of children running here and there to see what was being prepared.

"Oh my," I said, and nudged Adriana. Cardinal Barbo had a temporary fountain constructed in the square in front of his palazzo, the Borgia bull eleven feet tall with pipes cleverly installed so that it would dispense something later, gushing out of its mouth.

Wine or water? The children who were watching the craftsmen preparing were highly curious.

A little further along another palazzo was decorated with enormous banners, the Keys of St. Peter displayed with the bull on a field of green. A huge banner above it read, "Caesar was a man. Alexander is a god!"

I crossed myself quickly. That sort of hubris invited the Furies. I wasn't about to take a chance on whether or not they were real. At least Rodrigo hadn't claimed it himself. Pope Alexander VI was God's earthly habitation, not God himself.

Adriana shook her head. "Rodrigo has every bit of attention he craves. No one will ever ignore the pope!"

I looked at her sideways. "What do you mean?"

"I've known him all my life," she said. "He was a young clerk like your brother when I was a child and since we are cousins he was in and out of my father's house all the time. He could not bear to be ignored. It angered him so much to be passed over in favor of those less talented because we were not of an old Italian family."

"Did he make enemies with his anger?" I asked quietly. If he had been of a temperament like Cesare, I could see how it would happen.

Adriana shook her head. "The worse it was, the more genial he became. Always ready to buy a round. Always ready to loan a ducat or two to his tormentors. They never saw the daggers in his eyes." She looked out at the cheerful crowds. "Now he has them all where he wants them. They hate him and they're forced to kiss his ring. Or his ass, if he wants them to. He'll smile and call them brother and make them admit that he is their equal." She glanced sideways at me. "And they will never forgive him."

"They never will anyway," I said quietly. There was nothing in the world that Rodrigo could possibly do to make himself acceptable to the likes of Clarice Orsini.

"Being so public about you does him no good either," she said in a low tone. "'He has reduced a woman of noble birth to concubinage.' That is what is said."

"My family had no more money than his in Spain," I said. "Being able to trace my line back four hundred years gives me no particular virtue and it certainly isn't worth any cash. The people who flutter at my descent into sin ignored my family before because we had no money."

Adriana made a moue of agreement. "Money matters, my dear. Rodrigo has plenty of it. But it won't buy respect."

"His actions must buy that from people who care more about deeds than lineage," I said. *And hope there are enough of them*, I thought. Not being of an old Italian family might be forgivable to those who weren't old nobility, but I completely agreed with Adriana that having it known he had a conversa grandmother would be the end of him. She was not wrong at all. As long as that remained a rumor spread by obvious rivals like della Rovere, it would be ignored by most people. A marrano pope was, after all, absurd.

As we neared the bridge the crowd thickened and the guards had to work harder to clear way for the litter and keep people from pressing in on both sides. Adriana looked straight ahead as if she didn't see them, but I was prepared. I drew out a purse of silver soldi and smiled at the nearest child. "In honor of His Holiness Pope Alexander," I said, and tossed a coin. The child caught it, and everyone turned.

"It's La Bella Farnese," a man said. "The pope's woman."

I threw him a coin. "Blessings on this happy day!" He looked surprised, and then I could not see him behind the guards and bearers.

"A cheer for His Holiness!" I said and tossed four or five coins away and back. People scrambled, and I tossed another bunch as a cheer rose.

"Alexander!" someone yelled. Someone else took it up, and I tossed another handful in their direction. It did clear the bridge ahead of us as everyone dodged behind us.

I gave Adriana a radiant smile. "We could push and shove, or we could bring delight."

"You are a clever minx," she replied approvingly. "You won him with joy."

"I won him with devotion," I said completely honestly. "You, at least, should know the truth even if you don't believe it. I adore Rodrigo. I would be his if he had lost, and I would be his if he were utterly disgraced. You may believe I would scramble away from him like a rat from a sinking ship if he fell, but I would not. I have my honor, and I love with honor as much as Oriana or any such lady I might take for an example."

She looked at me and an expression of something like dismay crossed her face. "Oh my dear," she said, "to love so passionately is to invite heartbreak." She had been widowed while still in her thirties. I had never met Ludovico, for he had died before I came to Rome. There had been no one else for Adriana, not that I knew of.

"I know," I said, and squeezed her hand. "But I shall take you for an example of steadfastness." She was alone in the world with no child except Orsino, who wasn't much, and her cousin who gave her his daughter to care for. I looked out at the throngs, at the Castel Sant'Angelo bright in the sunshine, banners streaming from its parapets. "I hope you will always consider me your good daughter."

"Giulia." She squeezed my hand back. "You terrify me."

"I know." Adriana could not help it if she were frightened. She had more scars to pain her than I did.

Ahead, trumpeters blew a fanfare. On the walls of the Castel Sant'Angelo, an enormous banner was being raised, the keys of St. Peter above the Borgia bull. It made my heart lift to see it display against the flawless blue sky. Even Adriana's forebodings could not mar this day.

Chapter Fifteen

The places inside the basilica itself were reserved for prelates and clergy, with the exception of a few ambassadors. However, stands had been erected in the square outside for those whose birth or position recommended them. Donna Adriana de Mila and Donna Giulia Farnese, widow and wife of Orsini, certainly deserved seats, even if ours were better than our marriages would allow. They were in the front on the left, beneath a red and white striped awning to keep off the sun. There was no one ahead of us, so we could see quite well.

There were clerics everywhere. I tried to spot Alessandro but could not. He was somewhere among the clerks. Perhaps he was even inside. Or perhaps he was with the household? I did see Burchard. He was bustling around the basilica doors telling people where to go, his glasses glinting in the bright sun. The ceremony inside had already begun and he was bristling at people entering late for Mass.

People kept coming over to greet me. Captain Rizzoli stood behind me at the end of the row and one of his men was just to his left. I had bodyguards even in the stands. It certainly made my new status clear to me. From now on I must be guarded as the consort of a head of state.

At precisely noon the bells began ringing and the basilica doors were thrown open and the procession came out. First were pages and clerks in white and black respectively, then various bishops and prelates in purple and gold. I caught my breath. They were followed by the cardinals, each one with a dozen squires wearing their family colors. It was a living tapestry, green, gold, red, and every other color. I spotted the blue of the Sforza easily, the boys' tabards displaying the arms of the snake devouring a child, Ascanio Sforza walking behind them in his full red robes.

The bells tolled in joy, as they had tolled in sorrow a month ago when the Pope died. It was like Easter and Pentecost in one, solemn and yet utterly joyful. *The Pope is dead and he is risen. He has gone into the tomb and grace is vested in another.* Rodrigo. The censers came next, gilded thuribles swinging on their chains, a cloud of smoke smelling of precious resins rolling over all. Behind them came the Host borne aloft in its container of gold and glass. And then Rodrigo.

He appeared out of the smoke, his pure white dazzling amid the profusion of colors, floor length white cope heavy with bullion over layers of white brocade. He held a scepter in his white gloved hands, a little smile on his face. It widened as the crowd roared, their voices swelling at the sight of him, a smile of pure pleasure, a bedroom smile, intimate and hungry and feral and lazy with love. Our king, our lord, our sacrifice…. It moved everything in me to my knees. I would have gone to my knees in truth had I not been seated in a chair.

Behind him was a cardinal bearing the papal tiara on a pillow, not a tiara in truth but a crown of three tiers, solid, heavy silver and gold, jewel-embellished. A hush came over the crowd as though a vast hand had stilled it. I could not hear the words, for I was too far away, but I watched him as they lifted the tiara from its purple pillow and placed it on his head. I thought his eyes closed for a moment. Then he lifted his hand, making the cross wide in blessing, and the crowd roared with one voice as though it was their triumph. God had conquered death. The champion had won again. Their favorite had ascended. It was all those things in one. The trumpeters blew a blast. The cheer ran ahead of us, like ripples spreading outward from a stone dropped into water. The sky was flawless blue. The sun beat down. "His Holiness Pope Alexander VI!" the herald shouted.

Ascanio Sforza stepped forward and with his usual grace sank down on the step below him to kiss the toe of his embroidered white slipper. Rodrigo—Alexander—extended a hand and raised him up, Ascanio bending over it to kiss his hand. Rodrigo said something, and I saw Ascanio reply. Whatever it was made Rodrigo laugh, showing teeth for a moment. Ascanio leaned in and kissed him on the mouth. Then he stepped back, making room for the next cardinal.

In turn each of the remaining twenty-one repeated it, two pages helping Cardinal Gherardi kneel and rise. Della Rovere did it in the most perfunctory manner possible. That was trouble, I thought. Well, de Bastian had warned me. Orsini turned his head so that the kiss was on the cheek rather than the mouth as a good brother. I glanced at Adriana and she at me, but of course neither of us said anything. There were people in the row behind us.

I leaned toward Captain Rizzoli. "Excuse me, Captain," I said. "Do you know what comes next?"

He bent over. "The procession will form up. If you'd like to watch the departure, it will be next."

"Yes, thank you. I would," I said. The baby was quiet, presumably sleeping. It was very hot.

"Would you like water?" Captain Rizzoli produced a leather canteen slung against his back.

"Thank you so much," I said with genuine gratitude. It tasted of leather and wasn't cool, but it was indeed wonderful. I was not used to someone seeing to my comfort in quite this way. There was not a breath of breeze and the cloth of silver gown was quite warm.

I couldn't imagine how Rodrigo was managing in so many layers of brocade standing in the sun! They had at least changed the heavy crown for a miter. The procession was forming up to pass before him, and he watched smiling, not impassive but acknowledging those who called out to him with a blessing or a nod. Various ambassadors were first, and I noticed one preceded by a squire carrying a pillow on which rested a jeweled cross on a chain. "A present?" I asked Adriana.

She nodded. "It's customary for worthies to present gifts to the new Pope. From the colors, I'd say that's Milan."

The Duke of Milan was a Sforza, Ascanio's brother. They seemed to have cast their lot firmly with Rodrigo at the moment. "I see," I said. Rodrigo did love beautiful things, and valuables were always a nice thing for the giver to make the recipient feel indebted.

Rizzoli bent down again. "His Holiness will be preceded by thirteen companies of papal men-at-arms, followed by the members of his household and his kindred. That's where Donna Lucrezia will be. Then the bishops and their companies, and then the cardinals and their companies."

"It sounds utterly amazing," I said.

"One of the best parades we've seen," Rizzoli said. "And Rome has seen a few."

I smiled up at him. "Are your children watching? You have six, don't you?"

"Yes, Madonna," he said. "My sister and the three oldest were going to find places near the Lateran, toward the end of the procession. It should be something to see when he takes possession of the Lateran. That's where the last part of the coronation ritual is."

"So I understand," I said.

"Will you want to be there?" he asked. "His Holiness said that you might or might not come to the Lateran depending on how you felt."

"I think so," I said. I was hot but certainly didn't feel bad. On the other hand, it was going to be an hour before the procession entirely left and the Lateran was all the way across town. "We'll see."

"As you wish, Madonna," he said. "The litter is at your disposal."

There was quite a lot of dust. There were companies of foot and horse both, and since there had been no rain in a long time, they created clouds of dust. I could occasionally see Rodrigo through the crowd of the procession forming up. He stood on the steps, so he was elevated somewhat. He watched, the gold embroidery on the miter on his brow reflecting the sun, turning to speak to one of the cardinals for a moment, then to a page behind him. He looked handsome and self-assured, glittering from head to foot. Nobody had brought him water that I had seen.

Very slowly, the companies began to move. They would pass the Castel Sant'Angelo, then cross the bridge and make their way through the city streets to St. John Lateran. There would be a stop or two along the way, stations where various presentations were to be made. The entire business would take hours. After the back of the procession crossed the bridge, we could follow and either make our way home or detour past it on streets which were less busy, as I wished.

Slowly, like a vast, multicolored serpent uncoiling, the procession began to move. I caught a glimpse of Juan at the head of one of the companies of horse, clad in Borgia scarlet with the bull on his shining breastplate. He looked exceedingly happy. Rodrigo had probably put through an appointment for him immediately, a good beginning to a military career. The horses pranced, parade mounts showing off for the crowd, which cheered gratifyingly. Juan was a good horseman. A girl in the crowd threw a flower and he caught it, his horse stepping out of line as he bowed from the saddle and pressed it to his lips. Several young women shrieked. There was some of Rodrigo's charm, I thought. But adulation is a heady thing at sixteen, especially when one has not earned it oneself.

There were three carriages behind, each with shades against the sun. It was easy to see Lucrezia. She was seated to one side of her mother, Gioffre on the other side, and she leaned out beaming. She had an alms basket on her lap and kept throwing coins to the children who tried to run alongside before they were herded back by the guards. Her golden hair gleamed, loose across her shoulders, and her smile was radiant. Someone called out to her and she called back, waving and delighted. She had them in her hand, and how not? She was the princess of this fairy tale.

Adriana shook her head. "Lucrezia," she said.

I glanced at her. "She is behaving perfectly, and it is not as though other popes haven't had children. Franceschetto Cybo, for example! Everyone knew he was Innocent's son and he was at many official functions."

"Yes, but always with deniability," Adriana said. "Of course people knew, but no one had to admit that they knew."

I shook my head. "They love her. They love this."

"The commons who gather on the parade route do," Adriana said. "Not all of the prelates will. And the great families."

"I think the commons matter more," I said, conscious of Rizzoli at my other side. His family was not nothing. For that matter, my life was in his hands, not in those of contemptuous prelates who hated to kiss a Spaniard.

"That is what Rodrigo wagers on," Adriana said. "And I pray that he is right." Rizzoli shifted his feet, though his eyes remained forward and did not waver. Of course he could hear.

Now two squires were leading a white horse to the steps, its rich caparisons glittering. Not Memnon, I thought, Rodrigo's favorite Frisian, because it had to be a white horse for this, but still a perfectly beautiful gelding. One of the squires took the scepter, the other holding the stirrup for Rodrigo to mount, something of a feat in robe and cope and miter. It wasn't precisely graceful, but he did get up without incident, letting the squires spread the cope across the horse's croup so that the embroidery caught the light. Another cheer. You'd think the crowd had never seen a man get on a horse before! Rodrigo waved and smiled, and they cheered again.

He swung into line behind the prelates bearing the Host, two cardinals behind him and four squires flanking, each holding a corner of a white canopy that he rode under. Riario and Piccolomini, I thought. Well, they'd come over to his side early, and Riario's presence sent a message to della Rovere—his own cousin had supported a Borgia and been honored for it.

Of course that was inside intrigue. It was simply splendid. As the procession moved out, I could hear the cheers preceding it even over the joyous bells of St. Peter's. Another company of horse fell in behind, the papal army this time, with the Gonfaloniere following the first squadron. Bracciano wore red beneath his steel breastplate, his helm catching the light. He wore a sword, of course, and the richness of his horse-trappings was evident. He looked like a conquering hero, stern and proud. Behind him came several squires, one of them carrying a gift on a pillow which no doubt would be presented later. My blood suddenly ran cold.

It was a gilded box painted brightly, with figures picked out on it in gold leaf, something vaguely Egyptian about it. It was a lovely casket. And yet something swirled about it, some shimmer like heat over dark stones.

Bracciano turned, his eyes suddenly meeting mine. I saw the intent and he saw me see it. Did he invoke or merely play a role? "A red man out of the desert," I said. "Typhon." He nodded to me, a duelist's nod, the pleasantry of long adversaries greeting each other anew. I saw his mouth move. The name he spoke was not Giulia. And then he laughed, putting his heels to his horse and turning sharply into line, the squires falling in behind him.

A casket. A gift. A gift to pull one's soul within, to case Osiris in fine wood and pour in lead, a beautiful box that could not be refused. And why should it be? Why would Rodrigo see any harm in accepting such a gift? It was a beautiful chest the length of his forearm, not a dagger to the heart.

Except that it was. I sat stunned, watching the procession. A magical trap, not poison. And not demons, which could not abide holy ground, but an older magic, the magic of pure story. If Rodrigo raised one story, Bracciano would raise another, Typhon who murdered Osiris and scattered his body like offal and claimed control of the kingdom. What had he promised Typhon for this power? I had seen, two years ago, how he pledged his men to a demon's service for the information he wanted, never risking himself in the process. This time he had. What had he pledged in exchange for Rodrigo's life? I sat in the hot sun as the horsemen paraded past, frozen in place.

"Well," Adriana said, "shall we take the litter home, Giulia? It is very hot and some shade and refreshment would be nice." Around us, people were stirring and getting to their feet. The end of the procession was winding away. Either they would follow to the Lateran or go home. And where would the gifts be given? At the Lateran? That made the most sense.

"No," I said, standing up. "You go on, Adriana. Take the litter home."

She frowned. "There is only one litter. If you plan to follow the procession in it...."

"I'm not going to follow the procession in it. It's too slow." Stuck behind the horses in a litter, I'd be too late. Whatever was going to happen would have long since happened. People were clearing the stands around us. Captain Rizzoli was standing there looking confused.

"Giulia, I think you should rest. The heat is too much for you," Adriana said.

I leaned closer. "Adriana, in the name of God for once don't argue with me! I don't have time for this!" I took off my expensive pearl and gold cross necklace, handed it to her, and turned around.

"Now unfasten this dress."

She untied the laces. "Giulia, what in the world?"

"The cloth of silver dress is too conspicuous, and the necklace is too expensive." I pulled the beautiful thing over my head, leaving me in the pale blue gown beneath it. It was much lighter. "I have to go after Rodrigo. He's in mortal danger."

That caught Rizzoli's full attention. Perhaps he'd assumed I was simply too hot in the brocade. "Excuse me, Madonna?"

"Adriana, go home and wait for Lucrezia. I'm going after the procession on foot." I turned to Rizzoli. "We can go faster than the parade if we don't have the litter and we go around by back streets. They've got to stop at various stations and they'll be moving at a snail's pace. We need to get to the Lateran first."

"I don't know what…" Adriana began.

"I don't have time to explain." I piled the dress in her arms. "Bracciano. It's too complicated." Summer. Heat. Light without shadow. There were the ghosts of other cities here, other stories. We had played on this chessboard before, Typhon and I. There was a part of me that understood completely. I closed my eyes for a moment. *Dea Peregrina*, I said silently, *will you help me? And what will the price be?*

Your Rodrigo raised me up from the rubble. You have been my face, now and long ago. I will help, if you will allow me.

I took a deep breath. *Allow you to do what?*

To step into you when the time comes, she whispered.

As you did the other night. I understood, or thought I did.

Yes.

It was a Mystery, as Rodrigo said, a golden thread of truth that ran through all. I wasn't entirely certain what had happened, but it had been good. There was nothing in it that harmed anyone, and it had been beautiful beyond belief. And yet I could not think my way through this, tease it apart with learning and wit. I had to follow the compass of my heart. *I will*, I said.

I looked at Rizzoli. "Will you come with me? Just you. Too many men won't help and will slow us down."

"Of course, Madonna," he said. "And there are stout men there if we need them."

"I have no doubt they are worthy," I said, "But arms will not avail us now." I kissed Adriana's cheek. "I'll see you soon." I left her staring after me, for once wordless.

Captain Rizzoli fell in beside me. "What is going on?"

I looked at him sideways. "It's a very long story, Captain. And some of it you will not like."

"I don't like anything that involves murdering those I'm charged to guard," he said. "And why aren't more men useful?"

I stopped, looking at him. "The attack the other night, when His Holiness was at Donna Adriana's house—how do you think we escaped the assassins sent across the roof since they came after the house was asleep? And the week before, how do you think Cesare and I interrupted Silvia's murder?"

Rizzoli frowned. "I've been trying to work that out. Luck?"

"I dreamed a warning," I said flatly, "and it woke me in time." I had no idea how he would take that.

He nodded. "It makes sense that God would guard His Holiness thus, since it is His will that he be Pope." His eyes met mine gravely. "And you have had another such warning?"

"I had dreamed of a casket," I said, and I did not lie much. "I did not know what it meant until I saw it moments ago. It is the one that the Gonfaloniere means to give His Holiness at the Lateran. I do not know what means of harm it conceals, but twice these dreams have guarded his life. I cannot disregard this one."

"Poison, perhaps," Rizzoli mused. "A spring with poison on it that pricks when it is opened. Topical poison on the interior surfaces. Something like that. It would be safe to carry but not open."

"And I cannot prevent His Holiness from opening it if he

receives it without warning," I said. "So I must intercept him before he opens it."

"Of course," he said. "And you do not trust anyone else to take the message." Clearly he could dash across town without me.

"I do not think His Holiness will heed the warning unless it comes from me," I said. That was inarguable. "Or perhaps I can stop him from receiving the gift. I do not know how, but perhaps I can."

"Then we must get there as quickly as possible," Rizzoli said. He looked at me skeptically. A long run in the heat was far from ideal.

"The litter is too slow," I said.

"We have horses," he said. "There are several for the guard held close at hand in case they're needed. Can you ride?" He looked at my belly.

"I wouldn't choose this moment for a wild hunt across the countryside," I said. "But I can certainly ride through city streets at a decorous pace. It will be less taxing than trying to run all that way."

I waited while Rizzoli brought two horses around. I could hear the shouts of the crowd clearly, though the plaza in front of St. Peter's was clearing out. I thought perhaps the procession was stopped at the Castel Sant'Angelo for some activity there. I jumped at the report as the guns overlooking the river fired. *A salute*, I thought, *obviously they are firing a salute*. I took a deep breath. There were two cannons on the ramparts. Of course this was part of the celebration. And why was that a surprise? Some part of me was unfamiliar with cannon fire.

Is that so strange? You already carry someone else inside. It was like a whisper, like a dialogue with one's self, the hunch that says to take another route or the voice of memory. And yet not quite. It was no stranger than carrying the baby, knowing when it slept or when it bounced in joy. To share my body, to make myself a habitation, was nothing more than I already did. *It is nothing more than many women do*, she whispered.

I folded my hands across my belly, waiting for Rizzoli. *And that is what they fear*, I thought. *We did it first.* I thought she laughed. Something disturbed me, however. *Is Typhon real?*

There are always those who enjoy destruction, she replied sadly. *There are always people who, through fear or pain or selfishness, want to end everything they do not understand. Typhon always finds ready instruments. To destroy books so no one can read them, smash statues so no one may be inspired by them—those things are Typhon. Your Rodrigo has lifted me up. And so I will save him.*

What did Bracciano have to promise him? I wondered.

I do not know, she said. *But it must have been something of consequence.*

Rizzoli led up two horses, sturdy, solid geldings with the Borgia bull on their saddlecloths. "Here we are," he said. He cupped his hands for me to mount. It took me three tries. The gelding was much taller than my own palfrey, and my belly was in the way. He stood still while I got up, though. A well-trained boy, and hopefully gentle of gait.

Rizzoli looked concerned. "All right?"

"Yes, Captain," I said.

I had fretted that it had taken too long to follow the procession. I need not have. By the time we reached the Castel Sant'Angelo, the back of the procession was only on the bridge. At this speed it would take them two hours to cross town. We could follow at quite a decorous walk, detour around on other streets, and pass the procession easily. I said as much and Rizzoli nodded. "We'll go around to the north," he said. "That should avoid the worst crowds."

It did, though it was very hot. It was possible to tell where the procession was not only by the shouts of spectators, but by the clouds of dust. We stopped more than once to water the horses and ourselves at public fountains.

The Lateran itself was at the old city wall built long ago, its gate leading out into the countryside, and had originally been a Roman palace, so the story went. However, the old building had burned in the last century and been rebuilt. Hence it was new and well-appointed, one of the finest churches in Rome and the particular benefice of Rodrigo's rival, Cardinal della Rovere. Members of the household were already there preparing, and Rizzoli handed off our horses to a groom.

The procession wasn't far behind. Cheers heralded the front of it, bright colors somewhat dimmed by dust. The cavalry companies made a fine show. "I am looking for Bracciano," I said, craning my neck. And there he was, of course, looking stern and respectable on his fine horse. I did not see the chest. Where was it? Who had it?

The procession backed up at the Lateran, the crowd having to shift to make way for the various entourages, and I lost sight of him in the press. And there was Rodrigo. He was waving to the cheering people, not sitting impassively with due papal dignity. Instead, he smiled. Each time he lifted his hand in blessing, there was another cheer.

"What is—" I lost sight of him as the crowd was moved back to make room again, and I tried to work my way over to the right, where I hoped I would be able to see the portico. Unfortunately, far too many people had the same idea. And what was I going to do? Stop Bracciano from giving it to him? No, I somehow had to warn Rodrigo not to take it.

I pushed my way to the front. Too late. Bracciano was straightening from a deep bow before Rodrigo, a squire holding the painted and carved box on a pillow. Rodrigo smiled, nodding assent. No doubt he said a word of thanks. He did not touch it, but that was all it took to accept the gift.

I saw him sway, suddenly unsteady on his feet. Cardinal Riario caught him as he collapsed, the proceedings lapsing suddenly into chaos. It was slipping away from me. Everything was slipping.

And yet the stones beneath my feet knew the story. *A gilded box borne on the breast of the sea, a tamarind tree, pots of sprouted grain, the walls of a city white in the morning sun, a cave with the stone rolled away…*

I reached down, drawing from it, the world shifting before me. The Lateran and crowd faded like a dream, like something a thousand years ago or a thousand years yet to come, a shadow background. The city itself was a chessboard beneath my feet, bounded only by far horizons, myself the white queen on the board, the black rook holding the white king in check. Around us, the other pieces were frozen in an eternal moment.

He looked around, Bracciano and not. The red man from the desert waited behind his eyes. "Typhon," I said.

"You again." He didn't look surprised.

"Me. Again," I said. We faced each other on the board, a clear diagonal open before me. I walked it, my skirts whispering around my legs, a diagonal on black that put me between rook and king, my back against the white king's chest. "You may take the queen," I said. "And the king will take the rook on the next move. Too high a price, my lord Bracciano. Typhon will play you as you play your men. After all, are you any more than a gaming piece to him?" I was myself and not myself, Isis who countered Typhon, and Giulia who knew Bracciano's weakness.

And yet he had a line of retreat. If the rook withdrew to the side, no piece menaced it. I saw him decide. Was it worth it to lose his life to only take the queen rather than the king? Typhon might play with lives, but Bracciano valued his own above all, as Rodrigo had observed. I did not gamble with my life, not really. I knew him. I knew what his choice would be. I placed myself before Rodrigo knowing the outcome.

I saw him waver. I saw the moment Bracciano decided. He bowed, his hand to his breast. "You may claim Rome, but you cannot stop the fires. Destruction comes whether you wish it or not. You will be forgotten and wind will blow through your empty halls."

"We will see what I can do," I said. Or she said. We said.

He stepped back, retreating to the side on the horizontal, out of harm's way to a position that menaced nothing. The chess board faded. I stood in the square before the Lateran, Captain Rizzoli at my elbow in the press. If I swayed on my feet, surely it was the heat.

Riario was supporting Rodrigo, kneeling behind him and holding him in his arms. I saw a page bringing a vessel of water, and then they were clustering round and he was lost behind people. "Captain," I said.

"Madonna." Rizzoli's face was set and he started shoving a path for me to the front, some giving way when they saw the bright Borgia livery. It was slow going. The crowd was tightly packed. Some were pushing forward and others back. Rodrigo…. The vision paled next to the reality of seeing him fall. My heart pounded. Surely I had turned the evil. Surely.

The guards at the front to contain the crowd let Rizzoli through when they saw his colors. "…and this is Donna Giulia Farnese," he said, and pulled me behind him through the cordon.

I saw the white miter amid the red-robed cardinals. Rodrigo was on his feet leaning on a page, Riario splashing his face with water from the pitcher.

"…in the portico out of the sun," Cardinal Piccolomini said loudly. "We're all about to pass out."

And there was Alessandro amid the crowd of aides. He looked up and saw me. He began to make his way against the stream toward us. Rodrigo was being escorted into the Lateran, waving away someone's suggestion that he lie down. He looked somewhat damp. Riario must have practically thrown the pitcher of water in his face.

"Was that it?" Rizzoli said quietly.

"Yes," I said. A sense of unreality hung around me still. I looked around for Bracciano and found him entering the Lateran with the crowd of worthies. He was frowning. *Typhon has ceded the field*, she whispered. *Well done, daughter.* There was a kind of pride in her voice.

I took a deep breath. Alessandro worked his way around two cardinals to us. "Giulia, I didn't expect you. And you've changed clothes." Clearly he'd seen me in the cloth of silver earlier.

"It was too hot," I said. "And I was afraid of ruining it in the streets. What happened to Rodrigo?"

"He fainted," Alessandro said. "I'd faint too if I'd been standing in the sun for hours in all those layers. But it's cool in the Lateran. Do you want to come in?"

"Yes, please." I wanted to see Rodrigo myself, even if it was only from a distance amid the crowd.

We slipped in at the back of the portico, me and Alessandro and Rizzoli, standing against the wall beneath the arches. A choir was singing. Rodrigo was being escorted to a strange, low stone chair. The choir stopped as he reached it. He turned, then sat. It was oddly shaped, with a keyhole in the bottom and a back that inclined, low to the ground. A silence fell. He closed his eyes, almost lying in the chair. For a long moment we all waited thus. It seemed that the world held its breath.

And then Rodrigo got up. Smoke flowed from censers. One of the prelates intoned, "He raises him from the dust, and lifts the poor from the dunghill, that he may sit with princes and hold the throne of glory."

I blinked, seeing for a moment a gilded coffin as I reached down to take his hand where it lay on his breast, his eyes opening in wonder while above us the high ceiling echoed with tambours and choir. I raised him to stand beside me, the firelight washing over us from great cressets filled with fragrant oil. I knew that place as I knew my own name, as Rodrigo knew the halls of the Vatican. My heart filled with love at the sight of it.

The Serapeum is dust, she whispered. *But we are not.*

Rodrigo was standing now. The music rose in glorious harmony. Solemnly, a prelate presented him with the keys to the Lateran, Rodrigo's face grave. "His Holiness, Pope Alexander VI," he proclaimed.

"It's amazing, isn't it?" Alessandro whispered.

"And so beautiful," I said, leaning back against my brother as the voices of the choir soared to the ceiling.

Chapter Sixteen

I was exhausted by the time I got home and wanted nothing more than a light meal and then to go to bed. Maria fussed over me, saying that I had overdone it in the heat and I should have returned earlier with Adriana. "I had to see him crowned at the Lateran," I said, and she *tsked* at me.

"You see him all the time. No need to do yourself harm."

"You are perfectly right," I said, and let her tuck me in for a nap.

I woke to the bells ringing Compline. The stars were bright in the sky above the city. I went out on the balcony through the newly repaired doors and leaned against the rail. There were lights in the streets, not the roving torches of mobs but the lights of open tavernas, people strolling in the evening, celebrating, eating, drinking. Later there would be fireworks over the river, but I would watch from here. There wasn't a better spot, and it would be lovely to relax. I hoped that amid all the bustle Rodrigo would think of me, knowing how I loved fireworks, knowing I was watching. He would be on the battlements of the Castel Sant'Angelo with the dignitaries, watching the stars break over his beloved Rome.

There was a knock on my camera door. "Come in," I said.

Dionisio slouched out onto the balcony to join me. "It's a beautiful evening," he said. He looked a bit sunburned.

"It is indeed," I said. "How was the parade?"

"Wonderful," he said. "The Sarfati girls enjoyed it."

"I'm glad," I said. "I would be happy for them to join me out here for the fireworks if they'd like. You can too. And whoever else wants to." I sat down in one of the chairs at my little table. "We'll have a perfect view from here. Have you eaten?" Dionisio shook his head. "Then join me for dinner. We'll eat out here and enjoy the evening air." There were some things I wanted to talk with him about without the entire Sarfati family.

I asked Maria to send up our dinners when they were ready, and I settled in the chair enjoying the cooler evening air while Dionisio leaned on the rail. He looked at me keenly. "I'm guessing you wanted my advice on something."

"Your knowledge," I said. It was hard to put into words, hard to put a frame on these experiences, but learning was always the best resource. "Tell me about the Serapeum."

He shrugged. "I don't know a great deal about it. It was a temple here in Rome. The ruins were dug up ten years ago or so. I believe that's where His Eminence—I mean His Holiness—got the magnificent statue of Isis and Horus."

"Not that one," I said slowly, though of course it bore on the matter. "The main one. The basilica, as it were. The Mother Church. These temples must have been like that, like parish churches to the great temple that Plutarch speaks of."

"In the manuscript Mois Sarfati has," Dionisio said. "The temple that Ptolemy had the statue conveyed to." He leaned back thoughtfully. "It was in Alexandria in Egypt, of course. A number of writers describe the Serapeum as the most wonderful temple of Isis and Serapis anywhere, a magnificent place in a city full of wonders."

"Destroyed, of course." I felt it like an ache in my breast. "By an overzealous mob, as Rodrigo would say."

"In the fourth century? The fifth century? Something like that. But it stood for six hundred years or more. I'm not really a historian."

"What do we know of the rites there?" I asked.

"Not much." Dionisio shrugged. "We never do. And yes, I feel it too. The shame of the loss."

I glanced away, out over the city filled with lights. Would St. Peter's someday be no more than a memory where the rites were lost to time? *The Serapeum is dust*, she had said, *but we are not*. The soul is eternal.

I felt it like quiet music, looking out over Rome. It was peaceful, simply a knowing. I had stood in that temple in ages past, loved it and served the divine there, from acolyte in a choir of girls to high priestess in a cloak like golden wings. I had raised my lover from a gilded coffin to stand at my side, living Serapis as I was Isis, his hand in mine. There had been kings and princes, wars and dangers, and a vast library full of books, paintings and sculptures and dreams of measuring the stars. How did I dare this Rome? I had dared as much before. To remake the world, to conserve, to find again what was lost, to push even further than we had gone before—was that not the dream? Was that not Rodrigo's dream since he was a boy in Valencia? He followed the compass of his heart.

And I was what I was, and being so must learn to be it better, just as he did. Surely there was a way to reconcile all the parts of myself. I would stand behind him, my wings spread as his shelter, and we would reweave the world. All this went through my mind in a few moments sitting in the soft evening of the Eternal City.

"The Serapeum must have been very beautiful," Dionisio said.

"It was," I said. He looked at me quizzically. There was a sudden streak against the sky, then a burst of red light. The fireworks were beginning. "Oh, look!" I said.

The Sarfati girls and the little maids and Maria all came to the door and I motioned them out, Dionisio stepping back to let the short ones in ahead of him as the next one went up, golden flowers reflecting in the river.

I put my hand on the littlest maid's shoulder. "Remember this," I said, to myself as well as her, and she laughed, cheering as the fireworks lit the perfect summer night.

The next night was the coronation masque. There had been other masques at the Vatican before, but not in the last two years because Innocent had been too ill. I understood that in Sixtus' day there had been revels to rival the court of France, but that had been before I came to Rome, so I had never seen them. A masque to celebrate the coronation was a welcome return to court social life for many.

In my silver dress and silver mask, I felt that I had appropriate splendor, indeed! I arrived in a litter with Lucrezia, Adriana in another litter behind, the cortège escorted by ten guardsmen in Borgia red with steel breastplates. Lucrezia was all but bouncing to make the litter go faster. "Calmly," I said. "Or you'll tip us over." This was her first masque and she was terribly excited.

We descended from the litter onto broad stairs and joined the brilliant crowd making our way inside. The herald announced us according to our proper precedence. "Donna Adriana de Mila. Donna Giulia Farnese." He paused. We were theoretically Orsini widow and wife, decent noblewomen who could expect such invitations, but the technically lowest ranking woman in our group was now a de-facto princess courted by the lords of Italy. "Donna Lucrezia Borgia."

All eyes turned to her. Beautiful, fresh, golden-haired in a glittering dress, a crown of gilt stars in her hair, not yet thirteen, she looked exactly as one expects the princess to on the first page, before any of the travails of the story have begun. She entered blushing, holding out her dress to walk and smiling back to those around her, Adriana and I trailing her like the second and third ladies in the theater company whose job is to fill out behind the naïve heroine. The Era of Lucrezia had dawned. It certainly gave people something to stare at besides my belly.

The sala was decorated lavishly. On the far wall was what was clearly a new hanging, a banner of the Borgia bull surmounted by the Keys of St. Peter and the papal tiara. Rodrigo was definitely making a point.

We clustered on what would be the dance floor, acquaintances coming up to greet us like dear friends. "What a lovely dress!" was said more than once, meaning "Good Lord in Heaven he's spent some money on you!" I smiled and thanked everyone, complimenting their jewels and hair in turn.

Lucrezia tugged at my arm. "There is Cesare!" she said. It certainly was. He wore scarlet hose and a matching doublet so short that it left nothing to the imagination. Certainly everything was emphasized by the tightness of the hose and the scarlet codpiece. He wore his crossed belts with sword and dagger and a bronze mask with a stern expression. "Mars," I said.

"But who is the lady?" Lucrezia asked.

A lady in green hung on his arm, golden ribbons on her sleeves and a necklace of heavy gold links around her neck, each one wrought like a flower. A little gold mask covered her eyes, and her red hair was piled high in elaborate braids ornamented with a gold net. "Fiammetta de Michelis," I said, dropping my voice. "And you're not supposed to know her because she's a courtesan."

"A court-i-san," said Lucrezia prissily, tossing her head. "Like my mother. Heaven forbid!"

A thought struck me. "Did your mother feel bad about not coming tonight?" I certainly would have.

Lucrezia laughed. "No! She said things like this were one of the reasons she and Papa ended. She said I might want to go now, but I'd learn better once I'd spent some time with horrible people being boring."

"There is some of that," I agreed. "But remember the game

boards we talked about? This is where our game is played." Whatever homily I meant to deliver on politics, she was having none of it.

"I'm going to have Cesare introduce me," she said, and charged off between people like a terrier at a fair. Adriana went after her, leaving me penned in by the crowd. I turned, excusing myself to get out of the press. I looked up into an expanse of red velvet. The Gonfaloniere looked down at me.

"My Lord Bracciano," I said, inclining my head like a duelist.

"Donna Giulia." He did the same. "I had hoped that I might see you this evening."

My voice was cool, though I was in fact conscious of how far it was to Cesare or others who might be helpful. "I am always delighted to see you, my lord."

"It seems we have reached an impasse," he said. His face was stern.

"You mean you have run out of avenues," I said. "The casket was clever. But fortunately my master is well-guarded."

He raised an eyebrow. "Perhaps you and I might come to an arrangement."

"I am Alexander's," I said, "and not for sale."

The other eyebrow rose. "I meant on his behalf, of course."

"Of course," I said. I glanced around. Rodrigo had not yet come in.

"He has made donations to many from the kindness of his heart," Bracciano said. "Including to my dear cousin, Cardinal Orsini."

"He is generous," I said. I had arranged that bit of bribery, two properties the Orsini wanted. No doubt Bracciano was furious that his cousin had gotten them by making a deal behind his back. What price did Bracciano himself want to set?

He looked thoughtful. "Franceschetto Cybo, the late pope's son, has many debts."

I had heard as much from Fiammetta, that he owed Cardinal Riario a small fortune. "What a terrible problem for him."

"His father had given him governorship of several estates," Bracciano said. "Cerveteri, Anguillara, Canale Monterano and Rota. I have offered to buy those lands from him, thus resolving his problem and mine."

"Except for the problem that those properties are not his to sell," I murmured. "They're Church lands that he held as a vassal to the Pope, not free and clear as his own estates." I could not picture where all of them were, but I knew Canale Monterano at least. It was strategic to control of Campagna. Rodrigo would not want it in Orsini hands. But it was not in Church hands at the moment either, no matter whom it legally belonged to.

"It seems to me they are," Bracciano said. "And I have made a fair offer on them. A hundred thousand florins."

I blinked. That would clear all Cybo's debts and give him money to be going on with. It was also a huge sum for Bracciano, who didn't have as deep pockets as Rodrigo. Though, to be fair, a hundred thousand was an extremely substantial sum to him too. Someone must be putting up the money. King Ferrante of Naples? He would love to have control of holdings in the Papal States. And Bracciano's son was married to a Medici; her family might do it. But all of that was nothing if the Church contested the sale.

"So you would like the sale to go through," I said.

Bracciano smiled. "You understand me, Donna Giulia."

His price was four properties. Well, it was a reasonable offer. I considered how to phrase it. "So if I do this, and your real estate difficulties are solved, we will all be friends? No more unfortunate incidents?" As though Silvia's death was no more than an unfortunate incident! My blood boiled. I would have him for that, the callous death of a pawn he didn't even notice. But not today. Today I needed to protect Rodrigo. I could feel the strands of the future in my hands. I could push that death in the vision away—

not remove it, but postpone it. I could defer the dream of Babylon.

"No more unfortunate incidents," he said with a little bow. "They waste your time and mine." He glanced over my shoulder. Ascanio Sforza was making his way toward us. He and Bracciano hated each other.

"I will convey your dilemma to His Holiness," I said. "I feel certain that he will want to resolve this matter to the good of all."

"Excellent," he said.

Ascanio Sforza was at my elbow. "My Lord Bracciano, Donna Giulia, a pleasant evening, is it not?"

"Very much so," Bracciano said, his eyes on me rather than Sforza. "Donna Giulia, we have an understanding."

"Indeed we do, my lord," I said. He nodded briskly and disappeared into the crowd. I turned to Ascanio. "Are you my rescuer, Cardinal Sforza?"

He sketched a little bow. "It would be my honor. And it's Vice-Chancellor Sforza."

I smiled. "I have yet to congratulate you on your new position. My many felicitations, Your Eminence." He wore dark blue with gold and silver spangles and a pearl and gold brooch on his velvet hat. "And who are you this evening?"

"I am Jupiter," he said, his face clean-shaven behind his golden mask. "Planetary Lord of Riches."

"I see that you are," I said. He had certainly cleaned up in bribes, not to mention Rodrigo's house. I did wonder something. "What did you say yesterday on the steps of St. Peter's when you kissed him that made him laugh?"

Ascanio smirked. "I said, 'Of course, darling.'"

I laughed. "You are a very bad man, Your Eminence."

"So I have been told," he said. He looked at me keenly. "I don't have to tell you not to trust the Gonfaloniere."

"No," I said. "We are well acquainted." Rodrigo was trying to balance the Orsini and the Sforza. The Sforza had just gotten the

Vice-Chancellorship, which was certainly a reason for Bracciano to make peace. "He offered a truce."

"Interesting," Ascanio said. I could almost see his mind working. Perhaps he was considering which Sforza relation would make a good Gonfaloniere. He glanced at me. "Peace is God's will, is it not?"

"It is certainly Alexander's," I said. "It is to be his motto: *Pacis Cultor*, Maker of Peace."

There was a flourish of trumpets. The crowd parted. I stepped back, now in the front row beside Ascanio. "His Holiness Pope Alexander VI!"

Rodrigo swept in, blindingly sumptuous in a wide-sleeved cloth of gold coat over white and gold brocade, a gold mask of the sun bright with real gold leaf. I sunk into a curtsy, as everyone did. Rodrigo stopped unerringly in a glitter of light like the lead in a play, spreading his hands expansively. "My dear friends," he said. "My very dear friends, I am delighted that you have joined me this evening!"

As though anyone were likely to refuse the invitation! They might hate him, but a papal coronation masque was not to be missed. Across the aisle made by the crowd parting, I saw Lucrezia with Cesare and Fiammetta. Adriana had clearly not succeeded in preventing scandalous acquaintance.

Rodrigo was hitting all the standard notes, so honored, so pleased to share this celebration with such wonderful people. "I hope that you will enjoy this evening and remember it with delight," he ended. Rodrigo nodded to the musicians. "A *basse danse*, if you please."

Everyone looked about for partners, except those who had someone beside them. I saw Fiammetta speaking to Lucrezia, stepping back as Lucrezia beamed, clearly saying that Cesare should partner his sister on her first dance at her first masque. It was both clever and kind, I thought, to make a friend of her. Cesare bowed like a courtier, taking Lucrezia's hand to lead her onto the floor.

I had been watching them and not Rodrigo. He had stopped in front of me, a little smirk on his face, and held out a hand. Realization hit me. The cloth of silver gown, the moon mask.... He'd planned this, sun and moon, King and Queen of the Heavens. There was a sort of indrawn breath around the room. To single me out thus, the pregnant wife of an Orsini, pregnant with his child, the rumor ran, before all the great families, before all the ambassadors—it was not done. This was not one of Fiammetta's scandalous revels or a party with friends at the Vice-Chancellor's house. This was the most official of official parties, full of wives and daughters and mothers and sisters of the noblest blood, with all the ambassadors of the crowned heads of the continent. I had said I wouldn't be hidden. I did not expect this.

Rodrigo's smile grew. "Donna Giulia, will you do me the honor?"

"Of course, Your Holiness," I said, and put my hand in his. He led me onto the floor, the first couple in the forming set, and the music began. I sunk into the *reverence* as he bowed, and then took his hand again as we began the *pas simple*.

The music was loud, and the conversations around the room began again. I'm sure we were the subject of many of them. I looked at him, trying to keep my face neutral, but his eyes were laughing. He loved to surprise, and if he shocked as well, so be it. He'd won. We'd won. We deserved this triumph.

We walked through the stately measures, the most formal and graceful of dances, ideal for a woman in the seventh month of pregnancy. A barge could have done it, and I was definitely a barge. And yet. Oh, and yet!

When the music ended and he raised me from the *reverence* again, he did not let go of my hand. He held it elevated on his own and turned me so that we precessed together. Beneath the new hanging of the keys and bull were two chairs side by side on a little dais. My heart skipped. We turned, me at his right, and Rodrigo gestured grandly to the musicians. "Play!" he said. "Enjoy yourselves!" He handed me into my chair and sat down beside me.

The music began. Voices rose. The next set turned and danced, wayward stars in our firmament. "I will never forget this night," I said quietly.

"Nor will anyone else," said His Holiness the Pope with an impish grin.

The masque ended very late. Lucrezia and Adriana departed with several guards as well as Fiammetta and Cesare. Presumably Cesare would see Lucrezia home and then continue to Fiammetta's house. I remained.

This time it was easier to simply go into his rooms and shut the pages out, to latch the door to the camera and help one another out of our lavish costumes. There was a freshening breeze through the tiny window, the candle flame shaking. It felt good after so many days of heat.

"I think it's going to rain," I said as he undid the laces in the back.

"I'm glad it held off until after the ceremonies," he said. "But we need it now." I turned around and started on all his fastenings.

We put out the candle but left the window open, getting into bed with just the sheet. He lay on his back and I came to his side, my head on his left shoulder, his arm around me, familiar and comfortable, whatever current of strangeness rippled beneath the surface. He sighed.

"Are you all right?" I asked quietly. "When you fainted at the Lateran…."

"It was the heat," he said.

"Not entirely." He didn't answer. "But I have taken care of Bracciano's business."

"Bracciano." There was a wealth of annoyance in that. I didn't think he was taking it quite seriously enough.

"He meant to kill you," I said, lifting my head to see his face. "He found a different magic, one that would work on holy ground." I wondered how much to say, how much he wanted to hear. "I countered it." He said nothing. It was too dark to read his expression. "I have kept my word," I said. "There were no demons and I will not ever deal with them. I see things, and I mean to go on seeing them. I will not tell you things you do not want to know."

His hand tightened on my back. "I'm the Pope."

And could hardly have heresy shoved in his face. "Yes, I'd noticed."

Rodrigo took a deep breath, and I put my head back on his shoulder. For two years this had been safety and warmth. "Well," he said at last, "I suppose if God wanted me to be Pope, thwarting plans to kill me is God's will."

He had found a loophole, as he usually did. "God is generally opposed to murder," I said. "So it seems to me that stopping the murder of a priest counts as a good work." I warmed to the topic. "And thus all other spirits or people involved are God's instruments."

"True, stopping a murder can only be good."

It was time to press it home, to find a moral space we could both occupy. "I will not lie to you," I said, "and I will not tell you things unless you ask, unless it is a matter of life and death." Surely he of all people could understand! This mystery was mine. "I am a Dove. It is what I am. To listen, to hear, to be a voice...."

"The Borgia Dove," he said.

"Your Dove," I said as he brushed his lips against my hair.

We lay thus for a long moment, my hand open on his chest, his arm around me. Rodrigo sighed. "Ah, sweet," he said. "If I were a better man, this would be a purely spiritual love."

I lifted my face. "What, like Abelard and Heloise?"

"Perish the thought!" He burst out laughing. "I'm very attached to all of my parts."

He'd had a moment. It was a brief moment.

"I'm very attached to your parts as well," I said, sliding my hand down his belly. He laughed, as I meant him to, catching my hand and bringing it to his lips. For a moment, as he kissed my fingertips, there was that current of strangeness, like water moving against my legs beneath the surface. I wished I could see his expression. "Are you different?" I asked.

"You tell me."

"Yes," I said. "And no." I didn't really have the words for what I felt.

"Well." He folded my hand against his chest.

And yet there were words that were real and true. "I have always seen God in your face." I did not ask what he saw in mine. He had already told me when we spoke beside his statue.

"My Giulia," he said, and I closed my eyes against him. Outside, the rain began.

Epilogue

November 30, 1492

I dozed, propped up on pillows, thick pads beneath me to catch the blood, with her in my arms. She dozed too. I kissed her tiny nose a thousand times, so flat, so soft. Her fingers were perfect, her skin almost translucent. I kissed each finger a thousand times too. How had I made something so wonderful? We dozed together while Maria helped the midwife clean up.

The door opened. Lucrezia was back, looking tired but a little triumphant. She'd stayed with me almost the entire time. "Can Papa come in now?" she asked.

Rodrigo pushed past her without waiting. He wore black velvet, not anything he was supposed to be wearing, and a broad smile, which he wasn't supposed to be wearing either. He bounded across the room. "My sweet darling."

"Rodrigo." I couldn't help beaming back. "Have you been here long?"

"Lucrezia sent word to me when you were brought to bed," he said. "I came straight away. Are you all right, my angel?"

"Every last muscle in my body hurts," I said, "but she tells me I am the model of health, and that for a first birth it was remarkably quick and easy." I grimaced, glancing at the midwife, who seemed entirely unawed by the pope. If that was easy, I should hate to have hard, but one should simply be grateful for good fortune when it came.

"My sweetest," he said, then a run of other endearments, as he slid his arm around me carefully. "Let's see our girl. Oh what a beautiful little face! You look just like your lovely mother, my Laura." I smiled, putting my face against the side of his. "Oh your little eyebrows! Oh your little nose!" He took her with practiced hands, supporting her neck as he cradled her to his breast, her head in the crook of his elbow. "You are my perfection. You are."

I laughed. "She is."

"And you are my perfection too," Rodrigo said, putting his other arm back around me.

I leaned on him. "I'm glad you're here. Though you shouldn't be."

"That was the point of buying this house. So that I can see you and my girls."

"True," I said.

"And I must see you often," Rodrigo said. He kissed Laura's nose again. "A perfect nose." He glanced up at Lucrezia. "Just like Lucrezia's nose."

"We are sisters," Lucrezia said. "Of course we look alike. Though her hair is dark like Cesare's." She looked at Laura critically. "I think she will be very pretty."

"I am fond of her nose too." I rested my head on his shoulder. "The Pope's daughter." She was not supposed to exist, and yet how could God Himself not adore her as her father did?

"Our daughter," he said, and kissed my brow.

*S*hortly *after his coronation, Pope Alexander VI welcomed Jewish refugees from Spain into the Papal States.*

He also acquitted Pico della Mirandola of charges of heresy.

Coming soon:
the third book of the Memoirs of the Borgia Sibyl

THE BLOOD OF THE BULL

Jo Graham

Queen of the Underworld

Rome 1494: Giulia Farnese has risen to heights of power and influence as mistress to Pope Alexander VI, her beloved Rodrigo, but storms loom on the horizon. A French army is marching toward the Kingdom of Naples, and all that stands in their way are the fragile Papal States. If Rodrigo won't surrender to the French, he has enemies who are eager to see him deposed—even if that means the French sack the city of Rome and kill thousands.

Yet an even darker threat is growing. In Florence Friar Savonarola's movement is burning books and priceless works of art, determined to purify society and destroy the Renaissance itself. Giulia's own abilities as a seer make her a target for Savonarola's purifying zeal. The repentant concubine of a Borgia Pope would be the perfect tool to bring Pope Alexander VI to his knees.

In a web of deceit, assassination and betrayal, Giulia must face her most dangerous enemies without Rodrigo by her side. To prevail, she will need all her wits and courage to descend into the darkness of the underworld—and return if she can.

Acknowledgments

I would like to thank so many people for their support of this book, including my long-time readers who have encouraged me at every step. I would particularly like to thank my pre-readers Joss Davis, Victoria Francis, Jennifer Roberson, Lena Strid, and J.J. Taylor for their feedback as I worked. I am doubly grateful for Melissa Scott's insights and suggestions as the work unfolded.

I am also indebted to Samantha Morris, who has kindly shared her original research on the Borgias with me and steered me to various sources. Her work on Cesare Borgia was particularly helpful. I am also appreciative of Dr. Katharine Fellows, who shared with me her doctoral thesis on Rodrigo Borgia in his years as vice-chancellor, and her work on the Papal Election of 1492. All mistakes are of course my own. I would also like to thank my editor, Athena Andreadis, who has strengthened this book so much with her considered thoughts.

Most of all, I would like to thank my wonderful partner, Amy Griswold, who inspires everything I do. A million thanks to you!

About the Author

Jo Graham is the author of thirty books and three online games. Best known for her historical fantasy novels *Black Ships* and *Stealing Fire*, and her tie-in novels for MGM's popular *Stargate: Atlantis* and *Stargate: SG-1* series, she has been a Locus Award finalist, an Amazon Top Choice, a Spectrum Award finalist, a Manly Wade Wellman Award finalist, a Romantic Times Top Pick in historical fiction and a Lambda Literary Award and Rainbow Award nominee for bisexual fiction. With Melissa Scott, she is the author of five books in the *Order of the Air* series, a historical fantasy series set in the 1920s and 30s. She is the author of *The Calpurnian Wars* space opera series (*Sounding Dark, Warlady, Fortune's Favor*) and the *Memoirs of the Borgia Sibyl*. She is also the author of three pagan spirituality books. She lives in North Carolina with her partner and is the mother of two daughters.